BREW

a love story

TRACY EWENS

BREW

a love story

Book design by Maureen Cutajar
www.gopublished.com

ISBN: (print) 978-0-9976838-7-5 | 0-9976838-7-2
ISBN: (e-book) 978-0-9976838-6-8 | 0-9976838-6-4

For Michael.
Thank you for our love story.

The key to everything is patience.
You get the chicken by hatching the egg, not by smashing it.

- ARNOLD H. GLASOW

Chapter One

Boyd McNaughton was losing a lot of blood. At least it seemed like a lot. He wondered how much blood a man could spare before he passed out. Staring down at his hand, fascination quickly flipped to anxiety when he realized he didn't want to find out.

"Boyd," his pain-in-the-ass brother said, reminding Boyd why he was bleeding and pissed in the first place.

"I'm fine," he said, grabbing rags off the stack he kept clean by the tanks below the old Foghorn Brewery sign. He covered his hand, not ready to catch a glimpse at how not fine things really were. Boyd boasted a decent tolerance for pain, but this was pushing the limit.

"Come on, man, let's not do this. You're bleeding."

"As always, little brother, you get a gold star. Now get out of my way before I drop dead right here on the brewery floor. Imagine that insurance claim." He managed to raise his eyebrows in sarcasm as he pushed past Patrick.

"At least let me drive you. The color is draining from your face. Maybe we should call—"

Boyd was in his truck before he heard the rest of Patrick's assessment. He'd cut his hand. He wasn't having a heart attack. Sure, it throbbed and a drop of blood escaped his makeshift bandage and hit his jeans as he turned onto Washington, but he was fine, damn it.

The look of shock on Patrick's face was classic. One minute they were in a full-heat argument over quality vs. quantity, and the next, his brother's expression fell. Boyd noticed the blood and was more upset that he'd contaminated his work space than anything else. Then the pain kicked in and every petty concern slipped away. He became singularly focused on breathing and staying upright. Pain was powerful that way.

Had he not been the one presently staining his favorite pair of jeans, he would have found the whole scene funny. Stopping at a red light, he replayed the argument.

"You promised we'd be ready for bottles and kegs last week," Patrick said, doing that pacing thing that drove Boyd nuts.

"I don't recall promising. Did I pinkie swear?" he'd asked, focusing on adding more yeast to what he hoped would be his last batch. "I know I'm behind."

Patrick's hands slapped his sides and Boyd didn't need to look to know his brother was in the middle of a pseudo temper tantrum. Yeah, Trick was frustrated, but there was nothing Boyd could do about it.

The recipe wasn't right yet and if his time-obsessed brother didn't leave him alone, Foghorn Brewery would be pushing lemonade as their anniversary brew.

"Don't do this to me." Trick sounded defeated.

Boyd glanced up to find the also-predictable hand running through his brother's expensive haircut.

"I've got people lined up, distributors willing for the first time to carry us on a trial basis. I need to deliver when I said I'd deliver. I gave you a cushion because I know how you can be, but next week that cushion is up and you're still..."

Boyd had raised his brow, wondering if Patrick was going to go with "contemplating your navel," or—

"Messing around in your sandbox."

Of course, it was the "sandbox" today.

"You do realize that I'm three whole years older than you, right? That I taught you everything you know about the sandbox. I'm not responsible for your uptight attitude, but I'll say it again. I. Am. Older. Step back."

Boyd took in the aroma of the batch as it cooked. Lemon, still with the lemon. What was it going to take to rein that in?

"Boyd."

"Trick."

"You're acting like an asshole."

"Back at you, little man."

"How much longer?"

Boyd glanced up again. "How the hell can I make this any clearer? Are you thinking that I have a killer recipe waiting to brew but instead, I'm screwing with you? Do you think I enjoy having you flying around me like one of the witch's monkeys in that movie Mom makes us watch every year? I don't. I'm nearly there. I'll spell this one out for you too. There. Is. Too. Much. Lemon. I'm racking my brain, and you're not helping. It could be fixed and ready to brew by this afternoon. It could take me a few more days."

"We don't have a few more days."

Boyd had had it. "Fine. Then I'll piss in a bottle and we can sell that. So long as we make your precious deadline, right?"

"The beer has got to be good by now. You're obsessing."

"Good is not enough. Goddamn—" Boyd pulled his hand from the keggle and blood ran warm down his arm like something that should have been pleasant, but turned sinister. Everything went slow motion and it took his brain a few seconds to catch up.

As the argument that now had him trying to remember if the ER entrance was off McDowell or Maria Drive faded into reality, Boyd grazed the edge of his wrapped hand as he turned the steering wheel and flinched.

Petaluma was a small city, so there was one ER with an urgent care in the same cluster of buildings. Boyd had considered going to urgent care, but he was still bleeding, and truth be told, he was a little nervous. He needed both hands in proper working order and that lemon balanced yesterday. Was it his turn to carpool to baseball? Was he on the schedule for Friday or was it Colton's mom picking up his son today? He'd completely forgotten about Mason. His brain must be scrambled.

If it was his turn to drive the guys, he'd need to be stitched up and on his way by two. Boyd glanced at the clock on the dash. He had five hours. Was that enough time? He'd only been to the emergency room one other time, and that had taken at least three or four hours in the middle of the night. All he remembered were connected chairs, televisions whispering infomercials, and of course, the moment one-year-old Mason's fever finally broke and he fell asleep among the colorful giraffes of his car seat.

That ER visit had turned out well, and there was no reason to think this one wouldn't be the same, he told himself. As soon as the woman in the Prius figured out which parking spot she was taking, he'd park and let the professionals do their thing. The rag was almost soaked through and the duct tape he'd found under the seat of his truck was barely hanging on. Boyd's stomach turned at the stained material and what he imagined was beneath. It was likely a lot less gruesome than he pictured, but he wasn't taking any chances by looking now.

Maybe Trick was right and he was obsessing about the recipe. It was the anniversary brew after all, and Boyd had to admit there was pressure there. Although, he could never figure out if the pressure to create something exceptional was self-inflicted or if doing it better was why they were still in business. All Boyd knew was every morning, his first thought was some version of "knock on wood." Mason had turned thirteen a few weeks ago and Boyd made a living, a good living, making beer. He wanted to hit pause, keep everything right where it was, but he knew better. Things had a way of changing right from under him.

Shaking his head as he turned off his truck, Boyd pulled his keys free with his left hand.

First things first, his hand was priority. He slid out of his truck and bumped the door closed with his shoulder. The rest of it, including baseball practice, the lemon, and whose fault all of this was, would sort itself out once the bleeding stopped.

Ella Walters was about to hit a wall. She'd been awake for nearly twenty-four hours and hoped to God the eye drops she was fishing from the pocket of her scrubs would help to ease her scratchy eyes. Somewhere after the twenty-eight-year-old male with a kidney stone but before the seventeen-year-old female, who presented with three of her friends a little after four in the morning bawling that she was "dying," Ella had taken out her contacts and put on her glasses. When she worked at San Francisco General, she never wore her glasses. She hated having anything on her face in the frenzy of a trauma center.

Petaluma Valley was a slower pace, which she was beginning to enjoy. She was glad she'd switched to glasses because it wouldn't look good to be bumping into things when Julie Blake's parents arrived in the ER at seven thirty to claim their daughter. Julie's friends had all been picked up a couple of hours ago, which cut down on the drama significantly. Ella notified Julie's parents that their daughter was not, in fact, dying. She'd had far too many shots of Firewater, but she was now hydrated and resting.

"This time," the father said as he and his wife helped an almost sober and mortified Julie off the hospital bed. "This time, you're okay, but kids die from alcohol all the time. Do you hear me, Julie?"

The young girl nodded, pushing her matted hair from her mascara-streaked eyes as they passed the nurses' station and the ER doors closed behind them. The white walls and speckled flooring of a sterile space Ella knew better than any other was quiet again, except for the intermittent bump of the air conditioner and the rhythmic beeping monitors. Ella patted the shoulder of the unit secretary and told her she would be in the on-call room if they needed her.

The small room off the hallway and across from the vending machines was more like a large closet than on-call quarters, but Ella could have fallen asleep standing up by that point. The clean air of the small city and the easy life was making her soft, she thought as she opted for the timeworn chair over the wobbly cot in the corner. Easing onto the cool green vinyl, she rested her head back.

Before her eyes had a chance to slide blissfully closed, Bri burst through the door eating a bag of Sour Patch Kids and exclaimed she had important news. Ella, resolved that there were only forty-five minutes left on her shift, extended her hand. At the offered bag, she put a piece of candy in her mouth.

"God." She chewed enough to swallow without choking. "How do you eat those things?"

"Best candy in the world."

"That's not a candy. That's toxic waste. Look, your tongue is blue," Ella said, leaning up in the chair now.

Bri propped herself against the wall, crossed one flowery clog over the other, and stuck out her blue tongue. "My news." She chewed. "Baker, Dr. Baker, Dr. Where Does a Man Get Shoulders Like That—"

"Yes, Bri, I know who Dr. Baker is," Ella said. She would have laughed, but she didn't have the energy.

"He's getting divorced," Bri said, licking the sugar off her finger and putting the bag back in the pocket of her scrubs. Ella took off her glasses, pinched the bridge of her nose, and closed her eyes. When she opened them, Bri was waiting for a response.

Brianna Cramer, or Nurse B as most of the doctors called her, was the first person Ella met when she transferred to Petaluma Valley Hospital almost two years ago. She had wanted nothing more than a job and some solitude. She wasn't looking for a friend, but Bri was, and Ella soon learned that Nurse B often got what she wanted.

"You need coffee," she'd told Ella after their first shift. "I'm off now too, so I'll show you the best coffee."

"Actually, I'm going to go home and—"

"Coffee doesn't take that long," Bri had said with that defiant honesty Ella now loved.

They'd had coffee and Bri turned out to be a steady, this-is-how-it-is beacon in the storm that was Ella's life back then. She consistently wore some shade of pink nail polish and her hair was a dozen shades of brown. She had large, warm set-apart eyes and full lips Ella envied. Most importantly, Bri was a great nurse. She was technically proficient and cared about every patient who walked through the doors. Ella often questioned when her friend would run out of compassion.

Ella had believed she owed patients her skills and her focused attention. As a doctor, she was there to ensure nothing slipped by her and that patients left her better than they were when they arrived. Until Bri, she'd worked among like-minded colleagues, but that was her old life. She normally left the warm and fuzzy to Bri, but working in a smaller hospital called on parts of Ella that were untapped in the whirl of a big trauma center. Patients presented with less than life-threatening injuries and wanted to talk, know about what book she was reading or if she thought acupuncture really worked. Ella didn't know how to move through that kind of contact, but she was trying.

Bri and Ella became friends shortly after that first day over coffee and had never turned back even though Ella was surely hard to love during her first couple of months in Petaluma.

"Maybe I'm getting old," she said now, still trying to get the pucker of the candy out of her mouth. "I used to be the queen of the double shift. Two shifts, shower, and out with friends." Thirty-six was closer to forty than thirty. Maybe it had nothing to do with fresh air. Maybe this was her downhill shift, Ella thought.

"Wait, you had friends in the big city? Were they paratroopers or super doctors?"

Ella closed her eyes again.

"Ninja surgeons?"

She shook her head, eyes still closed.

"You're really no fun when you're tired, you know that?" Bri sat on the arm of the chair and mocked a whisper. "Back to my news. Can you believe that Shoulders and Perfect Teeth are getting divorced?"

Ella opened one eye. "Are we surprised by this? Baker is not exactly the model of monogamy."

"Oh, come on. Those are rumors."

Ella held her gaze and waited.

"You know something." She pointed at Ella and stood. "Who told you he was cheating on his wife? Why don't I know?"

"No one told me anything. It's obvious, don't you think? Does anyone really need that many extra blankets from clean linens? And why is the good doctor so helpful? Quickies among the water pitchers, my dear friend. No need for Sherlock on this one."

"Oh. My. God. That is... well, that's kind of hot. I want to be ravaged in a closet."

"Do you? By a married man?" Ella knew her friend and there was no way, but Bri hesitated and appeared to be entertaining the idea.

"With twin daughters and one more on the way?" Ella helped her along. *Christ!*

Bri finally shook her head. "Okay, yeah, that's gross."

"Took you that long, huh?"

"Those shoulders are so—"

"Bri," Ella barked, moving past her to the vending machines in the hall. Sleep was not happening and it was time for liquid assistance.

"You're right. He's a pig. Good for her, right?" Bri followed.

"There you go. There's the woman I love." Ella slid a dollar into the machine and pressed the button for Coke. She could be a commercial, she thought. Exhausted ER doctor invigorated by the fizz of caffeine finds the strength to—

"Dr. Walters, they need you," Bri said, now closer to the nurses' station.

Breaking free of her advertising dream, Ella popped open the Coke and drank half of it in one gulp. Setting her ice-cold goodness on the counter, she tightened her ponytail and waited for the twin tingle of sugar and caffeine.

"Two things," Bri said. "Campbell is running thirty minutes late." She paused, allowing Ella the expected curse under her breath.

She did not disappoint. "Son of a bitch," she said, barely above a whisper.

Campbell was coming off a three-day vacation, she thought but did not say. Bri could practically read her mind anyway.

"And... you have a hand laceration in four. Male, thirty-seven, with acute signs of a bad attitude."

"Perfect. Chart?" Her eyes cut to Bri, who scrunched her face and handed her a single piece of paper. She took a couple of steps back.

"Trina is still helping Dr. Briggs in Exam One. The guy who kicked through his sliding glass door. She said she'd be in as soon as she was free."

"Where's Wilma?"

"Sick."

Ella finished the last bit of her soda and threw the can in the recycle. "Looks like you and I get this one. Let me know when he's ready for—" She stopped. "Where are you going?"

Bri already had her keys dangling from one finger, her purse up on her shoulder as she threw another bag on top of that. "I'd stay to help, but if I don't leave now, I'll miss my flight."

"To?"

"Los Angeles. Hello. My brother's wife had the baby. Remember? I told you I was going down there for the weekend."

Somewhere Ella did remember, but all the hours and days were dancing around in her memory. Sort of like how Bri was dancing while she waited to confirm that outside of their friendship, it was all right for her to leave a doctor without an attending nurse and with a patient waiting to be seen. Bri mouthed sorry, still dancing in place. Ella laughed and shook her head, now fueled by caffeine.

"Go."

Her friend, who suddenly morphed from Nurse B to Baby Annie's excited aunt, leaned forward and hugged her. Ella wasn't a hugger, but the give-and-take of friendship won out and she allowed her arms to be pinned to her sides as Bri got it out of her system.

"When I get back, we're getting you some hugging lessons."

"Really? Is that something they're now offering at the community college?"

"It should be."

Ella pointed to the clock. "The airport, Bri. Fly safe. You can resume Operation Cuddle after you've seen your niece."

Bri hefted her bags one more time and was gone.

After a few brisk pats to her cheeks that Ella hoped restored some color, she pushed the cold metal handle of Exam 4. The caffeine humming through her bloodstream, followed closely by a serious longing for the egg-and-cheese bagel she was going to pick up on the way home as soon as she took care of Mr. — She glanced at the piece of paper, a sad substitute for a chart.

"Mr. Boyd McNaughton," she said and glanced up to find a bear of a man. He was tall, broad, and scarcely teetering on the edge of the narrow bed. Dark jeans and a flannel rolled to his elbows, he presented in what was pretty much the standard uniform for March in Petaluma. When she'd first arrived in town, she'd wondered how long anyone could live in a place so consistent, but it had grown on her and now, despite the occasional craving for superior sushi or an opera, she found she didn't miss Dr. Ella Walters, Head of Trauma, or all the drama that went along with that life. She was settling into being one of four full-time ER docs, plain old Dr. Walters. Ella had been raised to never accept being one of many and while she wasn't ready to say it out loud, she was content in the clean air of smaller.

"Yeah." Her patient shifted farther onto the metal frame as if he were sitting up taller in class, then flinched and cursed under his breath.

Full beard, but his brow was damp and what she could see of his face was pale. The guy was in pain.

Is that duct tape?

"Great. We at least have your name right. I'm Dr. Walters." For an instant, Ella moved to shake his hand, which was her usual rehearsed greeting. That was not happening with his injury, so she defaulted to what she knew. She washed up and snapped on gloves.

"Tell me what happened," she said, grabbing a folded blanket and gently lifting his forearm. She needed to get what seemed like an entire rag collection off his hand before she could tell what she was dealing with. Quite a bit of blood and yes, it was duct tape. Wonderful. She began carefully unwrapping his hand.

"Okay, well I tried to tell one of the nurses out there, but she ran off and stuck me in this room. Does anyone work here?"

Ella raised her hand, met his eyes.

"Right." He huffed and instead of releasing a breath, some of the tension, it all seemed to rattle around in his lungs. "I cut my hand."

"I can see that. On what?" She opened the rags to find a nice-sized laceration, about 53 millimeters from the side of his hand into the palm. After asking him to carefully test range of motion, Ella was confident she was dealing with a cut. A nasty one, but there were no particles embedded in the tissue, no broken bones or damaged tendons. She grabbed the saline and four-by-fours.

"A keggle."

Ella met his eyes. Dark green, thick lashes, and pupils normal. All good signs.

His expression indicated she should know exactly what a keggle was. Ella's stomach groaned. Bagel time was well over an hour out now.

She inhaled. "What is a keggle, Mr. McNaughton?"

He was seething, presumably at someone or something that had nothing to do with her. His attitude did not improve while she manipulated his hand, but suddenly the reluctant patient had an answer. Amazing what a little cold saline could inspire.

"I make beer." He winced but didn't pull away. "I was working on a small batch, trying to get the lemon under control because I'm using Sorachi Ace, which I haven't tackled since 2010."

Right when Ella thought he might be delirious and speaking gibberish, he huffed again.

"You don't need to know any of that. Point is, my candy-ass brother barged into my happy space with his 'we need this yesterday' bullshit. A keggle is a metal vat. You've seen a keg, like at a party or something?"

Ella nodded, tossing the soiled rags and holding fresh dressing to his hand now. She'd seen a keg in some movie she could no longer remember. He cut his hand on metal. That was all she needed.

"It's that thing, a keg. But mine is cut out on top. It's not finished off because it doesn't need to be. I like to get in there when I'm working. It's a huge pot. I don't cut myself on the edge. Ever."

"Until today," Ella said, meeting his eyes again.

"Until today." Frustration finally spilled off his shoulders.

He exhaled as she peeled back the compress. Things were looking better already, Ella thought. Jagged, but clean. He'd need stitches, sixteen or seventeen from the looks of it. She was approaching that glorious moment, in most emergency rooms, when the all-important doctor wished her patient well with a smile before handing him off to a nurse for stitching and after-care instructions. Any other ER and there would be no need to chitchat or put the patient at ease. She'd be less than fifteen minutes away from fluffy egg whites and melted Swiss on a toasted bagel, easy red onion, and avocado. But Trina had not even poked her head in, so to the disappointment of Ella's stomach, she was on her own. Which could be productive, she told herself. It had been awhile since she'd stitched anyone up. "Practice and patience are the keys to good medicine" was her first-year professor's motto. Right now, that certainly rang true.

Chapter Two

Boyd scanned the white walls hoping he could concentrate on something other than the antiseptic smell and the glint of all that metal on the tray next to her.

"Okay," Dr. Walters said, finally done with what Boyd prayed was the last round of poking and cleaning his hand. She pushed her glasses up on her nose and turned to a computer jutting from the wall.

"Was there alcohol in the keggle when you cut your hand?"

"Yeah."

"Good. I'm assuming everything in your... happy space is sterile?"

He nodded.

"Even better. When was the last time you had a tetanus shot?"

He tried not to squirm at the mention of a shot, but his son's last immunizations were years ago and it had been even longer since Boyd had been near a needle himself. Tetanus? Was that the big painful one or the one where they put the bubble under the skin? *Christ, that one was nasty.*

"No idea," he said, going for aloof.

She washed her hands again and with her back to him, Boyd noticed where her hair gathered at the base of her neck. Long. Her neck was long. In fact, everything on her was long. Even though Petaluma wasn't a small town, per se, it was a close-knit community. He was used to seeing familiar faces. Ever since he was a kid, anyone out of the ordinary was intriguing. That's why he was noticing her, he rationalized; she was unfamiliar. She might have lived here forever, he thought. How would he know? It's not like he hung around with the hospital crowd.

"Are you new?" He heard his voice before realizing his mouth moved.

"I'm sorry?" She was still typing.

"Nothing. How much longer do you think I'll be?"

She turned to him, a strained curve to her lips, and pushed the glasses up again. She was pretty. *What the hell?* Had she given him something for the pain already?

"I'll get you out of here as fast as I can. To be safe, I'd like you to have a tetanus shot and then I'll stitch your hand. I'm going to numb it first because I'll need to trim the skin."

That time, he did squirm. She noticed and placed a hand on his shoulder. She seemed almost awkward at the physical contact. Wasn't physical her business?

Whatever was going on with her, Boyd felt awareness. That was the only way to explain it. The sugar on her breath, the way her hair managed to look messy but contained at the same time. Her short nails and her narrow shoulders. Everything was in clear focus.

Obviously, he was in pain and she was a medical professional.

"Right, that explains it," he said out loud again.

"Explains what?"

"I... was saying it's great that you explained about the skin."

"You won't feel me trimming, but the cut is pretty jagged," she continued.

"Great. Less information is better."

"A couple more questions. Do you drink?"

"A little."

Dr. Walters's expression said she didn't want to be asking the questions any more than he wanted to answer. He guessed some guy with a cut on his hand was not the most exciting thing for an ER doc. They both wanted this over with, a common goal.

"Smoke?" she asked, eyes back on the monitor.

"Used to."

She closed her eyes and rolled her neck. *Now that was hot.* Boyd gave up trying to understand the sudden interest. All he knew was looking at her was more constructive than freaking out like a kid over some impending shot.

"Okay, Mr. McNaughton."

"Boyd."

"Okay, Boyd. I'm going to level with you. Connect, if you will. I'm tired. I'm sure a business owner such as yourself can appreciate exhaustion. I have no nurse, and I desperately need a bagel sandwich. It's clear you are the guy who rarely uses Band-Aids. You hate hospitals and the people who work in them. I get it, believe me, but I'd really like to stitch up that hand before the caffeine wears off and I get loopy and forget all the fun stuff I learned in medical school. I think you'd like that too. So, maybe you could help me out here by being a little more forthcoming?"

She attempted to mask her impatience with another strained grin, but Boyd recognized the look. He was on "thin ice" as his mother used to say.

"Maybe you should sit back, make yourself more comfortable?" she said.

"That's not going to happen until I'm out of here."

"Noted. On a scale of one to ten, one being a nuisance and ten being excruciating, can you tell me your pain? Minus your anger at the candy-ass."

"Six."

"So, pretty painful."

"I said a six, that's middle of the road."

"Yes, it is." She appeared to tab through a few more fields on the computer. "But men tend to feign a high threshold for pain, so your six is closer to an eight." She put the buds of her scope into her ears and took them back out.

"This is only a suture," she mumbled, seemingly going through a mental checklist. "I do need a temp though, so open up." She pulled a stick attached to a curly cord from a box on the counter. Right when Boyd thought he couldn't feel any more awkward, she placed what he now recognized as a thermometer under his tongue. Holding the thermometer secure in his mouth, she checked her watch. She smelled like vanilla, or maybe pralines. She'd recently had a Coke, he could smell the syrup. Fancy watch, he noticed. Definitely not a local.

The stick beeped. She took it from his mouth, ejected a plastic piece into the trash, and returned to the computer.

"Are these questions for the pain medication? What if I don't need the meds?" he said.

"I'm sorry?" Ella hit the enter button and returned her attention to him.

"I don't need anything for pain. Can someone stitch me up?"

Ella nodded. "That someone will be me and these questions should have been asked when you first arrived. I'm sorry, we're playing catch-up here. Everything has steps. We don't have to like them, but I need to do them."

Boyd took in a breath and let it out slowly. He was rushing her, and he hated it when people rushed him. It wasn't her fault he'd cut his hand or that for some reason she didn't have a nurse.

"Brett's Bagels, is that where you get your bagel?" he asked, hoping to change direction.

She smiled, a completely unplanned smile, and holy hell they were suddenly somewhere outside the sterile walls of the hospital. Pretty wasn't the right word. Her face was sunshine peeking through pine trees on the best camping trip. The creases at her eyes spoke to her long nights but took nothing away from her flushed cheeks. She was beautiful and he wasn't making her job any easier.

"Best bagels in town," she said, as if he'd handed her one wrapped in their signature white butcher paper.

"Only bagels in town," he finished Brett's tag line. That almost curved his lips into a smile too. Almost. "I brew beer, so I do a fair amount of testing on the job, but I don't drink more than eight ounces a day socially, maybe sixteen on weekends. I smoked a pack a day from sixteen until the baby... until I was twenty-three. I want to smoke every day, but I don't. Better?"

He was rewarded with an even deeper smile. He must have lost more blood than he thought because he could not remember the last time he'd noticed the specifics of a woman.

"Yes. Thank you. I'll be right back and we'll get you stitched up."

He scooted farther back on the bed. He would be here for a while and that was all there was to it.

True to her word, Dr. Walters returned and gave him a quick shot, the needle not nearly as long as he'd imagined. When she started stitching him up, or "trimming the skin," as she'd put it, Boyd looked away.

Curiosity got the better of him a few minutes in and when he glanced over, his eyes met hers over her dark-rimmed glasses. She was probably checking to make certain he hadn't passed out. Lights now brighter, he figured out the color of her eyes at last—stout. That last detail arrived unwelcome. It hit too close to home, too close to his life's work as their worlds somehow meshed for a moment.

Boyd knew his place and he turned away, bringing his attention back to the water safety poster on the opposite wall instead of the stitches or the contrasting flecks in her eyes. His hand was numb, but the tug of the stitches was unnerving. He might have to kill Patrick with his left hand when he finally made it back to the brewery.

There were half a dozen shades of stout, and his thoughts betrayed him again. It was one of his favorite brews. Her eyes were more of an oatmeal stout, deep brown with a hint of amber, kind of like last year's Golden Polish. That was a good year. Great beer. Great eyes. He allowed himself one more look.

Dr. Edwin Campbell finally showed up for his shift looking rested and tan. The big jerk. After hurried rounds of the whopping two patients they had, and returning a phone call from one of the guys in radiology, Ella changed out of her scrubs and threw the wide strap of her bag over her shoulder before backing out of the emergency room into the filtered light of an overcast afternoon.

Petaluma was special. For months after she'd arrived, she had missed the buzz of San Francisco. More accurately the buzz of Zuckerberg San Francisco General's Trauma Center, but she'd come to appreciate the recurrent flapping of the flags overhead and the hum of shop owners and locals readying for the day or closing for the evening, depending on which shift delivered her back out into the fresh air.

If San Francisco was a five-lane freeway during rush hour, Petaluma was a small country road. A detour, she thought, which was exactly what she had needed when her ordered and methodical world had tilted on its side. Until that tilt, she couldn't remember a time after graduating from UCLA Medical School when she hadn't been at General. She interned there summers while she was in school and served her entire residency under the talent of their trauma team. The training and experiences had made her "one hell of a doctor" according to any of her colleagues. The accolades should have bred arrogance, but Ella grew up in a family that caused her to question her every move. There was little margin for error as far back as the second grade, so she was more than prepared for the rigors of medical school.

Ella was practically born to lead a trauma center until the day, 9:53 in the evening to be exact, when what she'd known for certain turned fuzzy. Once the dust settled, she retraced all the pieces to understand how she'd arrived at such a place in her life. After some time and distance, she'd come to believe it was difficult for anyone to see around a lie, but even two years out, her conscience still hinted that she'd played a part in keeping the deceit alive.

Ella possessed a lifelong need to dissect the "how" and "why" of things. She'd been born with what her high school biology teacher termed "intellectual curiosity," but the day she left for Petaluma had nothing to do with intellect and everything to do with getting out from under the weight of disgust before the shame swallowed her whole.

She paid the girl behind the counter at Brett's Bagels and dug into the brown paper bag before she started her car. The first bite was heaven and when she washed it down with strong coffee, all was right with the world. Closing her eyes, she allowed the warmth to ease her exhaustion, but in the next moment, she put her seat belt on and drove home before she fell asleep in the parking lot.

Everything about her life in San Francisco had suited her. Her work was intense and rewarding. Cherry on top, she was in a relationship with an exciting man who was equally as committed to his career. On the surface, a full and accomplished life stretched out before her and when one of her pillars crumbled, she realized the whole thing was interdependent. That, and all her adult years had been spent sterile and cold. She was a name tag, a curriculum vitae and predictably, she drew those same types of people into her circle. Once Ella had examined all the pieces, the shock that she was made of the same material as her father nearly brought her to her knees.

"Never shit where you eat, Ella Marie," had been her father's advice, which was delivered via speakerphone and always with a dash of reproach. "This is no one's business. You are the head of their blood and guts department. Keep that position, do you hear me? It's certainly not your fault you're a silly woman. Roll of the birth dice, dear. No need to throw away your perfectly pricey degrees."

She understood that most people would cower at his comments. Ella had certainly seen enough of her father's associates recoil, but she was used to it, had been raised on it. For an instant, she thought to mention that her father hadn't paid one cent for her education. That she'd earned a full ride and worked through college and medical school, but there was no point. The man was an unyielding wall, devoid of any warmth or shared experience. Before she succumbed to the same fate, she had resigned—to the utter disappointment of her department and much to her father's fury.

The better part of the two weeks that followed had been a blur. Sleeping on her couch and then the floor, the still-fresh shock overshadowing the logistics of uprooting everything. By the time the last of her boxes were loaded onto the moving van, she had found enough footing to propel herself north and settle into the riverside town of Petaluma. That was over two years ago and while the sound of a helicopter overhead still made the little hairs on the back of her neck stand up in exhilaration, the human being in Ella, the woman, had no regrets.

Pulling up to her house, she realized she thought more about the past when she was tired. She had taken a scalding hot mental shower years ago that should have erased the parts and pieces of a life she no longer wanted to miss, but the mind was fascinating in its capacity to hold on to memories. Fortunately, the heart was resilient. Through pain and scars, it kept beating. Ella had seen it firsthand. A seemingly dead heart could spring to life in an instant under the proper care.

She clicked the button to lock her car and tossed her breakfast trash into the green can she'd left on the curb before work. It was empty now and she should have left it there and gone straight to bed, but Ella liked a tidy home, so she mustered the strength to pull the can to the side of her carport. Enjoying the sound of the chirping birds overhead and the smells of early spring, she pulled open her black mailbox, grabbed the stack of what felt like mostly catalogues, and shuffled up the small walk to her "little cottage," as her mother, another thoughtless soul, had put it when she'd viewed Ella's home online.

It was quiet on her street. She valued the extras in her life now, the stability of being alone. She dropped her bag by the front door, tossed her mail on the table, turned the lock, and barely made it into the pajamas hanging on the hook in her bathroom. After brushing her teeth, she ignored the urge to floss as she climbed under the covers and buried her face in the relief and isolation of her down pillows. There was no way of knowing her last thought because before her mental list of what she'd done right and wrong in the last twenty-four hours had a chance to take hold, Ella was asleep.

Chapter Three

B oyd dropped Mason off at school thirty minutes early the next morning to make up a test he'd missed the week before when they'd taken off Friday to go camping. They'd given up on hopes of the perfect attendance award by the fifth grade. Boyd believed in a few mental health days a year. It was as important that a kid knew how to tie a fly onto his line as it was that he understood things that happened hundreds of years ago. Education was essential, but so was living. It helped that Mason was a good student and could afford to miss a day here and there.

The early drop-off meant Boyd could get into the brewery early, clean up, and hopefully start his new and final batch before everyone else had their first cup of coffee. When he arrived at work, it was as though nothing had happened the day before. There was a note from their housekeeping service that they'd done an "extra cleaning and sterilization" on his brew room. One of his other brothers, Cade, had spent a few hours taking apart some of the equipment and cleaning. He'd left a note too.

Boyd was grateful he could get started even earlier and glad Patrick had not helped with the cleanup. That meant Boyd could still be annoyed with him for at least a few more hours.

His mood a bit lighter because his hand had stopped aching and he had what he hoped was an answer to the overaggressive lemon in his brew, Boyd milled the grain and decided to create a real batch. He'd had enough fun with the keggle for a while and he was feeling confident. While he waited for the grain, he glanced up at the back wall of the closest thing he'd ever had to an office. It was more like a warehouse, with one exposed brick wall that was older than Boyd, hell, older than their father. His eyes combed over what he and his brothers termed the "journey wall."

There were line sketch drawings from their dad, who helped redesign the new space, and a couple of their first beer recipes pinned to a board. All the fancy finished stuff hung in Patrick's office. Boyd preferred the scraps of paper colored with smudged jottings of original ideas. They showed the work in progress. Among the sketches were photographs, mostly black and white, of him and his brothers, often with Mason on one or the other's shoulders, at various points along the way. He even had an early head shot of their youngest brother, West, before he made it big. Boyd loved every image. Not only because it showed their bond and their business, but because it showed his son growing up around men who loved him.

Foghorn Brewery was the best thing the three oldest McNaughton brothers had ever done save the truly kick-ass two-story tree house they'd built the summer before Boyd went into high school. The thing had electricity, thanks to their father. While Boyd had hoped to share it with his own children someday, he had no way of knowing back then that he would be a father before he left college.

Not that he was complaining. Mason was an unbelievable kid. He'd changed Boyd's life in every way for the better, and the adoration Boyd felt when his son was born nudged him to be a better man. He'd also grown up faster than most guys his age.

"Being a dad will keep you out of trouble." That's what his parents said the Christmas he came home, less than a year shy of graduation, to deliver the news.

Boyd was the oldest of four boys, so it was no surprise he was the first to foray into fatherhood, but he grew up in a somewhat traditional home. His dad cursed like a sailor when he was talking to his foremen or some "incompetent moron of an electrician" anytime one of his jobs was late. Still, in the McNaughton world, people got married, bought a house, decorated a nursery, then had a baby.

Things didn't work out that way for Boyd, but it made no difference to him or his family once Claire, his college girlfriend, became pregnant. Most of the time, he felt like the luckiest guy in the world. And now that the brewery was seven years and running, he was glad he'd been smart with his money because it ensured Mason would want for nothing.

It could be said that the arrival of Mason McNaughton was the reason Boyd and his brothers sat down at Flips, the local bar at the time, one early summer evening and planned what would become Foghorn Brewery. Boyd had been putting his degree to use as a freelance engineer, but projects were inconsistent and he didn't want to touch his savings for day-to-day expenses. His brother Patrick was due to graduate the following May and already had a job lined up with an ad firm in San Francisco. Cade was fresh out of junior college and working as the bartender for some hipster hotel in the city too. But that afternoon, they allowed themselves to dream. This time, instead of a tree house with a skate ramp on the ground floor, they were figuring out money and making adult plans well outside of their comfort zone.

It would take three more years before what they'd scribbled out even remotely resembled a legitimate business, let alone a brewery. Two weeks after Mason started kindergarten, Patrick decided he'd had enough as an ad man and joined Cade, who had already moved home to manage Flips after the owner, a high school friend of their dad's, fired his existing manager for skimming the till.

Patrick and Cade rented a house less than five minutes from where Boyd and Mason lived. It was as if the stars had aligned and it was finally time. Foghorn Brewery started making beer that year.

The mill stopped grinding with a familiar hollow scrape and Boyd turned off his memories. It was time to get back to work, time to make the wort. He'd add the Citra once everything was in the tank, and that would take care of the lemon. The missing ingredient that had cost him almost a week of trial and failure was going to make his best damn beer to date. Fitting that it would be their anniversary brew, and right on time for the opening of the Tap House. Boyd felt like he was back in his groove; the rhythm of his work and all the steps were falling into place. He remembered what the doctor had said. "There are steps to follow whether we like them or not."

Maybe it was the blood loss or that he'd still been thinking about meeting Dr. Walters, but after he'd relayed the whole story to Mason, save the part about her eyes looking like Golden Polish, Boyd couldn't sleep. Around two in the morning, he gave up trying and climbed into the shower. There, under the beating water, he knew Citra was the answer. He'd thanked God, or whatever was up there, and gotten dressed.

Making beer had never been complicated for Boyd, but as each year went by, he felt the pressure to top himself, stretch what he knew, and pursue more exciting combinations. It was good work and kept him on his toes, but when his mind drew a blank, it could be grueling.

"How's the hand?" Cade asked, standing outside the bay door and covered in sawdust. He looked like a troublemaker who had blown up the wood shop. Boyd noticed the expanse of his brother's chest, which appeared to grow larger every time he saw him.

Did the guy live at the gym?

"Don't bring that crap in here," Boyd said.

"Aww. What was that you said? Thank you, little brother, for cleaning my equipment after I slashed the crap out of my hand because I got all jumpy about the lemon and a big bad deadline." Cade shook his head, thankfully outside the door, and the sawdust flew off the long center patch of his hair before he flipped it back off his face.

His brother's hair was buzzed on the sides now, but in deference to the long hair he used to sport, he left the center strip untouched. Boyd thought it resembled a limp Mohawk and made his observation known often, as was the McNaughton way.

"Thanks for the cleanup." Boyd met Cade's eyes with an expression of sincerity. That was all he was getting. "I figured out the lemon. Spontaneous brew day happening right now."

"I can smell that. Trick was worried about you."

"I'll bet. The hand is fine. Go away." Boyd held up his bandaged hand and turned to his computer to monitor the temperature.

"How many stitches?"

"Seventeen."

"Damn."

"Yeah."

Everything was on track. In twenty minutes, he'd have wort. That would cool and he'd have beer a few hours after that. If all went well, he might even make the tail end of Mason's baseball practice.

Cade cleared his throat. Still there.

"What the hell? I'm good. Go... cut some more wood. What are you doing over there anyway?"

His brother smiled that same grin he'd flashed when he was a little boy. It was more dangerous now and sort of antihero, to use one of Mason's comic book terms. Cade was the tatted up, rarely-on-the-right-side-of-sane McNaughton brother. He was a good guy, but sometimes his glinting green eyes spoke to high school detentions and missed curfews. Their mother called it trouble, their youngest brother, West, who was an actor called it his "hell, yeah" face, and on more occasions than any of them could count, women at Flips called the look "wicked." But they usually said it in a way that meant they'd been in Cade's bed. Boyd hated the look because it meant his brother was gearing up to be an even bigger smart-ass than usual.

"I'm showing concern. And if you must know, I'm making a frame for the dartboards."

"Well, look at you, Martha Stewart. And don't show concern. I'm fine. Had a shot and everything. Now get out. I've got work to do."

"Holy crap, a shot?" Cade practically squealed like a toddler and turned to leave.

"Nice shirt, by the way."

"Right?" He whipped back around. "It's one of my new favorites."

25

Boyd shook his head as his brother stood with an expression of pride most grown men wouldn't share over a T-shirt that read Namaste at the Brewery. It was one of Cade's tamer choices. Foghorn restored and moved into the historic chicken hatchery in the center of town close to two years ago. Petaluma's history was rooted in chickens and farming, so it seemed natural when they started a brewery to name their beers after chicken breeds. There were some crazy names. When the hatchery came up for sale, they jumped on it to complete their whole chicken theme. It had cost them a fortune, but with the help of two second mortgages and their brother the movie star, they'd made it work. Now, the brewery was "hopping," as Patrick liked to joke.

"Hopping. Get it? Hops for beer," he'd said the day he showed them the grand opening artwork.

Christ, Boyd had no idea how he put up with all of them. That wasn't exactly true. He loved them deep in his bones and from the time they were little, he'd taken the job of big brother seriously. The fact that they'd all worked together and helped him raise a son was never lost on Boyd. They loved him back tenfold, even Patrick. Even though that little shit was getting the silent treatment for at least the rest of the day.

"I'll let you go," Cade said, still standing there, arms splayed, admiring his shirt.

Boyd laughed. No matter the day, the fight, or the number of stitches, Cade had a way.

"Okay, yeah. Good talk. See you around, Stitch," Cade said.

"Don't."

There was the look again. "Too soon?" He turned and walked back to the Tap House. "Glad you're okay," he called out, hand raised.

"Me too," Boyd said, returning to his work, still smiling.

Following one glorious day of doing nothing but sleeping and binge watching *Sherlock*, Ella decided her second day off needed to be productive. So, she showered, dressed, and even put on a little lip gloss. She had grocery shopping to do and needed to catch up on the reading assignment for her continuing education credits. Every three months, no matter how brilliant a doctor was, they were required to teach something and learn something. "Give and Grow" was the term after she graduated. It seemed every physician she knew whined about the time it took and the inconvenience. Ella enjoyed learning but would admit it was difficult to switch gears and return to books after spending time in the real practice of patient care, especially trauma. A lecture on pain management seemed removed compared to a gunshot victim screaming at the top of his lungs.

Ella preferred practice and procedure to theory. But, she hadn't seen a gunshot wound in over two years and while it was morbid to want that kind of violence, she wouldn't mind something more than a hand laceration every now and then. Looking to the table where she threw her mail, she noticed her phone vibrating. It was Vienna, Ella's "tied for best friend" as she put it when she and Bri were together, texting to ask if she wanted to join her at Knitterly.

Two people bailed on the 11 a.m. Cricket Loom Weaving class. Sistine asked if we wanted in. Yes?

That sounded like more fun than the grocery store or "Pain Management and Appropriate Treatment for the Terminally Ill." Her stomach growled as she slid her glasses on and she texted back that she'd pick her up at the bakery. She needed food and Vienna owned Sift, the most amazing bakery, even trumping the ones Ella had left behind in San Francisco.

Throwing a book into her bag, she decided to go to the grocery store after class. That should assuage some of the guilt, at least the simple kind brought on by skipping out on chores for time with her friend and baked goods.

When Ella arrived at Sift, Vienna was behind the counter observing Pam, her first official employee, ring up a customer. Ella slipped past the line and into the black, white, and bright yellow dining space of Sift. She took a seat at her favorite round lacquered table in the corner next to an abstract painting that reminded her of dancing tulips. Sift was not only a joy to look at, it was a feast for the senses even before anyone took a bite. Butter, cinnamon, and even banana. Waiting for the crowd to die down, Ella found herself wrapped up in her book and was startled by Vienna's voice.

"I didn't know you read Stephen King. How did I miss that?" she said, setting a French press of coffee and a warm chocolate croissant in the center of one of Vienna's delicate mismatched plates on the table in front of Ella.

Ella flipped the book jacket to hold her place and noticed her friend decked out in a black-and-white apron, her hair back off her soft features in what Ella now knew was a goddess braid. Honestly, Vienna's hair was an accessory all its own. "I used to read him all the time. He's wonderful and this is his new one. Hardback. Don't you love real books?"

"The only hardbacks I read are the book club selections because Mrs. McNaughton likes the pages."

"Me too."

"That does it. You should be in the book club."

Ella loved the idea but wondered if there was something strange about being in a club with Boyd McNaughton's mother. She was overthinking—she'd promised herself to cut down on that.

"He's scary though, right?"

"Twisted and intelligent. There's a difference."

Vienna pressed the plunger in the coffee, poured them both a cup, dusted off a smear of flour from her apron, and sat down.

"How's Pam working out?" Ella asked.

"Good. I can rest for a few minutes and have coffee with you. I get to go to a loom class in the middle of a Sunday. She's perfect."

"Thank you for bringing me food."

"You are most welcome." Vienna's eyes shifted to the register and back to Ella.

"I wasn't going to mention this since you're working, but you're happy. I mean you were happy before, but this is a new level, don't you think?"

Vienna put her hands to her cheeks and beamed. She was a gorgeous woman on an average day, but now that she was in love, she was virtually ethereal.

"That bad, huh?" Ella said, smiling and pulling off a piece of croissant.

"That good. He's great." Vienna sipped her coffee.

Ella laughed. "He is. I take it the thing with his friends got better?"

"Not exactly, but they're going to have to get over the fact that he has a girlfriend now. He can't be a bachelor forever."

"True. And you bake. I mean that's major."

Vienna nodded. "I bake and I'm good in bed."

Ella nearly spit her coffee across the table. She should have been prepared for that one. Vienna certainly wasn't shy, but something about the declaration among sugar and pastry made it seem all the naughtier.

"Does Petaluma's fire chief agree?"

"He came over on Friday and stayed until his shift started this morning."

"Oh, well no wonder you're glowing."

She wiggled her eyebrows over her cup. Ella shook her head as Pam asked Vienna for a price confirmation on morning muffins. Vienna confirmed and stole a piece of Ella's croissant.

"How about you? Any new prospects I need to know about? You know Thad has a friend who is—"

Ella held up her hand, and Vienna laughed.

"Do I need to say anything or is the hand enough this time?" Ella didn't talk about her love life, or like life, or even her lust life. To Bri and Vienna, she might as well be a born-again virgin. Physically that rewind was, of course, impossible, but Ella had been in neutral for over two years now, and it was working for her.

"No, I understand the hand. I mean, I don't understand it, but there's no arguing with it. I don't see why—" She sighed and finished her coffee. "You have to get lonely. No way you'll ever admit it, but as your friend, I need to keep asking."

"Well, there's a creepy guy in chapter two of my new King book. He might be my new book boyfriend."

Vienna sighed. "Well, maybe fiction is safer than what's out there in the dating world."

"Ah, ah, we do not say the D word. Besides, you probably snatched up the last dreamy, throw-me-over-your-shoulder guy in town." Ella tried for humor to deflect off a subject she knew most friends discussed.

She enjoyed talking with Bri and Vienna about their love lives. She'd laughed and cried with them, which was more than she'd ever done before moving to Petaluma. Ella was working on connecting, and it had made all the difference in her life, but she wasn't ready for full disclosure of her heart. She made great progress sorting through her feelings, but the truth was she was still embarrassed by her past and questioned if her friends would see her differently once they knew.

Vienna beamed at the mention of Thad and stood. "I'll let you avoid the D word once again because you've given me the over-the-shoulder visual, but someday I'll get into that heart of yours, my friend."

Ella took the last bite of her croissant, wiped her fingers, and made a show of opening her book and returning to her devious book boyfriend. She peeked over the cover as Vienna laughed.

"Impossible. You are impossible," her friend said and slid back behind the counter while Ella rejoined the safety of Stephen King's imagination.

Vienna and Ella met during a kickboxing class at the Y. Ella had been in town less than a month when she took a flyer off the post office bulletin board. Vienna nearly roundhouse kicked her in the jaw that first day, and they'd been "up for anything" partners ever since. Vienna Platt had a zest for life, a positive vibe that had been as refreshing as Bri's strength. Ella knew all about the human mind and the methods for avoiding depression. She'd spent a life needing no one, seeing it as weakness. It was not a mistake that her first steps in Petaluma were to confront the overwhelming sense that she needed help, support. It had proved a tough hurdle for her to clear, but she'd been given two women who asked to be her friend. They practically demanded it.

In that first year, Ella took up every class, went to every event she could find, including the Ugly Dog Contest, all to escape herself. In the process, she learned to make soba and crochet and with practice, she'd mastered a roundhouse kick nearly as impressive as Vienna's.

Looking back on the singular purpose she had when she'd arrived, she could have made so many wrong decisions in the heat of anger and self-loathing. She could have popped pills, which became her mother's crutch soon after finding lipstick on her husband's collar, or she could have allowed her heart to completely freeze over like her sister Becca. Even outside her insane family, Ella had seen doctors self-destruct. No matter the mistake, she wouldn't allow that to happen.

Life's tornado swept her up—along with everything she thought she wanted once upon a time—and deposited her in the heart of a place she was beginning to think was right where she belonged. Practice and patience, she reminded herself as she realized Vienna was now by the door gesturing it was time to go. Practice and patience were the keys to good medicine and maybe even healing herself.

Chapter Four

Boyd had already tasted what they were tentatively calling "Shamo," named after a Japanese chicken with a long neck. According to Patrick, the label was going to be epic.

"The chicken already looks like he walks upright, so we added some biceps and a tattoo. It's genius," Patrick had exclaimed weeks before he'd climbed up Boyd's ass about the deadline. And now, as he leaned against his work table, Boyd could rest easy that the beer behind the label would be epic too. Of course, his brothers still needed to do a taste, but if they didn't like it, they were assholes. Especially Patrick, who he hadn't seen or spoken to all weekend. Smart man.

"Are we done fighting?"

Speak of the devil. Boyd heard his brother's voice but didn't turn around. "It's Monday. You back for more, little brother?"

"How's your hand?"

"I'm no longer answering that question. Stitches come out the end of the week."

"Good. I'm sorry."

Boyd glanced over his shoulder, surprised by the simplicity of Trick's usual embellished words. His brother could have easily pulled from his arsenal of sarcasm or charm, but when Boyd met his eyes, they looked as tired as his own, and with that, he forgot to be pissed.

"Me too," Boyd said. He knew Patrick's job wasn't easy. Dealing with schmoozers and distributors was Boyd's worst nightmare, but he wasn't about to get into a my-job-is-harder-than-yours debate. "I might, maybe, minimize your deadlines and the pressure you're under."

"Most of the time." He smirked.

"Yeah, well it's done. The beer is done." He knew his brother understood that was his apology. Boyd had recognized the urgency and fixed the problem. That was all Trick was going to get. "Do you want a taste?"

"Um... Yeah, I want a taste. This better be good. Keeping me waiting with all your temperamental creative garbage."

Boyd laughed. They were nearly back to normal. He handed him a pint glass.

Patrick was an expert at knowing what people wanted. Boyd crafted the beer, with some input when he was in the mood, but Patrick knew what would sell. Pissed Boyd off to no end, but he listened because there was no sense in owning a brewery if no one liked what they were putting out.

"Darker than I thought it was going to be, but clean. More of an APA than an IPA."

Boyd scoffed because he hated being confined to labels, but they'd already had one fight this week, so he let it go. "I'd still call it pale, but maybe more toward American, like you said. Midrange."

"Good size head."

Boyd nodded and returned to his computer as the glass hit his brother's lips. He hated the first taste of any batch, but especially one he was this psyched about. Sometimes it took him a month of experimentation before he finally drew up a recipe. Especially for summer brews, because he tended to lean toward heavier lagers. Light and or fruity took a herculean effort. Every brewery, and there were more and more these days, did an IPA. Most of them were all right. Boyd didn't brew beer for it to be average. He wanted a creation, which was complicated further with larger batches. Patrick wanted something for the upcoming tap house and a local distribution route he'd spent years working on.

His brother set the glass down on the work table next to Boyd, the unofficial signal he was ready to share his thoughts. Patrick wasn't smiling, which wasn't a bad thing. He was thinking. A good sign. If he didn't like it, didn't taste all the layers Boyd intended or the hell of a finish that was sheer luck, Boyd would start over. He'd be butt hurt, but all three of them had to love what they offered up to the public or the endless hours were for nothing.

"No grapefruit," Patrick said.

"Nope."

"Sorachi Ace and..."

"Citra," Boyd added as if he were revealing a trade secret.

His brother took another sip.

"What's the ABV on this?"

"Five point nine."

He nodded.

"Are you going to tell me what you think, or stand there swirling it around like it's friggin' wine?"

Patrick laughed. "You must like this one. Sorachi Ace is a risk. Remember that one Plymouth Brew House tried a couple of years back?"

Boyd remembered but didn't say anything. He never commented on another brewery's output in case there were beer gods somewhere waiting to screw with him.

"There's no grease, and it's got the right amount of bitter," Patrick said.

"You like the finish? The finish is what makes it. Well, that and the smell."

"Fresh-cut grass."

Boyd grinned. "Yeah, that's right, little brother. Fresh-cut grass in time for summer."

"It's a hell of a beer, Boyd."

"I know."

"Yeah? You seemed a little nervous."

"Right. The day you make me nervous is the day I—"

"How'd you balance the lemon? I mean, it's almost tropical."

"The lemon in the Sorachi was a bitch, but then I figured it out. Citra makes it even and gets rid of the bubble gum."

"Bubble gum?"

"Yeah, I taste bubble gum when it's off. No bubble gum."

Patrick finished his last sip.

"Are we still calling it Shamo?" Boyd asked, relieved both because the first taste was over and he wasn't fighting with his brother anymore.

"Well, we were going to go with Shamo because the Sorachi is Japanese, but now that I've tasted it, I think we need to address the tropical."

"Tropical what?" Cade asked, joining them with a glob of mustard on the corner of his mouth and an overstuffed hoagie sandwich that was practically begging for a plate. Boyd remembered he hadn't eaten since Mason handed over his toast crust before getting out of the truck at school.

Boyd poured another pint and gave it to Cade.

"Ah, Frankenstein is finally out of the lab. Is it any good?"

Patrick nodded.

Cade, only driven by taste, finished chewing the bite of sandwich and took a big gulp. There was no need for him to look at the color or texture. He served beer and once the remodel was finally finished, he would run the Foghorn Tap House. Cade could pair any beer with any food from prime rib to a Snickers bar. He never cared about appearances, so long as the taste was there. Boyd knew already that Cade would love the finish.

"Oh, hell yeah." He wiped the back of his hand across his lips. "Well done. I get the tropical now and the dry finish. Nice. Shamo Sunset."

"We can add some water and a sunset to the label. I held the final print until we tasted it," Patrick said.

And with that, they'd created another beer. Boyd felt his shoulders drop and his chest relax because once again he'd been given a reprieve. Whatever shoe or change was on its way was not dropping today, he thought. He knew they'd all considered leaving in a cloud of frustration at least a dozen times over the last seven years, but the three of them knew that like a great rock band, it would be the death of their brewery. They were each vital and as Boyd poured another round, he knew he'd stitch his hand up a hundred times for moments like this with his brothers.

Ella finished a twenty-nine-mile bike ride, showered, and loaded her breakfast dishes while brushing her teeth. Monday mornings were her favorite. Things felt right at the beginning of a new week. She packed her lunch and grabbed an apple out of the fruit bowl on her small round table in the alcove of her kitchen. Her house was clean, laundry done, and it was time to go back to work. She wasn't ready for another double, but she was more than ready to get back into her scrubs. She had no idea how people worked from home. She'd no doubt start alphabetizing her spices if she had one more day off. After watering her one plant, Ella smiled at her tidy home and grabbed her keys.

"How is that even possible?" Bri asked as Ella handed over the bag of salt-and-vinegar chips she'd agreed to pick up on her way in. "No one likes Monday. That's not even a gray area or a minority opinion. No one. You are completely alone with your Monday love."

Ella shook her head. "I think a lot of doctors like Monday. I like them because weekend shifts are usually chaotic, people out getting into trouble, you know? Monday is a new week. Everyone returns to their responsibilities and order is restored."

Bri stared at her and crunched into three chips at a time. The ER was empty so she had joined Ella while she put her things away in the locker room. "No one," Bri repeated. "There are coffee cups about it, memes, T-shirts. The hatred of Monday is an American pastime."

"I thought that was baseball." Ella pulled her hair back with an elastic at her wrist and closed her locker.

Bri kept crunching. "Yes, baseball, apple pie, and Monday loathing."

"Well, I like it. Maybe it's left over from working in a big hospital. Mondays were tame." She put her stethoscope around her neck and walked into the hall.

"Forget about work. Don't you hate that the weekend is over? Even if you're working a Saturday or Sunday shift, there's still a weekend feel when you get off. Sleeping in, a larger newspaper, brunch. Remember when we went to Wishbone for brunch a few weeks ago?"

Ella nodded before adding a stuffed bunny and a coloring book she'd brought in for the collection box. The hospital was putting together spring baskets for the kids in pediatrics.

"We had yummy food and Bloody Marys. Wasn't it hard getting up the next morning, having to shake off the fun of the weekend?"

"I had orange juice and worked that night." Ella patted her on the shoulder as the glass doors buzzed open and an older man leaning on his son or grandson slowly approached.

Dehydration, Ella thought but held judgment until she had more information.

"Duty calls," she said to Bri as Wilma, the triage nurse, asked the gentleman to take a seat for her initial assessment.

Ella turned her back, still eavesdropping to see if she was right, but Bri kept on espousing the evils of Monday, a perfectly decent day.

"Never confuse having a job with having a life," Bri said softly next to her as she threw out her empty chip bag.

Ella instinctively rolled her shoulders as what felt like judgment settled at the back of her neck. Familiar, but less hurtful.

She stopped listening to Wilma and met Bri's eyes, unable to determine if she'd meant the comment as a jab. "Do you think you're the first person to tell me I work too much?"

"No, but you can't like Monday. It's a cry for help."

Ella shook her head. "You're a crazy person."

"True, but I'm your crazy person and this"—she extended her hands to include the whole of their department—"can't be something you look forward to after pancakes and time with your girls."

"I like my job."

"Too much."

"Oh, okay. And you determined this how?"

"When you said Monday is your favorite day of the week."

"This is ridiculous." Ella heard Wilma take the patient to Exam 1.

"You are comfortable commenting on my lack of drawer organizers, my need to hug, and my attraction to cruel men, except for Sam."

Ella and Bri bowed their heads. "Sam was a wonderful man," they said in concert.

"I'm admittedly an open book of mess, but I'm calling you out on Monday. Stop it."

"I'll review your objections," Ella said.

Wilma handed Bri the chart.

"Do that," she said and walked toward Exam 1. "Any guesses? I know how you love this game."

"Dehydration," Ella said quietly.

Bri opened the chart shy of the door and gave Ella the thumbs up.

"Knew it," she said to herself as the door closed behind Bri.

Ella leaned against the wall and crossed her arms. Her initial pride at her on-site diagnosis turned to angst. She was pathetic; hospitals were her life. She spent more time sanitized than she did in the sun. What did that say about her?

"Hey, Wilma. Do you like Mondays?"

The tiny blonde wheeled around in her chair. "Is that a trick question? No one—"

"Likes Monday. Right, I know. No. One."

Ella considered why she preferred work over her downtime. She guessed, as with all things, it was rooted in her upbringing or her past experiences. Most likely, she didn't know any other way. Even before she knew what work was, she'd preferred school to summer, study hall to recess. Bri was right—what the hell was wrong with her?

Ella patted her hair and tightened her ponytail when Bri emerged and called her into the exam room. This was officially not a good Monday.

Chapter Five

By Friday, Ella had shoved the conversation with Bri to the back of her mind. That afternoon, one of the doctors from urgent care had to leave because his wife went into labor, and Ella agreed to fill in. She was on call anyway and didn't have set plans for her day off.

Oh, shut up Bri.

The overhead clock flipped to one o'clock and Ella made another circle through the empty back exam area. She was dressed in business casual and a lab coat, which was a nice change. The urgent care was frequently short-staffed, but the birth of a child carried some weight even among doctors.

Why did it seem like everyone was jetting off somewhere, in love, or having babies but her? Maybe she should plan a trip someplace sunny and warm. Unexpectedly memories of the last time she was on a sunny, warm beach came to mind, and she decided she'd stick with the Petaluma River for now.

Urgent care was adjacent to the ER. There was rarely a true emergency, so they were pretty much the same thing. Except the vending machines in urgent care accepted credit cards and seemed to have an endless supply of Dots. Ella wasn't certain if it was years of being told they would rot her teeth or that they were always well stocked, but she loved Dots.

A red one had settled into her left molar as Felix, the triage nurse from the front desk, notified her she had a patient. Ella wiggled her tongue to dislodge the candy and pondered what she could possibly be treating at one in the afternoon. Maybe a school kid scraped his knee getting off the bus, or a teacher had a sinus infection and her primary care doctor couldn't fit her in?

Bri's words creeped back in again. Maybe Ella did work too much, because she enjoyed guessing what was behind the exam room door almost as much as she liked piecing together diagnoses. Although, she was rarely right with the door game.

Adding another "not even close" to her record was Boyd McNaughton. He stood propped against the bed as he had been about a week ago when she'd stitched up his hand.

"You work here too?" he asked, flashing a hint of a smile and in a much better mood.

Ella ignored every cliché to keep herself from going all *Grey's Anatomy* on the poor guy. Turned out after a few nights of sleep and some sexy talk with Vienna over a Cricket Loom, Boyd McNaughton was an attractive man. Dark wavy hair, huge shoulders that would put Bri's misguided fantasy about the scuzzy, adulterer Dr. Baker to shame. His eyes were deep set and green. Were his eyes green last week?

Hello, paging Dr. Walters. We are not good at picking out men, remember? Check the guy's hand and turn it over to the nurse.

She didn't even work urgent care. Maybe this was a sign... *oh no you don't*. This was not a sign or fate or any of that other stupid crap that leave women with puffy eyes and crumbs in their beds. Damn Vienna and her shower stories.

He needs his stitches out and you are a physician. You've been in people's chests as they were wheeled into the operating room. Massive car pileups, crushed bones. Remember the guy who pulled a knife on you when you told him his brother had died in the ambulance? Remember that? You're a badass, Ella. This man is not attractive, do you hear me?

She stepped closer and took his arm. He smelled like a spice cabinet. *Son of a bitch.*

"Not usually. I'm filling in. Dr. Brandis is about to be a father."

"Yeah? Well, I guess doctors get to have babies too." Their eyes locked and for a moment, it felt like they'd both realized how babies were made. Redirecting her attention back where it belonged, Ella checked for redness or infection. Nothing.

"Looks good," she said.

"Great. Can we cut these off?"

She glanced over her shoulder, still holding his arm because the warmth and smell of him didn't belong anywhere near a sterile exam room. She felt an unexpected pull toward something messier, less cold.

Being near him was suddenly like watching trees sway in the wind from a window or the sound of birds singing on a porch. He seemed to embody everything she wasn't, and that unnerved her. Scanning for any nurse on duty to save her from her obvious hormone or sugar imbalance, Ella found no one. Not a soul. What was it with nurses and Boyd McNaughton?

"Yes. All healed up. Let me get—" She craned her neck one last time. She could feel the steady pulse at his wrist. Her eyes traveled up his massive forearm to the velvet dust of hair that disappeared into the rolled cuff of his sleeve. Honestly, she needed to stay tired because this was ridiculous.

"I'll do it myself and get you out of here," she said, happy to return to the mechanics of her job.

"Perfect." He scooted forward and Ella washed her hands.

She'd snipped the first stitch when the door opened and a young boy said, "Dad?"

Ella glanced up to find a kid with the same dark waves barely above his eyes, bright white Adidas, and a backpack that was slipping fast off his shoulders. He was lanky, a fairly typical preteen or teen until the eyes. The eyes were a dead ringer for the man she was unstitching. This was Boyd's son.

"I'm getting my stitches out here. Don't you knock? Who raised you?"

"Some guy who smells like beer."

"Watch it."

Ella went back to removing the stitches. She was certain this child's mother, Mrs. McNaughton, would appear any minute. Ella had been lusting after a father, someone's husband.

Dear God, it's like I am prewired for disaster.

"Sorry. You don't smell like beer all the time. Uncle Trick said you were here and I"—he stopped at the sight of Ella's work—"Holy balls that's nasty."

"Mouth," Boyd said, glancing at his hand and then quickly back at the wall.

His son turned his back to them. "Okay, this is better. I can't see anything this way. Man, this place smells like the new toilet bowl cleaner we started using." His backpack dropped to the floor next to him.

Was this kid at home everywhere?

"I needed to talk to you right away. I was at school today."

"That's a good start," Boyd said.

"She comes up to me during lunch. Like out of nowhere, and I've got my tray with the Friday burrito that kind of looks like a scab. Not the point."

Ella peeked up again like he was some television show she couldn't stop watching. He was facing the wall and somehow managing to have a complete conversation with himself, all the while assuming his father was listening. Ella went back to work.

"The food doesn't matter. The thing is, she scared the balls... I mean she scared me and I dropped the tray right at her feet. It went splat and I froze like one of Grandpa's rabbits. Then I bolted out of the cafeteria. I'm done-zo, right? I mean complete loser move. I ran."

"Well, it's hard to make dumping a burrito at a girl's feet look cool. To be clear, we are talking about *she* she, right?"

"Is there any other she, Dad?"

Ella wanted to look up again but kept snipping.

"No. Maybe she... won't remember tomorrow?"

"I rode my bike all the way here and that's what you've got?"

Boyd hissed a little as Ella pulled the second-to-last stitch. "Mase, she freaked you out and you dropped your lunch. It's not like it's the end of the world."

Mase, cute name, Ella thought right as he peeked over his shoulder, the need to see his dad apparently overriding his squeamishness. Boyd must have noticed the lost look on his son's face because she could virtually see him backpedal to connect. "It probably would have been cooler to say something and blow it off, but you were nervous. She'll get over it."

"I blew it," Boyd's son huffed.

"Not true," she said as if to herself, and both father and son grew quiet. Ella pulled out the last stitch.

"Did the doc say that?" the boy asked.

Ella nodded, surprised they'd heard her.

"This is Dr. Walters. Dr. Walters, this is my son, Mason."

"Oh, right. Sorry. Nice to meet you. Are you done with my dad?"

"Nice to meet you too, Mason. You can call me Ella. I'm nearly finished." She placed her scissors on the tray.

"You don't think I blew it?" He moved closer to her, his expression as if she were a fortune-teller with all the answers he needed.

She was far from that, Ella thought. She shook her head.

"No, I don't think you blew it." Pulling off her gloves, she had no clue why she was so compelled to respond. She certainly wasn't an expert on relationships, high school or otherwise.

"How so?" he asked.

"You were nervous. Girls like that."

"They do?" Boyd and Mason said in sync.

"How do you know?" Mason asked.

She wondered how to answer that question coming from a young boy. She would have been insulted if a man had asked.

"Mase, she's a woman," his father helped.

"Oh, yeah. But she's old."

Boyd closed his eyes. "Sorry."

Ella laughed. "That's okay. He's right. I mean, from his perspective."

"How old are you?"

"Not another word." Boyd held up the hand not being bandaged. "Back on the bike. Look both ways and I'll see you at home."

"No, no, wait. This is good." Fidgeting now in a valiant effort to postpone his dad's next words, he pulled over a chair. It got caught on the strap of his backpack and dragged that along. Ignoring it, he sat. "I'll be good. I'll sit right here."

Boyd looked at Ella, eyes pleading.

"I don't mind. Mason, I'm thirty-six."

"Really?" They both said in concert again.

"Wow, do you two practice this at home?"

His son laughed. Ella had forgotten what child laughter sounded like. It was as if even more trees and birds and sun-soaked breeze blew through the antiseptic air. She found herself wondering if Dr. Brandis's wife had had the baby yet. Were they sitting in awe of the change in their world? Did people recognize that the air changed as soon as a baby was born, or did it take years before an energy like Mason came into being? Ella had delivered a few babies in her career, most of them under less than optimal circumstances, but she'd never thought of them as little people. Standing in front of her now, eyes wide with questions, it was hard not to notice and enjoy a kid like Mason.

Boyd tried not to react to her first name or acknowledge that the name Ella Walters suited her. It rang regal and efficient. It wasn't often that Boyd met a woman like Dr. Walters, and that was exactly why he needed to finish up this little visit to the urgent care and be on his way.

"Ella," Mason said.

Boyd cleared his throat and his son glanced over.

"Sorry, Dr. Ella. I wasn't meaning disrespect about your age. You don't look as old as my dad. He's only a year older than you and he's, well, you look great, for an older person, girl. You know what I mean."

Boyd noticed his son's feet move beneath the chair as he witnessed a young man slowly backing out of an insult. It was entertaining.

"I do. Thank you for the compliment, and you're forgiven. Can you hand me that tape over there? One more step and you can have your dad back. Sounds like you guys have some strategy to work out."

Mason handed her the tape and plopped back down in the chair dramatically. Ella's smile wasn't strained or awkward like it was the first time they'd met. She'd either gotten some sleep or she was more comfortable around kids.

"Don't shy away from the nerves. It's a sign that we fluster you, and that's flattering in and of itself." She washed her hands and applied another pair of gloves.

Did her hands ever chap from all that scrubbing?

"See, guys have it all wrong with the casual and cool routine. Women like real and vulnerable. It's attractive."

"Even tray dropping?"

"Oh, especially tray dropping. That's a complete breakdown of control."

"Huh." Mason nodded like he was listening to a seminar, and Boyd hid his smile.

"I guarantee she was on the bus thinking about you."

"Serious?"

Ella nodded.

"You're tall," Mason said, his mind seeming to wander off, as it did, in a million directions.

"I am. Five nine."

"My dad is tall." Mason glanced at the doctor, who suddenly seemed uncomfortable. He had a way of putting things right on the table without regard for interpretation. Boyd loved that about this age. Before high school, kids were right on the edge of self-conscious, and it wouldn't be long before he would change again. Lately Boyd tried to memorize every phase, but it was impossible.

"You're pretty tall too. How old are you?" Ella finished taping his hand and changed the subject. It was well played.

"Thirteen. Just turned."

47

"God help us all," Boyd said as she snapped off her gloves again.

"Do you have any brothers?" Mason asked, and Boyd recognized his son's move into twenty questions.

Ella shook her head. "A sister. Older. She lives back home in LA."

"Huh, you're from LA? How long have you lived here?"

"Almost two years."

"Are you ready to go back to LA yet?"

Ella laughed. "Not yet. It's nice here."

"What kind of doctor are you?"

"Mase, I think that's enough. I'll bet Dr. Walters needs us to get out of here."

"What? It's not like we talk with doctors all the time, or females. We are like a den of dudes." He laughed and shrugged his shoulders as if he was already comfortable with a stranger. "That's what my Gran says when we're all together and she's the only girl."

Boyd raised his eyebrows and questioned where all of this was coming from. Turning his hand, which no longer felt so itchy, he envied Mason's ease, especially around the one woman Boyd had even bothered to notice in years. He doubted his son even realized he was talking with a girl right now, smiling and being himself without breaking a sweat. There was no way to show him that without getting an eye roll, but it was the truth.

"I mean, except Mom, but she's... different," Mason said.

Boyd could tell the good doctor was trying to figure out that last part. He couldn't blame her.

"I'm an emergency room doctor. I worked at San Francisco General Hospital, and then I moved here," Ella said quickly and efficiently as if she were reading from a cue card.

"Why?"

"I... wanted a break."

"General Hospital like the soap opera?"

"How do you know about soap operas?" Boyd asked, standing from the bed now.

"Gran watches *General Hospital*. It's awesome. Someone's always crying or taking off their clothes. You wouldn't believe what they show on TV."

"Great. Are we done?" he asked, making a note to talk with his mom.

Ella nodded and the corners of her mouth quirked. Her mouth. Feelings Boyd had long forgotten rushed to the surface of his skin. Jesus, maybe his son's adolescence was contagious. Thankfully, this was the last time he'd need to see Ella Walters.

"Okay, we've wasted enough of the doctor's time. Let's get home."

"I'm an only child," Mason said as they walked out.

"Oh, so lucky." She walked with them, seeming more at ease and lighter again.

Boyd had watched people humor Mason throughout his childhood to varying degrees, but she was genuinely interested in talking with him.

"You think?" Mason said.

"I do. You'll have to meet my sister sometime. Believe me, you'll be grateful for the solitude."

Mason laughed, and Boyd lost his focus one more time before moving his son in front of him and closer to the front door. He'd seen Mason with his mom. Claire was good with him during the short periods of time she was around, but like Mason told the doctor, his Gran called them a den of dudes. Boyd's father also had a saying: "If it ain't broke, don't fix it." He and Mason were fine. Now that his one and only medical emergency had passed, things would be back to normal.

After quick goodbyes and practically tearing Mason out to his truck, Boyd changed the subject and offered to buy pizza for dinner. Single dudes could have all the takeout they wanted.

Chapter Six

*E*lla contemplated returning her sister's call and the two text messages that followed, but she couldn't muster up the strength. She knew that would sound awful to anyone who hadn't met Becca, or Rebecca Walters-Blanchforth as she routinely introduced herself, complete with a noncommittal handshake. Ella and her sister were two years apart and back when she was Becca, they had a bit more in common but still nowhere near the sisterly bond represented in movies and television shows. Ella and Rebecca, an almost forty-year-old woman who at their last family event pondered over her second glass of wine, "Wouldn't it be divine to own a little shop on Coronado to tinker with?" now had nothing in common.

There was no one to blame except their parents, of course, but Ella found blaming the dysfunction on her upbringing boring. There was nothing she could do about the lack of love and overabundance of spine-straight structure, so somewhere around twenty-five she chose to count herself as a survivor and move on with her own life. Time spent with her parents was limited and nonexistent during those lucky three hundred and however many days they were busy "living their second half." Ella had hated the absence as a child, but as an adult, she coveted any distance from her mother and father.

Her parents, known to the world as Dr. and Mrs. Langston Walters, had a toxic relationship according to some online worksheet Ella found herself taking last December when her mother had called her a "callous deserter who was going nowhere fast," after she'd purposely booked a double shift so she didn't have to return home for Christmas. "Extremely Toxic," the results had declared. As a rule, Ella avoided all things extremely anything since breaking free of San Francisco.

Outside of the occasional outburst over something they needed, her parents didn't seem to care. Her sister, on the other hand, made things more difficult. Ella had attempted an on-again-off-again relationship with Rebecca outside of their upbringing, as adults, but it never worked. They'd been pitted against one another growing up, and some habits were nearly impossible to unlearn. Turned out trust and nurture needed to be taught among siblings, Ella had learned in her freshman year psychology class.

Her mother and father must have skipped that part of parenting and jumped right to which daughter was the favorite of the moment or who was "dragging the family name through the mud." The latter was usually Ella's department, which allowed Becca to flit around on a cloud of favored that only expanded as they got older. Truth was, Becca Walters had been a privileged girl trapped in the ignorance and indifference money allowed. Rebecca Walters-Blanchforth was a bitch.

Ella was certain her sister would say the same about her. She'd spat it to her face on at least two occasions, so Ella didn't feel guilty for simply thinking it. Her family was what it was, and Ella usually kept the whole mess tucked away unless her sister called or texted. That's when it all came spilling out like an overpacked box. The latest spill was her sister's relentless drive to plan an anniversary party for their parents. Ella was certain she had "assigned tasks" and that her sister was steaming at being ignored. Ella picked up her phone, her thumbs hovering, and set it back on the coffee table, opting instead to finish the last chapters of her book. Stephen King, even with half the cast of characters dead, was less daunting than her sister, let alone trying to understand how their parents' marriage was something worth celebrating. She'd call her tomorrow.

The phone vibrated again. Ella planted her feet on the ground in front of her couch, sat up straight, prepared for confrontation, and touched the green button on her phone.

"Hel—"

"You know, E, I get that you have some delusion that you're better than the rest of us, but it's rude. You're rude," Becca spewed.

Ella tossed her glasses on her coffee table and rubbed the pressure point between her eyes.

"Are you there? Effing Christmas, did you hang up on me?"

"I'm here, Becca."

"Are you sick? Why are you whispering?"

She wasn't whispering. She was merely trying to counter the noise her sister had forced into her peaceful home.

"I'm fine. What do you need?"

"Need?" she scoffed. "Darling, I need exactly nothing. I'm simply hoping you will acknowledge you are a member of this family for approximately four hours on May seventh. That is the moment, forty-five years ago to the day, that our parents vowed to love and cherish each other. Do you think you can grace us with an appearance?"

Ella's eyes were still closed, as if that would keep the impending nightmare at bay. "Sure. What do you need me to do? Are you're putting the whole thing together?"

"I gave up relying on you a long time ago. I have a staff. It's going to be amazing. All I need you to do is show up in something other than those pajamas you wear to work and try to be nice to Mom and Dad. They want you there."

"Do they."

"Of course they do. E, every family has... a dynamic. I don't know why you're so hard on ours. Some of Mom's friends are flying in, all of Dad's colleagues, even a few of the now extremely accomplished women we went to school with will be there. Basically, anyone who is anyone in our circle is gathering to celebrate."

Becca was in what Ella referred to as her Fairy-tale Mode. It was an affect she adopted, usually in between her lunches with the ladies or her all-important causes, that included a complete rewrite of their childhood. She recast everyone as whimsical characters and, as expected, made herself the princess. Everything was perfect, occasionally she slipped in a "mommy" or a "daddy," and Ella played the role of the evil witch, the one with the wart on her nose, or the one who shoved children into the oven. There was no way to snap Becca out of it, so Ella conserved her energy and played along.

"It will be fantastic. I received the invitation. It's stunning."

Her sister released a soft "humph." At least she'd stopped rambling.

"Thanks for checking on me. I'll be there."

"Why are you so... snide?"

"Okay. Let's wrap this up. I'm happy you're happy with the way things are going. Wish your staff well. I'll see you in—"

Becca had hung up. Peace and quiet, finally. Well, quiet at least. It would take a very long bike ride before peace was restored.

Boyd, Patrick, and Cade stood on the main floor of what in two weeks would be the Foghorn Brewery Tap House. The floors were concrete and the old bay doors that were rusted and barely moveable when they bought the place were now refinished and fitted with heavy glass windows from top to bottom. They overlooked a beer garden that Cade had been dreaming about since that first day they met to talk about starting a business. Boyd surveyed the beamed ceiling, exposed vents, and polished wood. The far wall was repurposed wooden egg crate pieces, some of them still with old logos. The place was coming together. They turned to face Cade's pride and joy—his bar.

"I might cry," his younger brother said, gliding his hand over the glossy pale wood surface.

"Don't," Patrick said, handing him a beer. "You don't want one?"

he asked Boyd.

"I'm good." He took in the smell of polish and ran his boot along a crack in the floor that Aspen Pane, their Wonder Woman disguised as a business manager, termed a defect. Cade declared it was "purposefully placed character." The petty arguments didn't matter now because the place was going to be a hit. Boyd could feel it, and somehow the looming success made his mind spin. What did that mean for the brewery? Would he eventually need to hire someone to help him, and how would he keep the quality from going to hell if he had to rely on other people?

"Maybe he's losing his hearing," Cade said and chomped into what Boyd recognized from the menu as their buffalo chicken wrap.

"You with us, old-timer? The mugs are staying where they are, but once we get the pints, pilsners, and tulips, should they hang or stack?" Patrick pointed behind the bar.

"Does it matter? How are you hanging a pint, or a pilsner? Leave them in the washing crates behind the bar or chilled."

"Glasses need to be on display. It's a thing."

"Then it's your thing, no need for my input. I'll bet after the first week, Cade will have them wherever it works for him and his bartenders."

Cade barely caught a piece of chicken before it fell to the floor and popped it into his mouth.

"How is it that you eat all the time, but I'm the one creeping closer to a dad bod?"

"Sex. I have a lot of it," Cade said through his chewing.

Patrick and Boyd both stared in bewilderment, wondering how their brother managed the simple tasks of life like grocery shopping and paying the electric bill. The man was a muscled adolescent.

"With yourself?" Patrick asked, and Boyd laughed like they too were kids.

"No, Brothers Monk, not with myself. I date and that often leads to sex. You two should try it."

"How the hell much sex are we talking about here? I saw you eat two burritos for breakfast a couple of hours ago." Patrick said, wide-eyed.

Cade wiggled his brows. "Wouldn't you two like to know."

"No, nope, we do not want to know. No one wants to know," Boyd said.

"And I'm not a monk—I had a date last night," Patrick added, overly defensive as usual.

"Really, how'd it go?" Aspen said over the pencil in her mouth as she carried a box into the bar. She put it on one of the round high-top tables and pushed the pencil into her hair.

Those must be the labels, Boyd thought before Patrick practically dropped his beer.

"Fine. Great, if you must know," Patrick said to all of them, avoiding eye contact with her.

"Oh, I'll bet. Sex?" Cade asked, oblivious or not caring that they were in mixed company. "Don't answer that." He tossed the last piece of his sandwich into his mouth and wiped his hands. "The answer is no."

"You're an asshole." Patrick reached into the box and pulled out a roll of labels. Boyd noticed the familiar butcher paper color and walked behind the bar.

"What? Boyd's the one who wanted to know about my hot body. He's the girl. No offense, Aspen."

"None taken. Feel free to discuss all hot bodies in my presence." Aspen handed Patrick two pieces of paper.

"Good?" she asked him.

Patrick was still turning the labels in his hand, and Cade leaned over his shoulder.

"Yeah, better than good," Patrick said, shrugging their brother off. "They're perfect. Worthy of the beer, Boyd."

Boyd glanced up from checking out the taps. He wasn't all that interested in the bottle labels. They were clever, but he tried to stay out of the hype and promotion because he believed it messed with his creativity. If he ever started pandering to public perception or tried to create a taste around some image, he'd be doomed. Call it superstition, but he believed to do his job well, he needed a kind of vacuum. He had a feeling that might become more difficult as the brewery grew.

"Looks good," he said to appease his brother. "You decided against cans."

"It needs to be in a bottle," Patrick said.

"Agreed."

"Cans are making a comeback," Cade added. "How about you, Boyd, any dates... sex?"

"Nope. Still a monk." Boyd turned one of the beer mugs in his hand and started thinking about fall and what he was going to do for a stout this year. Now that he'd solved Lemongate, it was time to create again.

"Mason tells me you and the ER doctor are getting cozy," Patrick said.

"The one who stitched his hand?" Cade asked.

Patrick nodded. "Mase stopped by while our dear brother was having his stitches out and the doctor gave the kid some advice on girls. There were some sparks between the adults, from what I hear."

There was no way his son used the word "cozy" or "sparks." His brother was fishing, and Boyd was about to remind them both who was born first in the family.

"Seriously? Why am I the last to know?" Cade asked.

"Because there is nothing to know. Trick is making shit up in his mind. He does it for a living. Ella did take out my stitches because she's a doctor, and she gave Mason some advice on girls, well, advice on 'she.'"

"Ella. Pretty name," Cade said, moving to Patrick's side.

Yup, they were squaring off.

"She's blond, according to our astute nephew, and tall."

"Tall, huh? I'll bet she'd be perfect for Thad. He's single. Right, Aspen?"

Aspen, being female and smarter than the two lugheads combined, didn't even acknowledge the question.

Boyd leveled a stare at his brothers and tried not to laugh as they stood shoulder to shoulder. "Is this the part where I get jealous and say, 'No. She doesn't like Thad. I want her.'?" He smacked the back of

Cade's head. "What is this, amateur hour?"

Patrick laughed.

"She is beautiful," Aspen said and Boyd, who'd almost made a clean escape, knew he was in trouble. "She's in our book club now. Vienna from the bakery invited her. Apparently, she reads Stephen King. I remember your mom tried to get us to read Gillian Flynn last year, but that's the closest we've come to dark. Anyway, she hangs out at the bakery a lot if you're looking to casually bump into her."

All of them stared at Aspen. Boyd didn't know where to begin. He had no idea his mom was in a book club, let alone that she liked dark books. Hell, did he know anything anymore?

"Our mom is in your book club?" Patrick beat Boyd to the question.

Aspen nodded after opening her yogurt and taking a bite. "She's one of our founding members. She does our taxes every year. Of course she's in the book club. Sistine is the president, and then me, Vienna..." She took another bite and glanced at the ceiling as if she were putting together an organization chart on the fly. "That's right, then Vienna recruited Bri because she comes into the bakery every once in a while. She's a nurse at the hospital. Another connection to Ella." She took her last bite and shrugged. "So, that's a pretty extensive network. Weird how things are connected, right?"

Yeah, weird. Boyd and his brothers seemed equally stunned at the things that went on without their knowledge.

"What are you guys reading?"

"Well, it's a... women's book club, so we're not guys."

Patrick rolled his eyes and stuck his hands in his pockets.

"Mostly fiction." She peeled a banana and bit into it. "We like a little bit of everything."

They all nodded, and Boyd tried to remember the last time he'd read something that wasn't eighth-grade required or on the internet.

"Oh, and my brother is not her type," she added.

"Why not?" they all asked, including Boyd, who couldn't stop himself.

"He's too... pretty. Women like her don't go for muscles and perfect teeth. Do you ever notice that? Most gorgeous women look for something else in a man."

"What about Giselle and Tom Brady? They're both pretty," Cade said.

"Yeah, but I'll bet she's more turned on by his career, his drive, than his looks. He's an isolated example of a hot football player."

"I don't get all the fuss with him," Patrick said.

"No?" Aspen closed her laptop, stood, and tossed her lunch trash. "I do. Me and thousands, let's make that millions of other women and likely quite a few men, we get it." She patted the box with the labels as if to say her work was done.

"Thad is dating Vienna. The doctor is all yours," Aspen whispered to Boyd.

"I am not interested in—"

"Shh, I'm not all that romantic, but you might want to think on this one. I mean strictly from a supply-and-demand point of view. What are your other dating options? The snack bar moms?"

"They're married."

"Exactly. This is a small pond, Boyd. Keep your options open."

"Is that your professional advice?" he asked and couldn't help but smile.

"It is," she said before turning to bump Patrick's shoulder. "Don't worry, you'll catch up. Google Tom Brady or my favorite—sweaty Tom Brady—you'll see what the rest of us are fussing about." With a sarcastic grin, she walked away.

"Hey, any idea when we're getting the rest of the glasses?" Patrick called to her.

Aspen pointed over her head as she pushed through the door. "Ask your bartender. He's in charge of the aesthetic glassware, remember?" Even with her back to them, Boyd could tell she was rolling her eyes, and then she was gone.

Boyd loved that woman like the sister they all needed. She was the real deal, as their dad liked to say.

Patrick crossed his arms and leaned against one of the stools, trying for cool and failing. Boyd muffled a laugh, but Cade let his go and said, "She's got your number, Mr. Smooth."

"Always has been immune to the Patrick McNaughton charm,"

Boyd added, and just like that, the focus in the room shifted from two against Boyd to two against Trick. The beauty of three, Boyd thought. It wasn't so easy when their youngest brother, West, was home and things were even. Boyd would take whatever advantage he could get so long as he didn't have to discuss Dr. Ella Walters or the fact that Mason hadn't stopped talking about her advice.

Chapter Seven

*E*lla had managed to quiet a toddler with a raging ear infection when Bri came into the exam room. "You have a visitor."

"Be right out," she said softly, handing the little man with heavy lids back to his exhausted mom. Ella took her gloves off and washed her hands.

Bri stood by the door.

"Okay, Amanda. That should help with the pain while the antibiotics kick in."

"Thank you," the mom whispered. Her son, red cheeks dotted with tears, was finally asleep on her shoulder.

Ella nodded, turning to the computer and finishing her notes. Near the top of her list of reasons she loved being a doctor was the ability to alleviate pain. She'd witnessed discomfort on all levels, and having the knowledge to quickly assess and relieve was rewarding. She also enjoyed watching a beating heart in her hand, but that likely only happened once in a career. Lately, her job consisted of less life-threatening injuries and more tear-soaked eyelashes.

Had Mason ever been to an emergency room as a baby? Ella wondered if Boyd had brought him in alone. Sat in one of the plastic chairs, worried and solitary.

It made no sense that she thought about him or felt a loneliness for a man she barely knew, but once again the brain was a mystery. Ella had been restless when she first moved to Petaluma, but the rhythm of the town had settled over her now. Maybe noticing Boyd, questioning if he noticed her now that Vienna had informed her there was no Mrs. McNaughton, was another part of that rhythm. Her mother would call it settling for less, but Ella wholeheartedly believed it was a shift in energy.

She hit enter and refocused. "The nurse will be in with your discharge papers and prescriptions," Ella said. "Be sure to give him the antibiotic until it's finished." Ella left the room, guiding the heavy door to a quiet close.

Bri was right at her shoulder. "It's a young boy."

"I know. Nathan. Cutie, huh? Double ear infections." Ella flinched and patted her pockets for her lip balm.

"No. I mean that little guy is cute too, but your visitor is a kid."

Ella had almost forgotten about the visitor. "Is he a patient?"

She shook her head. "Looks fine. Maybe not a little boy. He's probably a tween or a teenager." They were walking and as they passed the nurses' station, Ella saw Mason. Slipping the lip balm back into her pocket, she scanned the waiting room for Boyd.

"Hey. Are you... everything okay with your dad?" she asked.

"Yeah, why?" He adjusted his backpack and appeared to stand a little taller, as if the mention of his father was juvenile for a guy who saw himself on the cusp of chest hair.

"I was wondering because... are you hurt?"

He checked himself out. "Nope. I'm good," he said and winked at Bri. Ella closed her eyes as Bri turned, laughing.

Leaning on the counter, attempting to appear casual and hoping to God this wasn't some sort of runaway situation, Ella started again.

"So, what brings you by the ER in the middle of the afternoon?"

"I thought we could talk."

She nodded as if it was the most natural thing in the world that a child she met only a week ago wanted to "talk." His face was serious. He sported worn-out Vans and sparkling dark green eyes bigger than his father's, now that she noticed the details. "Great. Are you... wanting to volunteer at the hospital? Did seeing your dad in here stir the need to help others?"

The pause was familiar, Ella realized. Bri and Vienna had the same vacuous look anytime Ella told a joke. Jokes were not her strength, neither was casual.

"No." She sensed he wanted to add, "Why the hell would anyone want to work in a hospital?", but the kid had manners. She could tell the first time she met him. "I have"—he leaned closer in confidence—"some more questions for you. You know, I need advice."

Ella tried not to look surprised or amused because he was serious. She remembered being a teenager. Everything was serious back then before she grew up and realized she hadn't even scratched the surface of that descriptor. But Mason was a joyous thirteen and obviously believed he'd found the inside scoop on the females he'd recently discovered.

"Oh, sure." Yep, she was a physician who readily agreed to talk girls with a teenager in the middle of her shift. If she ever decided to go back to San Francisco, it was unlikely they'd take her at this point. She was not only soft but connecting now with people who weren't even her patients. Ella didn't care. She liked Mason and wanted to help. "Let's go sit down, so we have some privacy."

Once in the back corner of the waiting area, Mason slid off his backpack and placed it on a chair. He took his phone out of his back pocket and put it in the front of his backpack. He seemed like a man getting ready for an important meeting who did not want to be disturbed. He sat and Ella took the seat next to him, conscious that she would have to leave if anyone came through the sliding doors. For the first time since she'd moved to Petaluma, she hoped for a slow afternoon.

"I'm assuming this is about 'she'?"

Mason nodded and pulled a pack of gum from his front pocket. He folded a piece into his mouth and offered the pack to Ella. She took one, did the same, and extended her hand for his wrapper. After throwing their trash away, she sat back down without a word and waited.

"I'm sitting in class today. We have Spanish and Math together, but this was Spanish. We had to get in these groups to go over a story we read in Spanish. Total pain in the... total pain."

Ella nodded. The gum was good, Big Red. She hadn't had gum in a long time, let alone gum with sugar. She assumed all kids these days chewed sugar-free gum. Not that she knew a lot about kids apart from how their insides worked. She returned her attention to Mason.

"The teacher picks four people as capitáns." He caught her eyes to make certain she was following him. "That's Spanish for captains."

Ella's expression widened in interest. "I figured."

"So, *she* gets picked as a capitán of one group because Senora Blakely loves her. But that has nothing to do with my question. *She* picks Eden first, that's her best friend."

"Understandable."

"Right, but here's where it gets weird. She bumps Eden and they both look at me. When I look up she looks away, but Eden is checking me out like that guy who wanted to see in Dad's camper a couple of years ago when we were crossing the border after camping in Mexico. Suspicious, you know?"

Ella laughed, but Mason shot her a look that nothing, absolutely nothing he was saying was funny. She cleared her throat.

"Then they both do that thing I hate where girls laugh like you're the stupidest idiot in the room. She didn't pick me. Josie picked me and then we kicked their asses, I mean their... bottoms"—he rolled his eyes—"with our reading and review, but that's not the point either. Can you help me out here?"

Ella chewed her gum and tried to think and act cool at the same time. Mason had somehow marked her as an authority, and she didn't want to let him down. Considering she was a newbie in the connect-and-be-human department, the pressure was on. "By *she*, you mean the girl, right? She is the one who broke eye contact, not the friend."

"Yeah."

"What is she's name?"

"Chloe," he whispered as if it was top secret. "But I don't like to use her name in case someone is around, ya know?"

"Understood. That's a beautiful name though."

"I know." His eyes went a little fuzzy and Ella felt she'd been given a gift—a glimpse into a young man that her thirteen-year-old self would have been reluctant around too.

"Okay, so she picks her friend first and then they bump shoulders and look at you?"

"Yeah."

"And then she looks away. Does she smile first?"

"I can't remember. I mean not a real smile because I remember those, maybe a little smile. She wasn't giving me the death stare. That's something, right?"

"Yes. Good sign. So how many more students did she pick for her group?"

"Three. All the groups had five, so she had three more picks."

"Did she pick all girls?"

He nodded.

"Oh, I like her."

"That's good? All girls is good?"

"I think so. If she'd picked another boy in the class after the whole bump and little smile, then I'd say she's a game player."

"So all girls means?" he asked, leaning on his knees now.

"She's not ready for boys yet, so she stuck with her girls."

"Not ready, what does not ready mean? She's not allowed to talk to me?"

"She's your age?"

"Yes."

"She's young. I'll bet she's a good student. She's focused on herself right now, and her friends."

He nodded, popped his gum.

"I'm guessing that's why you like her. I bet she's not all about the makeup and Instagram. She's smart and so are you."

"Wow, you're good."

Ella leaned back and crossed her clogs in front of her. There was something about Mason that demanded fun. "I try," she said.

"So, what should I do?"

"Be her friend. Don't go all goo-goo eyes on her. See past all of that and get to know her. Girls love being seen for more than their pretty parts. Some of them are never recognized for more than their hair or their legs. That's why they get trapped when they're older. They think it's all they have to offer."

The look on his face reminded her of a cartoon character. Stunned and blinking.

"What if I don't know how to be her friend, or she doesn't want to be my friend?"

"Oh, she does. Breaking eye contact and the little smile are dead giveaways."

"They are?"

Ella nodded. She wasn't lying. She'd spent a whole semester on body language and diagnosis. In most cases, looking away meant "denial of the symptoms." It wasn't a reach to assume Chloe's little teenage heart was going a mile a minute.

"Do girls know they're strange?"

She nodded again, this time popping her gum before remembering she was at work. Ella uncrossed her legs and sat up.

"I need to get back to work, Mason. I think you're on the right track, but you should bring the crush part down a notch. Talk to her like a person first. Ask her a question or her opinion. Something simple, and don't wink. No winking, understand?"

He stood, and Ella fought the urge to pat him on the head or ruffle his hair. The kid was cute. It was flattering that he'd rode his bike all the way from school to ask her advice, but she realized he didn't see himself as a cute kid and tried to respect that.

"What's wrong with winking?" A deep, smoky-around-the-edges voice asked from behind Ella. A smile pulled at her lips before she could stop it, and Mason noticed. He glanced between her and the door, as if not understanding why a woman would be smiling at his dad. Ella steadied her expression; she couldn't explain it either.

She turned to find Boyd leaning against the opening to the empty waiting area. He raised his brow. "Winking is out, huh? Is there a manual you could provide us guys, Doctor?"

His presence seemed to take up all the space between the hard chairs and magazines. When she was alone with Mason, she felt fun and confident in her advice. Now it was as if the walls were somehow closer. There was a hint of annoyance in his expression, as if she'd knocked on his door unannounced or "pissed on his parade," as Bri often said. She took the gum out of her mouth and threw it in the trash.

"No manual. Simply friendly advice. Most men can't pull off winking without it being sleazy. It's a bit like women in four-inch heels. Hard to manage without practice. My opinion, of course."

Boyd's left eye barely closed, it was a nanosecond of a blink followed by an almost imperceptible upturn of his lip. "Got it," he said and pushed off the wall to join them.

Heat rushed up her back and she exhaled. "Okay, well, that was a good wink."

"Show off," Mason said as his dad stood next to him.

Boyd shrugged as Ella tried not to laugh. There was something about watching the two of them. Joy and yearning stirred in the same familiar part of her chest and she was like a kid, nose pressed to the window, wondering if she could join in.

Boyd tried like hell not to picture her in four-inch heels, but he'd been around long enough to know that the male brain wanted what it wanted. The image, while well worth the awkward pause, was thankfully fleeting.

"Mase, thoughts on why you're hanging out with Dr. Walters when you're supposed to be at baseball practice?"

"Emergency. Couldn't be helped. I texted you."

"Yes, you did. But I didn't see it until your coach called wondering where you were."

"He never even plays me. I don't know why I'm on the team," he said mostly to Ella.

Boyd was thrown by the three-way dynamic.

"I think my coach thinks because my dad is big, I'm going to hit like a growth spurt or something. Yeah, not going to happen." Mason pulled on his backpack and Ella stacked the magazines between two chairs, but Boyd saw the smile she was attempting to cover. Time to go, some sane part of his brain demanded.

"Okay, well the doctor—"

"Her name is Ella. She said I could call her that."

Boyd raised his brow in the scolding tone of the father he often thought he should be, but the kid was so funny most of the time Boyd had a hard time holding onto stern. "No, she's Dr. Walters to you because you're thirteen and she's—"

"Old. I know."

"Er... Old-er. Thank you very much." She bumped him.

They both laughed, and something twisted in Boyd's chest. It was a feeling he didn't recognize. Pride and longing mixed together maybe. Watching Mason with her somehow accentuated the one thing missing in his son's life. The piece no number of camping trips or late-night popcorn meetings could erase. Boyd felt an irrational urge to pull Mason toward him, away from an energy that seemed the perfect fit for a rarely acknowledged void. Having a mom on a limited basis was all Mason knew, and Boyd wanted to protect him from the wanting more he saw in his eyes. There was no sense in wanting more. They had been fine as they were.

Stupid reaction, he knew, but there it was clamoring in his chest. She was so relaxed with him and most importantly, she spoke to him like a person, an equal. Boyd had learned early in the parenting game that was rare among adults. There was often a need to treat kids like little toys or puppies in training. He didn't raise Mason that way and sometimes, like when he wanted control, it backfired. There were moments Boyd knew raising him as a little soldier would have been easier, but watching his son turn into his own man was worth the work.

Mason would go on, live past Boyd, and that filled him with pride. But his job wasn't done yet. If he was honest, it never would be, so their structure, their life needed to stay intact. That meant Dr. Walters had to stay where she was—there was no room.

"Okay, party's over. Please say goodbye to Dr. Walt"—Mason tilted his head—"Fine. Please say goodbye and thank you to Ella. Then throw your bike in the back of the truck. We'll get Chinese on the way home. You have a history test tomorrow."

"Don't you have to work?"

"I do not. I'll be spending extra time with my runaway son tonight. You and me, kid. Cuddling. Maybe after you study, we'll put on our footie pajamas and watch some Disney movies."

Mason cringed. "You're so weird."

"True statement. Get going."

Mason said his goodbyes and disappeared behind the sliding doors of the ER.

Ella followed behind, no doubt needing to get back to work. She stopped suddenly midstride and faced Boyd.

Christ, Aspen was right, she was beautiful. No makeup that he noticed, and she wore clogs. How the hell was any woman beautiful in clogs? It seemed unfair to the entire unsuspecting male population.

"How's the wound?"

Boyd held up his hand.

"Impressive stitching. I'll bet there's barely a scar in a couple of months," she said, more playful than he remembered her the last time they'd met. *Mason*. Kids had a way of loosening the grown-up out of people.

Their eyes met and he reminded himself that he didn't do this. The allure of women and the promise floating in their eyes didn't sway him in the least. For a split second, something flashed in her eyes and he'd have bet money she was struggling with the same pull, the same need to step closer, but insistent they stay right on their respective sides.

"I'm sorry about him," Boyd said, bringing the subject back to Mason. This was about Mason.

"No, you're not."

He laughed. "That's probably true. I hope he didn't take up too much of your time."

"He didn't. I enjoyed talking with him and he gave me a piece of Big Red. Quite an incentive."

"He doesn't part with that easily. More advice? Is that what he was here for?"

Ella nodded and Boyd ran a hand across his beard. The kid was one raging hormone, which Boyd could normally counter by getting him outdoors, but things had shifted lately and his teenage mind was a little more intricate.

"He's got it bad." Boyd might have imagined the jump in Ella's chest when he said that, but something happened.

"I can see that. Well, I hope my advice helped. You're right though. I do need to get back. Please thank him for me."

"For what?"

"Hanging out with him is doing wonders for my 'connecting with people' effort."

"You need to work on that? Connecting?"

"I've been informed lately that I'm... closed off. So, let Mason know the friendship is mutually beneficial."

"I wouldn't call it a—" Boyd stopped before he said something mean and selfish. He and his son were not an island. Boyd knew that, but sometimes he needed to remind himself. "I'll let him know."

"Thanks. Well, back to work."

Women enjoyed this, he decided. Once a man thought he had it all figured out, she changed, opened another door, and all hell broke loose. He tilted his head in goodbye. Ella Walters was a nice person, he'd admit that. The fact that he'd thought about her since the first time she'd stitched up his hand, her heart set on a bagel sandwich, was like the lemon in Shamo Sunset. It needed to be kept under control.

Ella thought they had left, so when the doors opened again, she stood, expecting a patient. Mason sauntered toward the nurses' station. "Dad said you're working on connecting, so I thought I'd give you a hug." Before Ella could say anything, he wrapped his arms around her waist. It was immediately clear that this was a child who was hugged and often. He squeezed.

"Are you going to hug me back?" he asked, looking up at her.

She patted him on the back and waited for the release.

"That's not a hug."

"Are you telling me I'm hugging incorrectly?"

"Nah, it's not wrong, it's just not a real hug. You have to get into it more if you're gonna make the other person feel better. Come on, hug it out."

Ella crouched a little and wrapped her arms around him. He was smaller than she'd thought under the bulk of his sweatshirt and backpack. She squeezed and in that simple gesture, the teacher became the student.

"Better?" Ella asked, letting him go and standing to her full height.

Mason shrugged. "It needs work."

"That's what I keep telling her," Bri said from the nurses' station.

Mason turned. Ella could tell he was going to wink but resisted. Instead, he smiled. He'd had braces, perfect teeth, she noticed. While he and Bri chatted, Ella wondered what it was like to raise a child alone. Did Boyd take his son to all his orthodontist appointments or did he have help? Did Mason's mom live in town? He'd mentioned her, so Ella knew Boyd wasn't a widower. Why was she even thinking about this? Was it possible to form a friendship around one piece of advice she hadn't meant to give? She supposed stranger things happened—people connected all the time under the unpredictable wand of circumstance.

"Are you going to Butter and Egg Days next weekend?" Mason asked.

Ella nodded as he backed toward the door.

"I'll be there, and I think *she* is going too. I'll work on the friend advice and maybe we can do some recon surveillance next week."

Ella laughed. "You better get out of here before your dad has to come back in and get you."

Mason waved overhead and was gone. The kid was charming and fun. Ella meant what she'd said to Boyd: Mason was intelligent, and she couldn't help but connect with him. Maybe that had been her issue all along. It wasn't that she was cold like her father; she simply needed to surround herself with the right people.

Chapter Eight

The next day, Ella took a deep stretch class with Vienna and Bri after work. She forgot her mat and had to borrow one from the studio, which smelled like broccoli and feet. Ella hated broccoli, and no one liked the smell of feet. Even Bri would agree with her on that one. Along with forgetting her own personal lovely-smelling mat, Ella had walked out of the hospital without her wallet and then had to turn back, giving her barely enough time to change before class started. Christ, it was a good thing she had tomorrow off because she couldn't seem to pay attention to anything.

That wink and the nearness of Boyd McNaughton replayed through her mind all night like she was some stupid teenager. She'd gone too long without human contact. What thirty-six-year-old woman was thrown by a wink? Boyd tolerated her because his son had formed an attachment, that much was clear. So why was she still thinking about the look on his face when she stopped short and all but plowed into him? His face was so...

She needed to get a grip. Where the hell was her broken heart when she needed it? After months of pain and crying following Marc's bomb drop, and through the year of anger after that, her heart had been front and center. A throbbing reminder of where she'd come from and why she was not equipped to choose men. As early as last New Year's, she and her heart had agreed that they were happy and never wanted to hand things over to another man again.

Right? Heart, are you listening?

Placing her palms flat on the stinky mat, Ella closed her eyes and found her heart steady and warm in her chest. She hoped it was listening, but the truth was there was nothing jarring or dangerous about Boyd McNaughton. She was certain he knew how to be naughty; that wink was a glimpse for sure. But he didn't lead with his ego or show interest in her at all for that matter. He didn't seem to need anything or even complain. The guy was raising a son on his own and running a brewery. All of that must come with baggage. Surely there was a story about Mason's mother. But he seemed solid, right in the center of his life and not needing anyone to make him feel good about himself, listen to his problems, or stroke said ego, at least not outwardly anyway.

It was refreshing and caught her off guard. And his son—what the hell was she doing hanging out with a newly minted teenager? She was in no position to give advice, and yet the simplicity of his dilemma was also new and innocent. It called to a time when emotions were wild and confusing. He was right on the cusp of feelings Ella had spent her whole life trying to figure out. But giving a young man advice on the young girl, a girl undoubtedly much like she was once, was so delightful. Ella didn't know how long Mason would need her assistance, or his father would put up with it, but for now it was genuine, shoes off, belly-laughing fun. The kind that a woman could get used to, a heart could settle into.

After class and a quick dinner with Vienna, Ella stood at the sink in her bathroom. She splashed water on her face, took off her sports bra, and sank into a hot tub of Epsom salts. Her muscles were sore and she needed to figure out what to get her parents for their anniversary. It was still over a month away, but it wasn't like she could hop on Amazon and have something shipped overnight. They weren't even the swanky boutique type. No, Ella learned long ago that any gift for her parents was a production. "An extension of intention and value," her mother had once said. "Gifts are so much more than spending money. They are a way of showing you know a person." Ella carefully sipped the hot tea resting on the side of the tub and questioned how she'd ever managed to get them anything with that kind of pressure. It was easier when she was younger because she made mugs or picture frames that the school would send home. She was never there to see her parents open gifts back then but did notice none of them were around the house when she came home for break. Even as a child, there were standards for praise.

Ella laughed at the absurdity, scooted up the slick surface of the tub, and tucked a towel behind her neck. Maybe she'd contact that rare bookseller the chief of pediatrics in San Francisco recommended three Christmases ago. She'd see if they could find a first edition of... *In Cold Blood*. There might be a subliminal message in there somewhere, but her parents collected books and while her father loved Truman Capote, he'd never been able to locate a first edition. That would be a coup.

"A genuine extension of intent and value, Mother dear," she said to her empty bathroom.

She'd call around tomorrow. On a sigh, she took another sip of tea and cracked open her pain management book in a concerted effort to get her continuing education credits done before the end of March. Perhaps reading about the terminally ill in a tub of salt would squash any romantic notions she had that Boyd wanted anything other than for his son to stop asking her for advice.

By the time Mason threw away the empty bag of popcorn, Boyd knew all the presidents and vice presidents. He hoped like hell his son did too. After checking his emails while Mason showered, Boyd did his usual nightly routine whereby he pretended to walk by his son's room and then spontaneously stopped to talk.

Bedtime used to be an event in the McNaughton house. He would read a story complete with different voices, tuck him in, and check that the bathroom light was left on. Those days were gone and while the memories pulled at his heart a few times a year, Boyd enjoyed the growing-up version of Mason too.

"So, did you get any good advice, other than not to wink?" Boyd asked as his son finished drying his hair and tossed the wet towel on the floor.

"Uh-huh. She's smart. And she likes you."

"Is that so?" Boyd leaned into his room from the doorway and picked up the towel. Handing it to him, he pretended not to be pumping his son for information, although he couldn't tell now if he was more interested in why Mason suddenly needed an expert opinion or the expert herself. "She can't be all that smart then."

"True. But she does." Mason slid his history book into his over-stuffed backpack and zipped it closed.

"Did you brush your teeth?"

Mason huffed. "Yeah, Dad. You don't need to remind me to brush my teeth anymore. I'm like practically an adult."

"Yeah, well Uncle Cade still forgets."

Mason's expression went from indignant to laughter, and Boyd was glad he still had some parenting skills left.

"Did you see how she got a little nervous when you winked and then... oh, how did she put it? Broke eye contact. That's it, she broke your eye contact. Did you see that?" Mason hopped into the dark navy sheets of his bed and hit the button on his iPhone docked on the shelf behind him.

"Can't say I did."

"Well, she did, and that's a sign that a girl likes you. Doc told me."

Boyd sat on the edge of Mason's bed, noticing something was missing from his bookcase. "Where'd your comics go?"

"I put them in a box in my closet."

"Why?"

Mason shrugged. "I don't read them that much anymore."

Boyd wanted to go to the closet and put them back where they belonged. But that wouldn't change reality—his son was getting older.

"So, do you think you're going to ask her out?"

"Who?" Boyd shifted out of his thoughts.

"Ella."

Boyd covered up the jump in his pulse at the mention of her name with a laugh.

"No. I'm good, but thanks."

Mason scrunched his face. "Why not? You don't have a girlfriend and she likes you. There's no way you don't like her. She's pretty and you winked at her. You never wink. So what's the problem?"

"I winked to prove a point. I was not winking at her. Speaking of girls liking you, how's Chloe? Anything you want to talk about?"

His son blushed and Boyd wanted to tell him there was no rush. He'd get his heart twisted into knots soon enough. Thirteen was a time to be selfish and get dirty. Damn hormones, Boyd thought. They took perfectly good bike-riding, fort-building boys and turned them into driveling idiots desperate for a look or a feel.

"Ella said to stop worrying about liking her and be her friend."

"Good advice."

"She said to ask her opinion or something about her."

Boyd nodded. He had to admit it was great advice. "What do you think about that?"

"I guess I can try, but my hands get sweaty and"—he shook his head—"I don't know. Maybe I should find a girl who doesn't make me so nervous for my first girlfriend. Besides, I think she likes Elton."

"The kid who wears shower shoes with socks?"

"He's popular."

Figured, Boyd thought. "So?"

"So, girls who look like Chloe like guys like that. He walks around like he's not in a hurry to be anywhere. I never see him with books. And his arms. My God, Dad, the guy makes me look like I'm five. I think he was held back a couple of grades. Chloe is forever talking about his hair."

"Is that why you texted Uncle Cade? You're consulting the family hair expert too?"

Mason nodded and flipped his bangs out of his eyes. "I need better hair."

"Christ."

"Language, Papa Bear. Language."

Boyd laughed. "Do you think new hair will make you feel better?"

"Yeah, I think Uncle's hair is cool."

"Good. That's all that matters. And to be clear, I get final say on the haircut. You are not walking around with a wilted Mohawk."

Mason laughed.

"Don't start doing stupid stuff for some girl. If she likes you for you then she gets to go out with you. If not, she misses out. Her loss." Boyd stood and went to turn off the light.

"Did Mom miss out on you?"

The question almost knocked him off his feet. He prided himself on knowing what Mason was going through or at least being in the ballpark. The mention of his mom was normal, but the question about the two of them together was new.

"I... neither one of us missed out. We got you."

"Yeah, but as a man. Did you want Mom to like you?"

"Mom does like me. But we're not in love with each other."

"Were you ever?"

Crap, he knew Mason. This question volley could go on for hours.

"Yes. We loved each other when we made you. In fact, maybe now is a good time to talk about how babies are made, Mase." Boyd sat back down on the bed as if to show he was settling in.

His son squirmed and pushed him off. They were both laughing. One minute he was so cool, talking about hair and on the brink of being a dude. The next, he was a kid. The "sex talk" was usually an easy out. Boyd knew it wouldn't be that way for much longer, but for now it was his escape when he didn't have the answers, which was becoming more and more frequent these days. He kissed his still-wriggling son on the forehead and hit the lights. Mason reached back and grabbed his phone.

"One more thing," Boyd said.

"Yeah."

"I have it on good authority that not all beautiful girls like the cool guys in shower shoes. Most of them go for the different guys, the ones with something else to offer. Don't you notice that?"

Mason's brows scrunched together. "Not... really. Look at Tom Brady and Giselle. Pretty even there."

Boyd shook his head. "Did Uncle Cade mention that?"

"No, why?"

"Never mind. Phone better be back on the charger by nine."

"Nine thirty?"

"Okay, but you best deliver an A on the presidents tomorrow."

"Done."

"Uh-huh. Love you."

"I know. You're not bad either." Mason smiled, and Boyd's heart melted like it did back when Mason only had one front tooth. No matter how much changed around him, some things stayed the same. Boyd turned off the hall light and went to his bedroom.

He'd lived alone with Mason for as far back as he could remember and that meant sleeping alone. Kicking off his boots, he lay on top of the made bed. Thirteen years was a long time to sleep alone, he thought. Why it mattered all of a sudden, he had no clue. He hadn't gone thirteen years without sex—now that would have been a tragedy. Hadn't it been his intention that he and Mason would make a life together alone? That must have meant accepting that he'd be sleeping alone. He had not thought much about it until he cut his hand and his son failed to see the inherent male dangers in a woman like Ella.

She was sexy and smart, which was a deadly combination. She appreciated Mason, which in a strange way both warmed his heart and broke it a little. His son didn't need a mom. He had one, even if she wasn't around all the time.

Ella wasn't trying to be his mom, Boyd corrected himself. She was... hell, what was she? She was being herself and for reasons he didn't want to understand, he couldn't shake the urge to step closer. Mason wasn't helping.

There may have been some flirtation when Boyd winked at her, but it was to prove her wrong, nothing more. At least, that was the story he was sticking with for now. He stacked the extra pillows on the empty side of the bed.

I have everything I need. Boyd practically said the words out loud. Then he turned on the television because it was too quiet.

Chapter Nine

T he next morning, Ella was at Sift and paying Pam for her chocolate croissant and a latte with three pumps of vanilla. Extra sugar and chocolate fixed things. It was science. She'd put in a few calls to book dealers and only had three more chapters on pain management to go. Ella planned on riding her bike that afternoon if the sun managed to burn off the clouds, so she let herself indulge.

Taking her seat, she had to admit if someone attempted to remove the chocolate croissant from her hand on a Friday morning, they were going to die. Probably a developing addiction, she thought, laughing to herself and taking out her textbook, but the best kind, she decided.

She'd just taken out the postcard reminder she'd received from the AMA, which now doubled as a bookmark, when she glanced up and saw Mason. He waved and lumbered over in that way young men did when they were still growing into their legs.

"Hey. Aren't you supposed to be in school?" Ella asked before taking a bite of pure butter and chocolate. She supposed it was bad form for a doctor to be eating this in front of a kid in the morning, but once her taste buds exploded with joy, she forgot to care.

"On our way. We need to pick up the cookies for my class."

"Nice." She wiped her mouth and wondered about the "we" in his statement. Boyd? A friend or girlfriend? Vienna mentioned Mason's mother didn't appear to be "in the picture," but that was all she knew. The McNaughtons, all of them, came in from time to time and Vienna had made Mason's birthday cake a few months ago when he turned thirteen. Red Velvet. Ella remembered because it was her favorite.

She wasn't certain why she cared about the "we." She wasn't one to snoop and Boyd, whom she'd decided to start referring to as Mason's dad since she was beginning to like the sound of his name, was unquestionably giving her the cold shoulder. That usually meant girlfriend, not that Ella's commitment radar was reliable. Why was she doing this? Thinking about any of this? She had sugar and coffee. Her life was set.

Vienna came up behind the counter. "I'm packing up your box now. Give me a few minutes. Do you want something for breakfast too? On the house."

"Sure. Hi, Vienna."

"Hey, cutie. Glazed doughnut?"

"Yes, please."

"Ella, did you pay for that?"

She nodded and took another bite. Vienna wiped her hands on a huff. It was a busy morning—good chance parties like Mason's needed extra cookies. Ella had been coming in long enough to recognize her friend's buzz and often took it as a chance to pay for something and even leave a tip in the jar by the register.

Ella could tell Mason wanted to wink, but he resisted as Vienna punched in something on the computer for Pam and then returned to the back.

One less future winker. My work is done here, Ella thought. That, of course, brought the best wink she'd ever witnessed to mind. Stupid wink.

"So, how are things?" she asked as Mason stood by her table and shifted his weight front to back.

His eyes traveled around the space in that way teenagers did when they felt the least bit vulnerable. "Do you mean with she? I haven't had a chance to try the friend thing. We're not friends on Snapchat."

"That or baseball or school. General inquiry."

"Oh, yeah. Baseball update: We still suck. I mean it's fine, but I'm not good. I'm thinking about field hockey once I start high school."

"My roommate in high school played field hockey all four years. She loved it."

"You had your own place in high school?"

"Sorry. No, I went to boarding school."

"Really? What's that like?" He sank down into the seat next to her as if she'd become ten times more fascinating.

"Um, kind of lonely," Ella said, telling the truth.

"Were you far away from home? Why did you go if you were lonely? Did you get in trouble or something?"

Ella hadn't had a lot of exposure to children. Her sister had a daughter, but she was, well, Ella didn't remember her niece ever being a child. Her name was Cressida. That seemed to come with a maturity right out of the womb. Other than her niece, most of the children Ella interacted with were sick or hurting. Mason was happy and so full of life.

"Yes, it was far away from my home. My parents live near Los Angeles in Brentwood. I went to high school back east in New Hampshire."

"Why did you go?"

She was hoping he'd forgotten that question. Mainly because she didn't know how to answer. What was the correct answer for a child his age? My parents are robots and should have never had children? Not ideal, so she went with Becca's Disney version.

"It's a tradition. My parents went, and so my sister and I went too."

"Huh. I'm nervous enough about high school. I don't think I'd want to sleep there too."

Ella laughed. "Good point."

"Where did you go to college?"

"Harvard and then UCLA for medical school."

"Oh, that's right. You had to go to more school after college." He rolled his eyes.

Ella rolled hers too. It was fun making fun of school for a change.

"All right, Mase. Sorry for the wait." Vienna handed him a pink box tied with string and then a white bag like the one Ella picked up on the mornings she worked.

Glazed doughnut, that sounded good too. Maybe next week, she thought.

"So, your roommate liked field hockey?" he asked after thanking Vienna.

"She did. She used to say constant movement was a high. Is that why you don't like baseball? All the waiting around?"

He nodded. "Never thought about it that way, but yeah. I get bored and then I mess up. I like basketball, but look at me." He gestured up and down his body. "That's not going to happen."

Ella laughed.

"Mase, are you baking the stuff yourself? Let's—" Boyd's voice rumbled through the tinkling sound of the bell on the front door, but he stopped when he saw Mason standing by Ella. Wiping his boots on the mat by the door, he visibly took in a breath.

Ella was used to men looking at her, assessing who they thought she was or more often doubting her abilities based on her looks. She'd worked twice as hard in medical school and busted her ass once she graduated to prove she wasn't some blond genetic lottery winner looking to land a doctor husband. Ironic she ended up with a doctor, and every stereotype was made worse by the way that turned out.

"Got it. I just got it. Vienna's a little nuts back there. She needed more time to pack it up. We've got time," Mason said.

"Sorry to keep you waiting, Boyd. Crazy busy this morning. Can I get you coffee and a sticky bun on the house?" Vienna asked.

Boyd hesitated.

"Fresh out of the oven."

He took off his baseball cap, morning hair all over the place. "Can't say no to that, but I'll pay for it. Thanks, Vienna." He turned to Mason, expression softened no doubt at the thought of anything Vienna offered fresh out of the oven.

"Look who comes here too—Dr. Ella from the hospital. Remember?"

Boyd nodded. "That was yesterday, Mase. I'm not senile."

"Not yet."

"Look at you all clever. How about you walk to school?"

"You wouldn't do that."

"I would *and* I'll take your cookies."

"That's cruel. Hey, Ella slept at her high school. She went to boarding school."

"Huh."

Their eyes met and she was hit again by the distinct feeling he wanted to avoid her. She wasn't a woman to take offense, but she was curious why he appeared to find her so distasteful. Maybe it was the whole doctor thing that threw him off. The boarding school tidbit certainly wasn't going to create any common ground.

"Yeah, and her roommate played field hockey."

"Interesting." Boyd took the bag and coffee Vienna handed over the counter. He offered her money and when she refused, he stuck it in the jar by the register.

"We're going to be late," Boyd said, no longer bothering to make chitchat with Ella.

Mason glanced at the clock on the wall. "Crap." He flinched. "I meant gee golly we better get going, sir."

Boyd shook his head and Ella tried not to laugh. Funny and smart, inquisitive and obviously a smart ass. His dad took him under his arm.

"Say goodbye to the nice doctor, unruly kid."

"Bye, Ella. I'll keep you posted. Maybe Dad and I should get your num—"

Boyd dragged him out the door before he could finish his sentence.

She was still grinning as she finished the rest of her sugar breakfast, and then it hit her.

Had Boyd even said goodbye?

This was not happening, he told himself as Mason turned up the music and continued babbling on about Ella and her boarding school years. Boarding school? Who the hell still went to boarding school? Gorgeous blond doctors with a great sense of humor and an affection for nosey kids, that's who. He knew he sounded ridiculous, but honestly, what the hell was a woman like her doing here?

"Ella went to Harvard. Did you know that?"

Boyd shook his head and tightened his grip on the steering wheel. That caused his hand to throb and then he thought of her again. Damn it, she was everywhere. He didn't need this, didn't want attraction anymore. He had work and his son. Women, other than his mom, Aspen, and occasionally Claire when the mood struck, did not factor into Boyd's equation. He'd need to figure out why Mason was so hell-bent on hanging out with the doctor. Yeah, that sounded good. "The doctor." That's how he should think of her from now on. It rang formal and so much better than the woman all disheveled with powdered sugar on her cheek. He knew where to file "the doctor," but Ella Walters was stirring up a whole mess of something he did not want to sort through.

"Yeah, she must be smart."

"Must be," Boyd said as he pulled into the school roundabout. "Okay, let's get in there and learn."

"It's Friday. No one learns on Friday."

Boyd moved to ruffle his son's hair and thought better of it. Mason's friends were waiting outside for him and the expression on his face said, "Don't do it, Dad. I'm not five anymore."

"Get out," he said in a Terminator voice.

Mason threw his backpack over his shoulder. "See you at three?"

"I'll be the one waiting outside my truck in a Speedo."

"That is so wrong," he said.

"Ya think? I don't know. I'm thinking an American flag one. Maybe with my work boots."

"How are you even allowed to be an adult?" Mason laughed, taking the cookies and sack lunch Boyd handed him once he hopped down out of the truck.

"I have no idea. They handed me a truck and a baby one day."

"It's a crazy world."

"Yes, it is. Be kind," Boyd said as Mason nodded to his friends and turned back one more time.

"Yup, I'll try. Be strong," he said, closing the truck door.

"I'll do my best," Boyd said through the window.

Their eyes held for an instant and then Mason was gone, joined by his friends and walking into school. Pulling away, Boyd allowed for the next car in line and swallowed back a lump in his throat. Two more months and his son would enter the summer before high school. Change was good, he told himself.

What do you want him to do, play with Legos forever? That's not what he wanted. He wanted Mason to grow up and have all the adventures imaginable. He was thinking too far ahead. Two months was a long time. Right now, they had a weekend and they needed to start working on a science fair project or he'd be up all night like last year when he was gluing cotton balls to poster board until 2:00 a.m. Weekend and poster board: that was as far ahead as Boyd needed to look.

Be kind, be strong. They'd been saying goodbye to each other that way since practically his first day of kindergarten. God, he loved that kid something crazy. He wasn't one of those dads to declare, "I have no idea where the time went." Boyd liked to think he was present for every twist and turn of Mason's life. He could remember most things, but lately little memories like the age he started walking or what his toddler voice sounded like were beginning to fade. Boyd supposed they had to if only to make room for the new memories, the details of who his son was becoming. There were times it seemed that to fully appreciate teenage Mason, he might need to say goodbye to toddler Mason. Like they couldn't both exist together.

Boyd pulled a piece of sticky bun from the bag Vienna had given him and tried to manage his mind the way he managed the recipe he needed to start working on once he got to the brewery. Balance — every change created something new. Change could be good.

Shit, I'm talking to myself now.

Chapter Ten

"Honestly, Bri, they're all starting to look the same," Ella said as she glanced up from her phone to find her friend in yet another sexy black dress. She and Vienna had agreed to spend the day shopping for a "dress that kills," but if she didn't find something soon, there were going to be casualties all right.

"No. This one has a keyhole back." Bri put her hands on her hips and twirled in the mirror.

Ella met Vienna's eyes right before they rolled.

"Oh, you're right. It *is* different," Vienna said. "I have an idea, let's think about whether a keyhole or the one with the single strap across the back is going to drop your date to his knees. While we're doing that, I need a large glass of wine and food."

Bri turned to them. "You're mocking me."

They both nodded.

"Change, Bri. You need to step away from the dressing room for at least an hour," Vienna said.

"Are you sure? I'm feeling this one."

"No, you're not," Ella said. "I'm with V. Lunch is calling us."

Bri took one more look in the mirror and disappeared into the dressing room. Ella and Vienna both closed their eyes. Food was moments away.

"Do you think I can wear any of these to Perfect Annie's christening next month?" Bri asked as she reappeared hopping on one foot and pulling the back of her shoe on the other. She'd taken to calling her new niece Perfect Annie or Brilliant Annie Pretty Face.

"Are you looking to get laid at the christening?" Vienna asked, handing Bri her purse.

Bri stopped, raised a brow, and pursed her lips. Ella shook her head and held the door open for them both.

They took their favorite table at Central Bistro and Vienna finally had her large glass of wine in hand as they looked over the menu they'd all but memorized by now.

"I'm so tired of dating, but I don't want to be alone forever. I'm not you, Ella."

"What's that supposed to mean?" Ella said.

"You're like a professional alone person. You bring your lunch, you don't fall asleep on your couch with Doritos stuck to your face. You're good at being alone."

"Well according to you, that's because I don't have a life and I have a strange affection for Monday."

Bri sipped her gin and tonic. "I explained that. It was a cry for help. V, have you heard about Monday?"

Ella laughed as Sistine and Aspen came in waving and the nachos were delivered. Ella glanced around the circular booth. "Why do you think we're all single?" she asked. All conversation stopped.

"Um... Well, technically I'm divorced, so that makes me a special kind of single," Bri said.

"I'm dating Thad, which means theoretically I'm not single. So... because I was waiting for the love of my life and he finally showed up?"

Sistine tilted her head in an "aw" gesture while Bri's brow furrowed.

"Oh, cut that crap out. If I thought you believed that and it wasn't your sex trance speaking, I'd have to smack you," she said.

"I'm single because... I don't know how to be anything else," Sistine said in a voice that spoke to her love of libraries. "I guess I like being alone? Is that an answer?"

The table nodded because as content as Sistine seemed, weren't human beings meant to pair up? Christ, that's what Ella had heard her whole life. Most of the time she too was content being single. In fact, until recently she rarely thought about it after the Marc disaster.

"Aspen?" Sistine said as if to take the focus off her.

Aspen glanced up from her phone. "Sorry. Single. Yeah, I don't need the aggravation. I have a good thing going at work. I have the occasional date, but I like my life, my work."

"Me too," Ella said.

"Clearly," Bri added.

Ella tossed a chip at her.

"I don't think that's true," Aspen said, giving her phone a few more taps and slipping it into her purse.

"Don't think what's true?" Bri asked over the chip she was crunching.

"That work is enough for Ella."

Ella felt the heat of the spotlight.

"I think you were consumed by work when you were at the big hospital, but now I think you want your job and other things. Isn't that why you moved here?"

"I... Yes. I wanted something different."

"Exactly." Aspen dipped a chip. "So, your usual 'it's all about my career' isn't the best explanation for why you're alone. What about Boyd?"

The table was still. Drinks midsip, a couple of mouths full. Ella felt the air rush from her lungs. This was why she didn't discuss her personal life. This was why she'd worked hard over the past two years not to have a personal life.

"What?" Aspen said as she chomped. "He's male and single. Ella already likes his son. Could be a good fit."

"Why do I suddenly feel like one side of a corporate merger?" Ella asked.

Aspen shrugged.

"Boyd's the hand laceration, right? With the cute kid," Bri said.

Vienna woke right up. "You know, I did notice some sparks the other morning when they came in for cookies."

This was enough. If Ella let them continue, it would be a matchmaker frenzy. "Did you? Because those sparks were from him hightailing it out of there as fast as his boots would take him."

Bri shook her head and finished chewing. "Seemed like he stuck around for a while when his son came to visit you."

"Mason came to the hospital again?" Aspen asked.

"Wait, I thought Mason was only thirteen," Sistine said.

Ella closed her eyes as all four women began trading comments and filling the others in on bits of information they'd witnessed. The now empty nacho plate was cleared, Ella ordered another drink, and there was finally a long-awaited silence as lunch was delivered and they all began eating.

Bri lifted her glass in a toast. "Aspen, I love you. I'm officially off the hook as the only obnoxious and nosy one."

The rest of the table laughed and Ella shook her head. "Couldn't let it go, could you?"

"Oh, hell no." Bri played with the straw in her glass. "I think Boyd is a perfect candidate."

"For what?" Ella's face grew warm.

"For some weekend... experiments."

"You are so wrong. The man has a child and he can't stand me."

"Not true," Aspen said.

Lord, this wasn't going to die.

"Do you have information you need to share?" Sistine asked.

Ella hoped she still possessed some intimidation and leveled her best cold-doctor stare at Aspen. Something needed to turn this conversation around.

Aspen shrugged again, didn't even flinch. Traitor.

"Not exactly information. Mason shares and his uncles listen. They were talking about Ella, and Boyd didn't seem uninterested." It felt like she was issuing a report rather than feeding the wolves, and then she returned to her phone.

"Well," they all said as if they were launching into a musical number.

"Oh yes, this is promising. I'm wondering if you have all forgotten the rule." Ella held up her hand, hoping like hell it still worked. It was all she had left. Aspen and Sistine appeared confused.

Bri rolled her eyes and swallowed another sip of her drink. "It's the hand again," she explained to them. "Dr. Ice here doesn't discuss her personal life. Although, I would like to point out that she was the one who asked the initial question about our single status."

"It was rhetorical. Like, let's discuss singlehood in general, in theory. You know?"

They all shook their heads and laughed again. Vienna high-fived Bri across the table. Traitors, they were both such obnoxious traitors.

"I'm sorry if I misspoke. I certainly understand not wanting to get into the mess of pounding hearts and all of that, but if you were looking to dive in, Boyd is a good guy," Aspen said to the table, but it was mostly directed at Ella.

"It seems that way. I'm glad I could stitch up his hand and meet Mason. He's adorable, but I'm afraid, ladies, that the juicy gossip stops there, so let's talk about something more interesting. Bri is going on a date tomorrow night with a former IRS auditor. Huh?"

The table erupted in laughter at Ella's failed attempt to redirect.

"That's right. I think he even worked in their corporate fraud department, so stay tuned for more on that hot-and-steamy developing story."

"Has he ever audited someone famous?" Sistine asked.

"No idea, but I'll ask."

"That's a pretty cool job. I mean it's not as fun as rock god or movie star, but it's different," Vienna said.

"True."

"Did you guys know that Boyd's brother is a—"

Ella held up her hand and Aspen stopped speaking, which based on what Ella learned from Bri and Vienna was no easy feat.

"Right, no McNaughtons. Got it."

Why was it so difficult for her to share her life with other people? Not even people, these were her friends to varying degrees. Maybe

Ella had never had friends on this level. All of this circled back to hugging and connecting with people over something more substantial than credentials and accomplishments.

The conversation turned to new wedding cakes Vienna was designing and the next book club meeting. Aspen excused herself to use her phone, asking for assistance with bail if she was arrested for "murdering Patrick McNaughton."

Bri sat back in the booth and grinned at Ella. She then gave an exaggerated inhale and exhale through her perfect lips. She drove Ella crazy with her touchy-feely crap, but somehow, she'd snuck under her skin and figured Ella out. Past what she put forward to everyone, Bri understood what made Ella who she was, and Ella supposed that's what being friends was all about. She took a deep breath and nodded to Bri, who raised her glass and returned to the conversation.

"Practice and patience are the keys to good medicine" was her first-year professor's motto. Today, that made more sense than ever.

Boyd had been at work since eight in the morning, save a break to pick Mason up from baseball practice, and now he was back at it again. He was almost done with his part of the to-do list before the Tap House opened. Plugging in the last string of lights that night, he prayed to all things holy that the thing lit up this time. It seemed crazy to him that one strand of lights made a difference, but Patrick assured him everything needed to be perfect. His obsessive brother hadn't steered the brewery wrong so far, so Boyd kept at it and if nothing turned on, he'd call the electrician to come out one more time. They had a few days left until opening, and as every small business owner would declare, a lot could be done in a few days. Still, he held his breath and hit the switch.

"Yeah. That looks awesome," Mason said, standing in the center of the restaurant and turning under the small pops of light. Boyd felt that skip in his heart again, the one that told him there would come a day when his son was grown and moving on to the challenges of his own life. The skip that said, "Slow down and drink it all in." Boyd listened to that advice, even when Mason was younger. He held him a beat more wrapped in a towel after tub time and tried to climb out of his own head when Mason needed to talk about something exciting at school.

Boyd was far from perfect. He didn't always have patience or the right answer. There were nights he put Mason to bed and questioned whether he had any clue what he was doing. But looking at his son now, growing taller and more confident every day, Boyd realized he must be getting some things right because his son was remarkable already. The thought made his chest swell with pride.

"Not bad, right?"

"This place is sick. Did you see Uncle Cade's bar? There are chickens everywhere."

Boyd smiled. "I know, he's already calling it his office."

"Badass office." Mason was still looking around in awe.

"Hey, my office is cool too."

He shook his head. "You have too many tanks and it smells funny."

"It rarely smells."

Mason pursed his lips.

"Half the time, fine, it smells half the time. But, I have copper."

"Yeah, yeah. I guess those old wooden barrels are cool. I'll give you second-best office."

"Because Trick's is..."

"Boring," they both said together.

"Did I hear you guys dissing my office?" He high-fived Mason's hand and pulled him under his arm. "I'm still taller than you, Little Man. And, I'll have you know we bought a new printer last week. Something like 250 color sheets a minute. It's impressive."

Boyd and Mason rolled their eyes. Patrick released his nephew and folded his arms across his chest.

"You got them to work."

Boyd nodded.

"Great."

Mason sat at the bar, spinning on one of the stools. Boyd knew he was anxiously waiting for the three vintage arcade games being delivered to the back room.

"We still need napkin holders," Patrick said, running his hand along one of the high-top tables.

"I thought Cade was putting a stack on each table with a brick on top?"

Patrick seemed confused. "I had not heard that, but I like it. Who's picking up the bricks?"

"Not me." Aspen flew in and plonked her laptop down on the bar. "Where's Cade?" She was typing furiously and didn't look up.

"Everything all right?" Patrick was somehow brave enough to ask.

"Well, now that's an interesting question." She flung her hair out of her face and met Patrick's eyes. "If you are comfortable opening a tap house with only mugs, without any other glassware, then we're good. I'll bet people won't mind drinking every beer out of a mug. I think Chili's uses mugs, so that's cool. Or"—she clapped her hands together as her crazy train pulled into the station—"maybe people won't mind cupping their hands. Even better, we could pick up some Solo cups. Boyd, are you good with people drinking your beer from a plastic cup?"

Boyd had seen this type kind of emotional explosion from his mom before. There were no right answers, so he sat on the stool next to Mason, who had ceased spinning and was now observing Aspen like she was another species. Field research, Boyd thought.

"What are you talking about?" Patrick said, the brave or stupid soul.

"Where is Cade?" she said again, slower this time, as if they didn't speak her brand of English.

"He went home. He was here early this morning for the refrigerator delivery. What's going on? How are we opening a tap house without glasses? Are you talking all glasses except for the few mugs?"

"We," she emphasized. "We were not in charge of the glasses. Remember several months ago when I found that great place in Santa Barbara and I wanted to order all of the glasses that day?"

They all nodded, even Mason.

"But no, that idea was shot down even after I got the guy to give us a volume discount." Aspen returned to her laptop and hit enter, hard. "That wasn't good enough, was it? No, Cade had a little friend, remember? Larson with the 'glass design' business, and I use that term loosely. She was supposed to provide an 'indie vibe' with her 'inspired' take on the traditional beer pints and tulips, remember? Because she had a great 'sense of aesthetics.'" Aspen was air quoting all over the place.

"I'm assuming she's not going to get them done. Have you found other glasses?" Patrick asked as if he was completely immune to all the quoting.

"No. I mean, I'm trying, but no one is going to fill a custom order in, what's left?" She checked her laptop. "Four days? I've been trying to see if Larson managed to complete any of the order, but Cade broke up with her or, 'let her down easy' as you... males say." More quoting, and even Patrick seemed a little nervous.

"So after that little plot twist, she's not returning anyone's calls. This"—she gestured up and down the bar—"this mess is why we don't mix business with pleasure." She put her forehead on the bar.

"Have you asked Sistine?" Mason asked.

Boyd was lost on how the knitting store woman could help, but after a pause, Aspen slowly raised her head.

"Her brother is a glassblower, remember?"

Aspen jumped from her stool and pointed at Mason like he'd won a game show. "You're right." She grabbed him and kissed him on the cheek. Taking her laptop, she turned to leave, mumbling to herself and then speaking aloud as if she were holding some kind of private and mobile meeting. Maybe with the voices in her head. "We need at least three hundred, but maybe if we rent some and her brother has some we can mix and—"

"Aspen."

She turned to Patrick. "I hate it when you do that."

"Say your name?"

"Silence me when I'm in the middle of my mind. It's like I'm a new puppy in your laundry room."

Boyd laughed. They'd known Aspen since they were in junior high. She was the valedictorian of their high school. Educated at Stanford. Why she hung out with them when she could be running some Fortune 500 business was beyond him.

"I don't have a laundry room," Patrick said, seemingly trying to assess whether their business manager had really lost her mind. "Do you have this? Do you need anything from me?"

Aspen laughed. "When was the last time I ever needed anything? I'll let you know in the morning. Maybe you can run by the party store for the Solo cups."

"This isn't funny."

"Oh, I realize that. Thanks for the great idea, Mase." She blew him another kiss.

Mason grabbed it and mimed tucking it into his T-shirt pocket. Boyd wondered if his son truly had issues with girls, because it sure as hell didn't look like it.

"Wait, where do you do your laundry?" Boyd heard Aspen ask as she and Patrick both walked toward his office.

"How did you know Sistine's brother was a glassblower?" Boyd asked when the two of them were alone.

"I ride by her knit shop on my way to baseball practice when we don't have carpool. The other day I went in because she has this huge weaving-looking thing in her window. I wanted to check it out."

"That led to her brother, how?"

"She gave me some sparkling water drink and some nuts. We sat and talked for a little while. She's super cool."

Boyd's expression must have hinted he was still waiting for the relevant part.

"We were talking about school and girls. She told me about her brother, who lost his arm in a motorcycle accident." Mason flinched. "He has this mechanical arm now, and I guess he crushes it with the women."

Boyd blinked and was still lost.

"She was telling me about him, jeez. He's different. Like me." Mason waved his hand in front of Boyd's face until Boyd caught it.

"Are you surveying all the villagers now?" he asked, trying to keep it light but a little concerned. "Are we asking all females for input now?"

"No, only a few."

Boyd laughed. "Well, good save with the glasses. Maybe her brother can help."

"I hope so. Aspen was all nuts. Women get so crazy."

"So do men."

"Yeah, but we don't talk as much."

Boyd supposed he was right. He wanted to tell him that was because most of the time men had no idea what they were doing, but that was a lesson his little man would figure out on his own. Besides, from the looks of things, Mason had it more together than all the McNaughton men combined, except maybe their dad.

The delivery truck pulled up, and Mason ran to the back room hoping to be the first one on the board for Galaga once it was plugged in. Boyd couldn't stop thinking about the committee of female resources his son appeared to be putting together. When had all of this happened, and when would this phase end? Boyd hoped with Sistine in the picture now, it meant Mason would move on from Ella Walters. That would make Boyd's life easier, at least that's what he told himself.

Chapter Eleven

By Saturday morning, the glasses crisis had somehow been averted. Sistine's brother agreed to sell Aspen everything he had and she rented the rest. She then promptly ordered the remaining glasses they needed from him, got her discount, and glared at Cade for a full day. When Boyd saw her earlier at the brewery, she was in a much better mood, which was great because the Foghorn Brewery Tap House was officially open following the 36th Annual Butter and Egg Days festivities.

Patrick's plan called for everyone to man the beer booth for a few hours in the afternoon. It was expected that over 30,000 people would attend B&E Days this year, and he wanted as many of those revelers as they could hold at the new tap house once things dwindled down around four. That meant a long day for all of them.

When Boyd was a kid, he used to think B&E was weird, but people traveled from all over the state for his hometown's special brand of history. It was now Mason's turn to roll his eyes and huff his way through unloading the truck and helping set up the booth. Once they were in place and grown men dressed up like sticks of butter or cartons of eggs began circulating, Boyd set Mason free from his duties so he could get something to eat.

Boyd had finished helping Patrick with the last of the signs and was putting on his apron when he spotted Mason making his way back through what appeared to be a giant grocery store dairy section come to life.

"Hey, Dad. There's Ella," he said, rejoining the McNaughton clan, now in full force, and biting into a piece of monkey bread he'd no doubt bought from Vienna's bakery, which had a line down the block.

"Where?" Patrick and Cade glanced in opposite directions like lost tourists.

Boyd handed a sample to a guy he'd talked to earlier while they were setting up. He was interested in next year's Foghorn beer lineup. After the sample, Boyd would hand him off to Patrick. Boyd could talk beer all day long, but if this guy wanted to know about promotion, he'd be disappointed.

"Over there," Mason said through another bite.

"The woman in front of Sift with Thad?" Patrick asked.

Boyd stayed busy, but he saw his brothers trade glances and look back toward the street.

"Damn." Cade was so subtle.

Boyd looked over. Ella was outside of the bakery with Thad handing out what looked like samples. Foghorn Brewery was handing out samples too, but it was beer. Boyd couldn't believe Vienna managed to get Thad, the town fire chief, to stand outside her sunshine-yellow bakery, let alone with a basket. That must be love, he thought, unable to avert his eyes.

Thad, or Thaddeus Pane as they knew him in high school, was rumored to be the most eligible bachelor among most of the female population of Petaluma. Thanks to Aspen, they all knew he was with Vienna now, and that seemed like life balancing out the good and bad.

When Thad was in high school, he wore his pants too short and spent a lot of time being banged into lockers. He was a classic underdog story. More accurately, a nerd to Iron Man story. Boyd liked underdogs, so he was happy for the Thaddeus he knew back then and the great guy they all knew now. Vienna baked like no one's business, and she gave so much of her time to the community that the mayor gave her a key to the city last year. If there was such a thing as a perfect match, Boyd supposed Thad and Vienna were it.

Reluctantly, he found himself doing the "glance up and quickly look away" game he should have outgrown after grade school. Ella wasn't wearing scrubs or a lab coat, which made Boyd's feigned disinterest more difficult. She was in jeans, a white T-shirt that looked soft, and a short black leather jacket that should have come across as biker, but on her, it read out-of-town beautiful.

Dr. Ella Walters. She even sounded like she was from the big city. She and Thad laughed with Mr. Graham, who owned the hardware store and was giving out egg-shaped measuring tapes. The three of them seemed amused at some story Thad and his biceps were telling. Aspen had it all wrong. Someone like Thad was probably right up Ella's alley. Kale eating and gym comfortable.

Yeah, not Boyd's style at all. He wasn't against getting his heart rate going, but it needed to happen outdoors. Hooking himself up to a machine never sounded fun, but looking down at the tight apron that hugged his middle, he struggled to recall his current fitness regimen because he didn't have one. Too much work, too much takeout, and too much being a dad. Boyd had let himself get a little soft, which hadn't bothered him all that much until he found himself staring across B Street at a woman he was positive looked incredible naked.

"Yes," Cade said, coming up next to him.

"What?" Boyd concentrated on filling the sample cups.

"Yes, your beer gut has grown."

"Shut the hell up."

"That's what you're looking at, isn't it?"

"No. I'm wondering how I manage to be the only good-looking one out of the four of us. That's what I was wondering."

"Uh-huh. So, the ER doc?"

"What about her? You know for a guy having so much of that calorie-burning sex, you seem awfully interested in my game."

"So, you're not looking over there, not looking at her?"

"No reason to look at her." Boyd bent to get more cups, more napkins. Anything, because his brothers smelled blood again and now that they'd seen Ella, he didn't have a convincing argument for ignoring her.

"Strange, Trick, that Boyd didn't tell us his ER doc had legs for miles."

"Strange indeed. Little man, did you say you and your dad were down at the ER last week?" Patrick asked.

Mason nodded, licking his fingers, clueless to the trap his uncles were luring him into. Ah, the innocence of youth.

"Was your dad talking with Ella?"

"Yeah, they got along great. She's funny. He winked at her and it was badass."

"Did he now?" Patrick said.

Pain. In. The. Ass.

"Cade, you have a line"—he pointed—"of potential patrons to help pay for your overpriced bar." Boyd stood clear of the small gathering of people reading the chalk boards propped near the samples station. His little brother was still focused in Ella's direction. Hell, Cade was likely her type too.

"I'm taking a break." Boyd untied the leather apron and set it on top of the stacked crates Patrick had set up for "ambience." He was beginning to hate that word.

"That's convenient," Cade said, handing out a couple samples of Shamo Sunset.

"Isn't it? Mason, stick around. I'll be back."

"Can I go see Ella?"

Boyd peeked over his shoulder in time to see the doctor toss her head in laughter and hand another sample to an older guy with a beak mask around his neck.

Christ! She really was everywhere lately.

If Ella had been in town for two years, why hadn't he noticed her before? Patrick and Cade both stared at him as if they somehow thought he was going to bound across the festival and pull her into his arms. For a moment of insanity, that didn't sound like a bad idea, but thankfully his sense returned.

"Okay, but stay where your uncles can see you," he finally answered Mason.

"Where are you going?" Patrick asked.

"I... have to make some calls and we're out of—"

Aspen moved between Boyd and Patrick to hand Cade the cashbox. "This is in case anyone wants to buy merchandise or the new T-shirts we had made for the Tap House," she said before dumping an extra bag of ice in the front display.

Both his brothers crossed their arms, and Cade smirked.

"What'd I miss?" she asked and followed all the eyes on Ella. "I told you she was beautiful. And funny too."

"I'm taking a break." He leveled a stare at both of his brothers. "And I don't owe either one of you an explanation. Watch the booth."

"Got it. We're on it, big brother completely unaffected by the gorgeous blond life-saving and also funny doctor. You do you and we'll keep an eye on things," Cade managed to say all in one breath.

Boyd wanted to flip all of them off, but there were families around and the booth next to them had baby chicks. Only a crazy man used obscene finger gestures in front of children and chicks. He felt dangerously close to crazy.

Maybe Ella's father was right. Maybe she was a silly woman because, despite a moment where she, Bri, and Thad clapped for the little kids dressed as various colors of chicks as they filed out of Copperfield's Books for the Cutest Chick contest, Ella couldn't take her eyes off the Foghorn Brewery booth. She was certain there were a lot of women drawn to that section of the festival, but she'd never thought of herself as obvious. The air was filled with barbecue, sunscreen, and spring. And of course, the cinnamon and sugar spilling out of Sift.

When Ella left San Francisco, she'd vowed to steer clear of the ridiculous. But there was something about Boyd McNaughton. She nearly laughed at herself it was so cliché. He'd come into her ER. People didn't meet like that. Maybe Bri was right—she needed to get naked with someone and start hating Mondays with the rest of the world before she entertained the idea that Boyd McNaughton and his fantastic son might be the type of people she'd been missing her whole life. She wasn't certain if it was his eyes, aged beyond his years, his broad, almost hulking frame, or that beard. What the hell was with the beard?

She glanced back one last time before agreeing to find a bathroom with Bri and caught his eyes. Eyes were cliché too. Damn it. He was walking away from the booth and dipped his head in acknowledgment. Not a word or a smile. Only a "yeah, I see you." And then he was gone into the crowd. She'd avoided his booth on purpose, which was silly, but she wasn't looking for trouble and she got the distinct impression the other day that Boyd wasn't thrilled with his son's new friendship. His life, their life, seemed self-contained. Ella both understood and respected his solitary purpose.

"Hey, Ella," Mason said, moments later after Pam arrived to give Vienna a break so she, Bri, and Vienna could go check out the pie contest. Ella waved them on and stayed put.

"Mason. Great to see you. This is so fun, right?" She took in the pre-parade festivities and frenzy.

"Yeah, you don't think it's lame?"

"This is most definitely not lame."

"I guess it's cool."

"Have you had the monkey bread? It's bad how good it is. I wanted to buy two, but people were watching."

"Our booth is over there. My dad took a break, but my uncles are there. Want to meet them?"

"Sure." So much for avoidance. She followed Mason and saw the resemblance in Boyd's brothers immediately. The taller one was a clean-cut and fancier-dressed version of Boyd. Same thick hair, but he was lean and his eyes were bigger. The other brother had a winding tattoo on his arm and his hair was cut short on the sides. He was built, lots-of-hours-at-the-gym built. And wearing a shirt that read "Foghorn Brewery—Cocks on Tap" above a sketched rooster on a bar.

Ella smiled. "Great shirt."

"Thanks." He extended his hand. "Cade." Firm handshake. Ella appreciated that and his blatant comfort with standing out. Was there one of every kind in the McNaughton family?

"I'm Ella, a friend of Mason's."

Mason beamed and nodded at his uncle. Ella couldn't explain it, but she was proud to be his friend. Honored that he wanted to be hers.

"This is my other uncle Trick. Well, his name is Patrick, but we call him Trick."

Patrick extended his hand.

"You must be the candy-ass."

"Sorry?" He chuckled.

"When your brother was in the ER, he said he'd cut his hand because of his candy-ass brother. You're marketing, right?"

Patrick nodded.

"Candy-ass."

"Guilty."

"Nice to meet you both." She was amazed at how easy it was to talk with all of them. "Are you the youngest?" she asked Cade.

"Second youngest. Our other brother lives in San Francisco."

Ella nodded and accepted a sample of beer Patrick handed her.

"My dad is the oldest. Then Trick and then Cade. My other uncle is a movie star."

"Seriously?"

Mason nodded. "Westin Drake. He's Nick Shot in the—"

"*Full Throttle* movies." She took a sip and nodded her appreciation to Patrick.

"You've seen them?" Mason asked.

"I have. A couple, but I can't remember which ones. That has to be awesome having an uncle in the movies."

"It is. He's cool."

"Hey, we're cool too."

"No, you're not," a voice from behind them said. Once again, Ella turned as Boyd appeared seemingly out of nowhere. Barely a smile on his lips and his hand on his squirming son's head. Mason broke free.

"Dad, Ella has seen Uncle West's movies."

"That is impressive." Boyd didn't meet her eyes. It was as if he was having a conversation with only his son.

"Yup, some of them," she said, wanting to make her presence known. It must have worked because he finally met her eyes, sort of.

"Nice. Do you like the beer?" He gestured to the now-empty cup in her hand.

"I do." The air crackled. Her shoulder barely brushed his and she willed herself to stay casual, comfortable. "Is this the famous brew you were mixing in the keggle?"

She should not have said that, referenced that, because he smiled. Holy wow, slow and easy as if he saved this particular grin for a few times a week and he needed to make it count. Warmth and male. Ella had been around some sexy polished men in her time, and this wasn't put on or practiced. It was almost organic and so rich that her head spun a little. Their eyes held.

"Look at you remembering the lingo. Yes, this is the famous brew."

Ella nodded, but before she was reduced to a bobblehead, she homed in on what she knew.

"Is the scar fading yet?" she said, instinctively touching his arm and lifting his hand as if they were back in the ER. Yet another mistake. Outside the security of the sterile walls of the hospital and without her rubber gloves, touching him felt like, well, touching. He twitched a bit at the contact, and she couldn't blame him. There was a charge between them every time, but now in the sunlight surrounded by family and fun, it was more of everything Ella knew nothing about.

Or maybe he felt nothing at all, she wondered. *Maybe he thinks I'm a complete weirdo for grabbing a virtual stranger in public.* She was clearly overdosing on contact and now needed to work on boundaries. "Oh, sorry. I don't know why I grabbed you."

"It's fine. The grab and the scar. Yes, it's fading. Both are fine." Boyd stepped behind the booth like he was afraid of her. Perfect. His brothers had returned to serving customers, but they were smiling as if they knew something she didn't. Or they were smiling because they thought she was a crazy person who manhandled their brother. Either scenario made her uneasy.

"Ella, want to go get more monkey bread?" Mason said, breaking her free of mortification.

"Will you say it's yours? Because I've already had one, and no doubt Vienna will give me a hard time."

"Okay." He laughed. "No one cares. I thought all adults stopped caring what other people thought. Isn't that like the only benefit of getting old?"

"Yeah, well some of us are late bloomers," she said.

"Dad, can I have money?"

"You have your allowance."

"Nice meeting you," she said to Patrick and Cade, who both invited her back anytime. They were still smiling.

"Boyd." She tipped her head in what she hoped was an I-can-take-you-or-leave-you gesture.

"Ella." He gave it right back, but she somehow believed him. As she and Mason walked away, he called them back. Mason turned and he handed him a ten-dollar bill.

"Buy Dr. Walters some monkey bread. Keep her secret."

"What's her secret?"

"All women have secrets. Hasn't she shared that little piece of advice?"

Ella swallowed. Christ, he was easier to deal with on her turf. "A monkey bread addiction is hardly a secret," she said.

Boyd smiled again, and this time he knew the potency. Was she that transparent? Until that moment, she'd thought herself immune to all things male. Boyd was harmless, she told herself.

Oh, you silly woman, her heart nearly cried out.

"Want to come with, Dad?"

"I think you've got this. Go easy on him, Doc."

Ella managed a smile, but almost tripped over her feet as she left with Mason, who she was beginning to think was the only safe male in the McNaughton family tree.

Chapter Twelve

Boyd's breathing had returned to normal once they were back at the brewery. Somehow, standing in the familiar was grounding and gave him a sense of what was real. Ella didn't seem real at all. He couldn't figure out where she'd come from or how in the space of a few weeks he'd found himself needing something more—No, that was the wrong word. He needed to brew, needed to hear his son singing in the shower, or see his family gathered around a table. If he had to make a list of can't live withouts, those would be his top choices. Ella was... she was a nagging craving that seemed more and more determined every time he saw her.

There was no question she liked Mason. Who could blame her? But that was the extent of this. He was a great kid, and lots of motherly types liked Mason. Not that she seemed all that motherly. Aw, hell, he was getting trapped in his thoughts again. Stick with craving. Potato chips, Vienna's sticky buns, and the local doctor.

Boyd tightened the loose screw on the door that swung to the back of the bar and stored the toolbox below the stereo. Cade was pacing and not eating, two things completely out of character.

"Pass-through fixed. I think that's it. The band is warming up."

Cade still looked like he was waiting for bad news.

"You okay?"

"Oh, yeah. I'm great, this is kick-ass, right?" Cade closed his eyes and leaned against the bar. "Any advice? Because I feel like I'm going to throw up."

Boyd rested his elbows on the bar next to his almost youngest brother. "Advice. Hmm... let's see."

He could tell Cade expected sarcasm. Sometimes it washed over Boyd—how old they all were, how much time had passed. He remembered when Cade got stuck in the seat belt in the back of their parents' Suburban and they had to cut him out. He'd been squirming around and trying to sit closer to the center so he didn't miss any of the action. The belt locked and trapped him in there. Their father had laughed so hard he had tears in his eyes until he found out it cost $350 to put in a new seat belt. Boyd didn't know it at the time, but that one incident encapsulated who his brother was. Kid or man, the guy was always plugged in and entertaining, scared to death he might miss something.

"You feeling the heat?" Boyd asked.

Cade nodded.

"There's no pressure. Be you."

His brother snickered. "Not sure how many bills that's going to pay."

"Oh, come on, you're smarter than this. You're the shit and you know it. You've built this and now it's showtime."

"We've built it."

"Yeah, but you're the yeast."

Cade lifted his brow. "Is there a punch line here somewhere?"

"No. I'm serious. You could argue yeast is the most important part in making beer. You can't technically have beer without water, hops, and grain, but without yeast, there's no action. I'm mean hell, hefeweizen isn't even hefeweizen without ale yeast. Yeast is the flavor, the style, and some would argue, the quality." Boyd bumped his brother's shoulder. "Don't worry about being something you think a fancy tap house needs. Do you and people will flock here, man. I promise."

Cade's eyes welled up and he quickly turned away. "What the fuck was that?"

Boyd laughed.

"Get out of my bar."

"All right, my work is done here." Boyd slapped his hands on the bar and backed away to go find Mason.

"Hey," Cade called to him.

Boyd turned around.

"You sure about all that stuff you said?"

Boyd nodded. "I'm the oldest, little brother. I'm never wrong."

Cade let out a breath, and Boyd felt that buzz knowing he'd helped. It was heady.

After about an hour of recon surveillance, as Mason put it, and no sign of Chloe, Ella went back to Sift to help Vienna and Thad clean up before the big brewery opening. Mason followed.

"Are you coming to the opening?"

"I might stop by," Ella said, picking up napkins and paper cups from some of the outside tables.

Mason pulled the trash bag from one of the metal cans and followed her around.

"You're pretty good at cleaning up," she said.

"Lots of practice."

When she glanced at him for confirmation, he added, "I help out around the brewery and I've got chores."

"What kind of chores?"

"Stuff to earn my allowance. Take out the trash, pick up my room. Dad does the laundry, but I make toast in the morning."

"Every morning?"

"It's kind of our routine."

"Do you have lots of those, routines? I only ask because I like my routines too."

"Yeah, I guess. We don't have lots of time in the mornings before school so I guess we do have a set thing. I pick out my own clothes though, thank God."

Ella laughed.

"He's fun, you know, and funny."

"Your dad?" Ella asked. She already knew who he was talking about, but she needed a minute to corral her thoughts.

Mason nodded and handed her the wet rag from the table they'd already wiped down.

"I'm sure he is. You all seem like you have a good time."

He kept nodding and seemed to go somewhere in his mind, as if he was searching for a way to help her understand.

"Mase, I can see why your dad is the way he is."

"You can?"

"Sure." She threw the last of the trash away. "I don't have children of my own, but it seems like an important job, you know. And he's good at it."

"I know."

"I'm sure he's given you great advice on Chlo"—Ella glanced around—"on she. Your dad knows you far better than I do and even though he's a dad, you might want to ask him all these questions you're having."

Mason shrugged. "He's good at a lot of things, but he's not good at girls."

"No?"

He shook his head. "I'll stick with your advice." Mason glanced back toward the Foghorn booth, which was now torn down, and Patrick waved him over.

"I gotta go." He handed her the trash bag.

"Have fun tonight."

"Okay, see you there. There'll be a pretty sick band and my Uncle Cade is a badass—well, he's cool."

"I'll try to stop by."

"Hey, thanks for calling me Mase. I think that means we're officially friends." He waved over his head as he ran back to his uncles. Ella hadn't even noticed she'd shortened his name, nor did she expect it to mean so much to a thirteen-year-old.

Ella drank wine. Her knowledge of beer extended to the massive beer aisle at her grocery store. She appreciated the funny names and the inventive beer labels, but as far as the taste, beer reminded her of medical school, specifically a bitter taste and all-day hangover. The sample she'd had of Boyd's beer was different, but she'd been too busy trying to regulate her breathing to pay attention. She didn't need to go to the Tap House opening. It was probably better to leave well enough alone.

"I'll pick you up in about an hour?" Vienna said, turning off the lights behind the counter as Thad collected the remaining trash bags and the one from Ella to take to the curbside cans.

"Isn't Thad coming?"

"He is. We'll come by and we can all walk together. Ooh, and maybe you'll need to stop by for a latte tomorrow to help your hangover after all of the partying and raucous fun we're going to have tonight."

"I doubt that. I have work tomorrow. You know, I should shower. You two go and find Bri... I'll meet you there." Ella had no intention of being a third wheel, and she'd honestly had enough feelings for one day.

"No, because you won't go."

"Of course I'll go. I attend all big events."

"Is this because of Thad? I can tell him to meet us there and you and I can walk over together."

"That's silly. I'm leaving now." Ella pushed on the door and allowed Thad, who was coming back from the trash, to pass.

"Okay, but if you're not there by six thirty, I'm calling."

"I'll be there."

"I thought you were going with us," Thad said, wrapping his massive arm around Vienna as they all made their way to lock up the front door.

"I am. I'll be there." Ella went up on her toes and kissed Thad on the cheek. The man was a sweetheart.

"You know how relentless I can be." Vienna locked the door and turned to kiss Ella.

"I do, indeed. I will be there, my dear Cookie Monster." Ella took in a deep breath of cool early-evening air and reminded herself that change was good. It had brought her to this town, her new home. Change had given her true friends and peace.

She'd been joined at the hip with Vienna and Bri pretty much from the moment she'd arrived in town. It was good that her friend had found someone. No doubt, it changed the dynamics, but it was time for Ella to slow down and figure out what lurked in the crevices of her mind when she wasn't running from double shifts to exhaustion on her bike. Her stomach turned. Vienna hadn't even said anything about not doing everything with her yet. She was projecting again, nothing had happened.

All she needed to worry about was getting home and pretending she wasn't looking forward to bumping into Boyd again. This time she'd be on his turf, and the thought of him in his element was intriguing. It might be fun watching him run away from her again, or figuring out why it bothered her so much.

Chapter Thirteen

The Tap Room opening was in full swing and exactly as Boyd had predicted. Cade was on fire: a natural entertainer with a gift for putting people at ease and showing them a good time. Their parents were sharing a high-top table with West and Meg, who came up from San Francisco. Boyd was happy to see his youngest brother, previously stifled by photographers and his own fame, finally at a place where the occasional whisper or iPhone didn't bother him. Meg was part of that, Boyd knew. It was easy to see she loved West, and that seemed to make all the difference in his life.

Patrick was across the room, handing out business cards to a group of men and women in similar casual, expensive cotton and trendy glasses. Aspen joined him, bringing over merchandise from behind the bar. No doubt the next big deal, Boyd thought and found he was smiling. Mason and a couple of his friends were running back and forth between chili cheese fries and the arcade games in the back. No girls had arrived, to his knowledge, and it was nice to see Mase being a kid.

Boyd leaned against the back wall that vibrated to the drums and bass of the band. He was absorbed in watching his world play out before him and didn't even see Ella walk in, which was a short-lived blessing. Once his eyes found her, he wondered how it was possible he'd missed her. She was still in jeans, a silkier top, and boots—half boots maybe. Whatever they were, she sported an impressive heel. Her hair was pulled off her face and looked like it was damp. That led to wondering if she'd taken a shower. Yeah, he was off to a great start.

He should just give up and stop trying to ignore the overwhelming need to touch her, finally know what it was to be close enough to hear her heartbeat, share breath. Ella joined Vienna, Thad, and two other women at the bar. She acknowledged Cade and Patrick. Boyd finished the last sip of his beer and moved into the crowd. The noise helped stifle his thoughts.

"Son." His father put a hand on Boyd's shoulder. "Could you please tell your baby brother here that I never walked around the house in my underwear?"

"You did," West exclaimed. "Remember when I had a sleepover on Halloween, Boyd? We were watching that movie where the babysitter was freaking out because the guy's in the house."

"*When a Stranger Calls*," their mother said. "I think I remember this, Rich."

West's hands were flailing and Meg was laughing. "Right? It was like one in the morning and you went to the door in your bedroom, circled around to the pool, and started banging on the sliding glass door."

Boyd laughed. "I remember this."

"We crapped our pants. It was pitch black and when I aimed the flashlight, there you were in nothing but your tighty-whities, jumping around like Bigfoot."

Boyd was practically crying at this point, as was the rest of the table, including their father.

Shaking his head, their dad finally caught his breath. "I guess I did do that, but I thought I'd put some clothes on."

"Nope," West said. "To this day, I don't know what scared us more."

"Hey, your father has a great body."

"Thanks, honey." He pulled their mom in for a kiss while Boyd and West both cringed.

"Where's Trick?" West asked.

Boyd pointed to the corner booth.

"Working a lot, huh?" their dad said.

Boyd shrugged. "Could be a while before he has such a large cap-tive and intoxicated audience again."

"True," West said.

"Speaking of beer," Meg said. "I don't even like beer, Boyd, and this is amazing."

He bowed his head. "Thank you."

West caught his brother's eyes and raised his glass. "Never had a doubt, man. Why are you without a glass?"

"Let me take care of that," he said and turned toward the bar. Swerving through the crowd, he came chest to chest with Ella. Her hands flew up as if she was deliberately trying not to touch him. Boyd was grateful because he didn't how much more of bumping into Ella Walters he could take. The guy at his back, the one who had pushed him closer to the woman he needed to stand clear of, stepped away.

Boyd should have backed up into the now-available space. He should have lifted his gaze from her mouth or the tiny freckle on the right side of her collarbone. He was an expert at doing what he should do, until now. He didn't back away. He stood there, willing his arms not to encircle her waist but relishing he was finally in the same space. She stayed put too. Was it possible she knew that being close to her was like warming his hands over a fire on a cold night? Their eyes met. What the hell was he going to do with Ella Walters?

The crowd moved again and they were hugged into the edge of the polished wood. They both turned to face the bar as if it was choreographed somehow and settled next to each other in the swirl of music and laughter.

"So, your brother really is Nick Shot," she said, a mischievous smile playing at the edges of her lips.

"Correction, my brother is Westin McNaughton. Not nearly as dangerous as Nick Shot."

"He always was the jealous brother," West said, now standing be-hind them.

"You wish. He waxes his ass, did I mention that?" Boyd said, not even bothering to turn around. West had an uncanny feelings detector. Boyd wasn't sure if it was all that time in Hollyweird, but the youngest McNaughton could spot bullshit a mile away, which meant he somehow homed in on genuine feelings. If Boyd turned around, there was no doubt West would see everything coursing through his chest. Yeah, he didn't need that right now. Boyd glanced at Ella and finally caught Cade's attention.

West put his arm around Boyd. "You seem awfully obsessed with my ass. You going to introduce me to your... friend?"

Ella laughed.

"You're an idiot," Boyd glanced over his shoulder.

"Probably." He extended his hand. "I'm Westin, the youngest of the clan. They'll try to tell you I'm the littlest. That rumor is a lie. Just want to put that out there."

"I'm Ella. Great to meet you, West. Thanks for the laugh."

"He's not funny. I'm the funny one."

"Yeah you are, old-timer. You're hysterical."

West pushed between them and ordered another round. Boyd would never admit it to himself or his pretty brother, but he waited for that sigh or recognition that most women oozed when they were around West. He was more in line with Thad the fire chief and while Boyd was not jealous, he was a realist. Women liked men who came across less like a dad and more like the cover of a magazine. It's not like he was testing her, that would be absurd, he was simply waiting for the inevitable.

No sigh. She craned her neck behind West and met Boyd's eyes. It was like she was checking on him or checking him out. Christ, he had no idea, but the whole thing made him dizzy. There he was, thirty-seven and dizzy. No wonder poor Mason dropped his burrito. This girl stuff was insane.

"Okay, well you two kids stay out of trouble," West said, his hands now full of pint glasses. "It was nice meeting you, Ella. And yeah, don't worry about that bald spot he's getting in the back here. I'll bet it's just a cowlick."

Boyd moved to bump him out of the way.

"Ah, ah, don't make me drop the merchandise. I heard a rumor you barely have enough of these glasses. Bad for business." West laughed and wove back into the throng of celebration.

The night sky above them, what Boyd could see through the wood beams, was dotted with lights, and the air smelled of delicious food and success. They were a hit, at least for tonight. He should finish out the evening in relief... should be reveling in the reward of their months of hard work, but he couldn't concentrate. A strand of hair blew across Ella's face and she gently tucked it behind her ear.

How was it possible she'd lived in Petaluma and he'd never seen her, he pondered for the hundredth time, following her gaze to Mason and his friends playing cornhole. She turned to him, laughter dancing across her eyes, and Boyd lost his breath.

"Do we know if 'she' is here?" Ella asked, leaning into him, the smell of vanilla and praline flooding his senses. That was the second time she'd done that, defused the surge between them with everyday conversation. Did she know how beautiful she was so she put people at ease before they made assholes out of themselves? Was the way his body reacted to her written all over his face?

He combed the crowd as if that might help remind him that she was there for Mason, that she was his friend, and that it didn't matter if her mouth tasted like vanilla.

"I don't think she's here. But, I've only seen her twice. Once from the car when I was dropping him off at school. She was handing out the school newsletter. The other time was at their seventh-grade play last year. She has curly hair. Oh, and I guess I saw her in the yearbook, but I don't think I'd recognize her from that picture."

Ella faced him to scan the crowd in the opposite direction at the same time the guy next to her decided to buy the bar a round. In his excitement to give away his money, he bumped Ella and she fell into Boyd. Her hands went to his chest this time and there they were again. Boyd nearly lost his mind. In the next second, as if she'd been shocked, she pulled her hands back.

"Sorry, I was—"

"It's fine. You're good. Excuse me."

How the hell did he own part of a bar now? They should have kept this thing a brewery, a quiet, solitary brewery. Now they'd invited fun and people falling all over each other. Mingling air and glances that felt like invitations. His heart pounded in his chest as he walked out of the crowd looking for a lifeline. For the first time ever, no one needed a damn thing. Figured. Even Patrick had joined their parents, and Aspen was now with Ella's friends. Boyd didn't look back. He needed more air.

There had to be something that required tending to. Hell, he sounded like his mom. Maybe Mason needed something. As if on cue, his son's laughter filled the edges of the space and Boyd noticed him high-fiving his friends over some cornhole victory, laughing in that way boys did when they forgot about girls. Boyd shoved his hands into his pockets, hoping to God he'd soon remember how to forget.

Ella toasted with her friends and watched Vienna hit the dance floor with Thad, all while keeping her eyes on Boyd. He seemed like a trapped animal as he disappeared around the side of one of the buildings. She finished the beer Bri had handed her and followed him. Zigzagging through the mass of people, she hoped she didn't run out of words because one of them needed to say something. She could go with safe and ask him why he didn't appear to like her, or she could take a chance and tell him the truth.

"Whoa, sorry." Boyd almost plowed her over as Ella came around the side of the building. There was no contact this time. Instead, he held her steady by both shoulders, as if she smelled. The guy was harsh on a woman's ego.

"I understand," Ella said, not certain that was even an effective opening.

"Understand what?"

"That being with Mason is your job and that the two of you are sort of a team."

"Did he tell you that?"

"He said you are his best friend. That you never let him call you that, but you are and that it has been the two of you for a long time." She paused, debating if she should say the next part. "I was trying to figure out why you had an issue with me, and I think maybe that's it."

"I don't have an issue with you. I don't know what's going on with Mason. He is suddenly—he seems to need something he didn't need before. I mean, of course, he needs his mom, I've read all the books, but he didn't appear to be missing anything outside of our family until—"

"Me." In his expression, she saw all the pieces of a man. He was a father first. That was all over him, but she wondered what that took away. Being a single parent couldn't be easy and even though he clearly had the love and support of his family, Boyd somehow looked alone.

"Not you. It's that he's getting older. He's not a kid anymore. I'm catching up."

"Is his mom..."

"She's not in the picture a lot."

Ella felt odd bringing it up, and he shut it down so fast she nearly missed the sting of pain.

"I had this thought," she said before she caught her breath and lost her nerve.

"Okay. I should get back to—"

"It looks as though you can't stand being around me. Every time Mason and I are having another one of our chats, you are quick to get out."

He was still holding her shoulders but said nothing.

"But then." Ella shifted her weight to one leg and settled into the feel of his arms, the heat of his body. She was surprised how easy the connection felt. God, she hoped she was right about this.

"Then?" he said on a breath.

"Then sometimes I catch a glimpse, or I notice you're looking at me before you have a chance to look away and I just..." Her body leaned into him all on its own like a moth to the energy that slid across his eyes.

"Just?" His hands held her the tiniest bit tighter, and Ella couldn't tell who was holding who at that point.

"I don't want to step over some invisible line you've drawn around yourself, but I feel things when I'm around you, Boyd. And I think that maybe you do too, that maybe you'd like to—" Slowly, she brought her hand toward his face. She didn't touch him, she honestly wasn't sure how to tackle a man like Boyd. His breathing was heavier now.

A loud noise from the Tap House startled them both and whatever was in his eyes slipped down her arms, along with his hands.

"Ella, I'm sorry if you think I don't want you around Mason. That's not true. You're his friend and—"

Another rumble that sounded like someone whacking the side of a metal can, this one followed by laughter.

"I need to get back over there." His eyes were everywhere but on her. "Are we good?" He nodded as if he were talking to himself. "Good."

Before she could say a word, he moved past her and she stood wondering why she'd followed him. The guy obviously didn't—

"Aw, hell."

She heard his voice, turned to see what was wrong, and found her entire body wrapped in him. His chest pressed to hers, arms holding her as his face dipped and he took her mouth. Her knees gave first, which was strange because she'd never been prone to fainting. Even in medical school. But they most definitely betrayed her now as Boyd's arm held her waist and drew her closer.

Sweet Jesus. She didn't even have a minute to process that she hadn't been wrong after all, that he did have feelings. There were no brain cells left for that thought. His mouth moved over hers as if kissing was something he'd taken the time to master. Pulling, his tongue slid across her lips asking for more and when Ella let him in, she realized she was shaking.

She'd been kissed before, hadn't she? She could have sworn there were memories of other men holding her like this, but she must have been mistaken. This right here was kissing. This was chest pounding, fists in hair. The man had taken her from irritation, right through confusion, and deep into need in less than a minute. All while standing under the stars with the rest of his world right around the corner. This was kissing, and she was certain she had never done this.

Someone called out a song and the music grew louder. Ella barely noticed until Boyd gently pulled his mouth off hers.

The only word to describe his expression was blissful. He was like a man fully satisfied after an incredibly long drought.

He smiled and she practically fell over.

"Yes, to all the above," he said.

She swallowed, not bothering to hide the shock. "What were the questions again?"

A laugh rumbled in his chest. With one arm still circling her body, he reached up and ran his thumb across her lips.

Not helping with the knees, Boyd. Go easy on a woman, will you?

"I have no clue what to do with this, but I didn't want you to think you were alone."

"And you were loud and clear on that point."

More laughter and a smile she'd never seen before. The man was potent when trying to avoid her. When he let out the happy, it was near deadly. He gently released her and stepped back, smile still in place until he bowed his head and appeared a bit lost.

"All right, so."

Ella's eyes widened. "So is right, beer man. Thank you for... answering my questions. I'll have to think of some more."

"Boyd," a rowdy voice called from somewhere in the night sky, "get out here, man, and tell Cade there's no limit on my tab, will ya?"

His eyes never left her as he slowly stepped back. "I should probably."

Ella nodded. "See you around."

He tipped his head in that way he'd done so many times before. She now understood that a gesture she used to interpret as indifferent dismissal was his way of saying, "There are no words."

After reaching out to touch her hand one more time, he walked back around the corner. Ella rested against the building and brought her hands to her face. She knew it was absurd, but she had goose bumps. She'd never felt anything so amazing outside the thrill of her job in her entire life. She wasn't some blushing teenager. She was a physician, a grown woman well past thirty with a heart firmly in the witness protection program.

But, he made her feel things that had her wishing he'd been her first everything. That he'd touched her brand-new heart before it broke and healed differently. There was something so pure and so sexy in the way he touched her. She took in the glorious night sky one more time and rejoined her friends.

Monday, easing out of this weekend, was going to be a tough go, Ella admitted. Not that she'd give Bri the satisfaction of that information.

Chapter Fourteen

Boyd thought about calling her, even entertained the idea of texting or using his own flesh and blood to casually bump into her again. It had been four days since he kissed her, almost five maybe. Every next move he came up with sounded stupid, so he did nothing. He'd kissed her and then they'd shared a little harmless eye contact for the rest of the night. That was it. Maybe she wasn't even expecting a call. She could be busy. It's not like they'd had some long discussion or slept together. Hell, that'd probably kill him.

He hadn't led her on. It was a moment of weakness and now things were back on track. Weren't they? He had a science fair to go to and she had... lives to save or books to read with his mother. He had no idea what she did in her free time. See, they barely knew each other. Everything is fine, that was his motto according to Patrick. Because of said motto, Boyd hadn't called. Which might or might not make him a jerk who kissed the hell out of a woman on the side of a building and then because he didn't know what to do with all the want, ignored her instead.

Shit!

He somehow found Mason among the maze of propped-up foam boards and lunch tables in the cafeteria of Petaluma Junior High

School. His project was number forty-three, Boyd remembered because he wrote it on the back in Sharpie at the stoplight before the school entrance less than ten hours ago. They'd fitted a wooden car with a solar battery and measured how much energy and the charge time it took for three different obstacles. Mason had wanted to do the beer-making process, but his science teacher said that was inappropriate.

Boyd learned after years of dealing with educators not to argue, but as the chill of the cafeteria air conditioning hit him, he noticed the kid two tables down from Mason did his science fair project on how to butcher a lamb. Boyd shook his head and questioned not for the first time about the general perception of appropriate.

"How's it going?" he asked, approaching Mason's table.

"Good. One of the wheels broke off when we were moving them around this afternoon, but I fixed it."

"How?" Boyd glanced at his model.

"Big Red." Mason patted his pocket.

He grinned. "Good thinking. Resourceful. I like it."

"Have you walked around yet?"

"I saw the lamb on my way over," he said quietly.

"Right? What the hell? I mean what the heck, and I can't do barley and water?"

Boyd shrugged. "Maybe once you get to high school."

"We have to do this in high school too?"

Before Boyd could answer, Cameron, Mason's second or third best friend—Boyd could never keep the order straight—joined them.

"Hey, Mr. McNaughton."

"Cameron. How's it going?"

"Well, my little sister ate a chunk out of my clay volcano, so there's that."

Mason laughed and exchanged some type of telepathic dialogue with his friend. "Dad, I'll be right back."

"Okay. I'll... walk around."

Boyd moved past brightly colored foam core and poster board, a parakeet, two lizards, and half a dozen models of the solar system. He nodded greetings to a few of the parents he recognized and when he found himself approaching the judges' table, he froze and tried to change direction. It was too late.

"Boyd," Angela Morse called out.

He closed his eyes for a second as if he could teleport like a *Star Trek* character. When that didn't work, he faced the two women who were now famous at the brewery. After countless stories, Patrick and Cade called them the mother hens.

"Angela, Stacey. Things look terrific. Great turnout this year, eh?"

"Thank you for saying so. Come here, you." Angela pulled him in for a tight hug complete with several pats on the back and the wafting smell of gardenias. Boyd pulled back, uncomfortable as always. "How are things with you?" she asked, and Boyd noticed she had a little bit of pink lipstick on her teeth, not that he was going to mention it.

"Oh, you know. Laundry." Lame answer, but he was still recovering from the hug.

"So cute that you do laundry. I can't get Steve to put his socks in the hamper let alone wash them," Stacey said, followed by grown-up giggling.

"What kind of fabric softener do you use? Or do you use those little beads? You do smell delicious," Angela added with a strange shrug, as if she were hugging him all over again.

Boyd could never tell if this was flirting or a weird form of nurturing. Whatever the case, it had been going on since Mason started kindergarten and got creepier from there. He didn't answer the laundry question, simply hoped the awkwardness would vanish.

"Mason tells me you're working yourself ragged getting the beer house—is it? Getting that up," Stacey added.

He took a deep breath, making a mental note to have the oversharing conversation with Mason again. "Tap house, it's a tap house and we are finally done. Thanks for asking. So, is the judging done, or do you have more work to do?"

"The judges are finishing up and then we'll tabulate. You know, Greg has a new administrative assistant and she is darling. Recently moved here from Idaho, or Ohio. I get those two mixed up. Anyway, I'd love to have you over for dinner so you two could meet," Angela said.

Greg was her husband and the CEO of a staffing company. This was easily his third administrative assistant in the last three years. The guy was either impossible to work for or kept hiring attractive assistants and his wife wanted them gone. Boyd was sure he had been asked to "drop by and meet" at least two others.

"We could do barbecue at my house," Stacey added, not helping.

Boyd was used to this routine. He'd been set up, cooked for, and coddled more times than he could count over the years, and he had to admit he'd mastered the art of excuses. Technically it was lying, he'd once had to explain to Mason years ago, "but it's either a little lie or hurt feelings. I'm going with the little lie," Boyd had said.

"Oh, barbecue sounds great. But I can't do anything until after graduation. Mason and I are working on a project with... Habitat for Humanity."

"Again?"

Crap, had he used that one already? He was slipping.

"Same one, it's a... continuation of the same project. They are an admirable organization, don't you think?"

Both women nodded. If they were suspicious, they were not letting on. Two of the jacketed guys with JUDGE on their lapels approached, and Boyd took that as his chance at a quick getaway.

"Thank you for the invite, ladies. Please thank Greg and we'll get together soon."

"But, it's only one night, don't you think—"

Boyd blended into the sea of other parents and kept his head down. He hoped random moms were less involved in his love life once Mason went to high school.

Almost back to Mason's table, Boyd nodded in recognition to one of the single moms, Mary or Marti, he could never remember, but he knew he liked her. Mason had gone over to her house a couple of times for her son's birthday. Boyd wondered if the dads treated her the same way as the moms treat Boyd. Were they constantly offering to fix her sink or carry her plants in from Home Depot? Such a bizarre world they traveled in, he thought. It was like they were in a land of starfish and they, him and Mary or Marti, were missing some legs. Like they weren't quite a full star and everyone else in the village was trying to repair them. Boyd could never tell if the gestures were out of kindness or fear that they too might someday lose one of their legs.

"You okay?" Bri asked as Ella handed the lady in Exam 2 with a broken pinkie toe off to her for discharge.

"Yeah, I'm great. I don't think Mrs. Beetle will need more than ibuprofen, but I put a script in there for six hundred milligrams so I don't have to worry about her taking too much over the counter. Please tape her up good and reiterate that she needs to be off her feet at least until the end of the weekend."

"Got it." Bri gave her that familiar look that said she recognized something was not right.

Ella gave Bri the chart and walked toward the nurses' station. She needed to hide behind her professional routine right now. She did not need a friend, nor did she need to feel anything at that moment. Everything in her head was upside down, and personal or not, that's what Ella loved about work. Calm in the storm, she told herself.

She sat in the break room eating a new ginger sesame chicken noodle pot she'd read about in some torture-yourself-until-you're-perfect-like-us magazine. She'd decided last night that she'd been eating too much barbecue or monkey bread, something. She needed to recalibrate and get back to a meal plan before she saw her family or they would certainly comment on her less-than-radiant hair or softer belly. Maybe she was adopted, Ella thought, opening her Kindle to chapter seven of *Needful Things* by Stephen King. No one in the book club had read anything by King, although Boyd's mom had mentioned being stunned to learn he wrote *Shawshank Redemption* and *The Green Mile*. That was how she hooked them to read one of his books for their club.

"It's not just gore, I promise you," she'd told them and then picked one of her favorites. She hoped they were going to see what she saw, but if not, she was still happy for the familiar distraction. Her phone was tucked deep into her purse and secured in her locker where it belonged. She was tired of looking at it and annoyed at herself that she cared.

It was one kiss. What grown person fawned over one kiss and sat around distracted, waiting for a call or a text? Someone who forgot she enjoyed Mondays, that's who. She read the same paragraph three times before tossing her Kindle onto the table in a huff of frustration.

"Is it keeping track of all the characters? Is that why you're throwing your Kindle? I know, right? Yesterday, I had to get Post-its and start writing them down. I'm already creeped out by this little store, I don't mind telling you. If this thing gives me nightmares or cuts down on the bliss of late-night internet shopping, I'm blaming it on you," Bri rambled as she sat and opened her store-bought sandwich.

She glanced over at Ella's mason jar of half-eaten lunch.

"Do I even want to know what that is?"

Ella took another bite. "It's good."

"I highly doubt that."

She laughed. If she were ever on a deserted island, Bri would need to be there if only for comic relief.

"So"—she bit into her sandwich—"let's talk about another developing story."

Don't go there.

"When last we saw our kick-ass doctor and hot bearded guy, they were playing tonsil hockey under a romantic starry sky. I'm guessing, since I've heard nothing else, that the customary call, text, naughty picture exchange, has not taken place?"

"I'm not discussing this."

"Oh no, you don't get to go back. You told me about the kiss, which shocked the yoga pants right off me, by the way. But you did it anyway, you opened the personal door and now I've got my foot in."

"So, I'm closing it now. Watch your foot. It was a moment of weakness."

"No fair." She tossed the crust of her sandwich in her mouth. They sat in silence.

"It was a kiss. I'm over it. I told you before, I don't date."

Bri nodded and sipped her Mountain Dew.

"I'm not some wide-eyed virgin. Life is messy, oh, and *The Notebook* was a preposterous movie."

Bri took another sip. "Yeah, that rain scene with the swans. Who the hell was that guy kidding? Almost as preposterous as the up-against-the-wall, hot-as-hell sex that followed. I mean, I had to shut it off after that nonsense."

Ella shook her head. "I don't know why we are friends."

"Yes you do. It's because I don't let you crawl into your weirdo Monday-loving ridiculousness."

"Could you stop with the Mondays. I love them. I will always love them."

"No, you won't. Not after a little roll around the barley with beer man you won't."

Ella laughed despite herself and of course, her mind filled with Boyd's face and the memory she'd tried to delete.

"Vienna would be telling you the same thing, but she's presently rolling around the firehouse or playing with the fire hose." Bri cracked herself up and started on the second half of her sandwich.

It was like a lunchtime comedy show right there in their little hospital.

"So, since I'm the only one currently searching for my fire hose, it falls on me to tell you that it's all right to be fluttery-eyed over your moonlight kiss. It's good that you're frustrated the stupid male hasn't followed up."

Ella crinkled her brow.

"Yeah, I know you're going to put on that, 'I'm far too educated and happy being single to care' routine, but you do. You do care, and I think it's great."

"Do you?"

She finished her Mountain Dew. "Yup. It's promising. Human." Bri tossed her lunch garbage into the trash, stood, and wiped the crumbs off her scrubs. "Now, would you like a hug?"

"What do you think?"

She sighed and washed her hands. "Fine, ice queen. Deny all you want, but there's a little pool of water around that heart, I can see it."

"That is not a good diagnosis, Nurse B."

"It absolutely is. You're melting. Good for you."

She blew Ella a kiss and went back to work. They wouldn't discuss it for the rest of the day. She knew Bri had said her piece and somehow, acknowledging the "developing story" made things lighter. Ella supposed it was good to feel something, even if it was frustration or confusion. There were upsides to being human, but the timing wasn't so great. If she was the ice queen, she was about to visit the ice castle. Her parents' anniversary party was tomorrow, on a Saturday—take that, weekend lovers. Further proof that nothing good ever happened on a weekend. Well, there was that kiss.

Ella rinsed her jar and put it back in her lunch sack. Kiss or no kiss, Mondays stayed.

Chapter Fifteen

*E*lla's plane put her in Los Angeles a few hours before the party. She checked into her hotel near the airport, keeping as much distance as she could manage. This was an in-and-out thing, she told herself. After hanging her dress in the small lacquered cabinet, she set the alarm on her phone, chewed on Vitamin C tablets, and took a nap. It felt like she was preparing for battle because she was.

The Uber pulled along the ostentatious curve of her parents' drive and in line with the rest of the cars waiting for the valet. Ella needed fresh air, so she told the driver he could make a quick U-turn and she would walk. He thanked her and seemed grateful to avoid the traffic jam of privilege. Rolling her shoulders back, she walked along the side of the pebbled driveway, avoiding cars and eye contact with any guests who might recognize her. She wasn't ready yet. She tried to breathe before she walked through the front door where the air supply would quickly dwindle down to nothing.

Pausing for a minute to collect herself and kick off a pebble embedded in the heel of her sandal, she remembered the year she received a locket from a friend in grade school. She must have been six or seven. The locket was glitzy and had a rose on it, she recalled touching her bare neck now as she stood to the side while guests arrived. Ella loved that necklace because it reminded her of *Beauty and the Beast*. That was until it turned her neck green. Despite the obvious ring around her neck, she refused to take it off. She wanted the necklace to be as beautiful as it appeared in the box. Her teacher finally told her it didn't matter how much she loved it—if she didn't take it off, it would hurt her.

This felt like that, Ella thought. Glitter covering ugly green, and all of it hidden behind a row of award-winning rosebushes. Finally in front of the sprawling home she'd grown up in—more accurately, where she'd spent a few holidays and the occasional vacation—she wondered if she was being harsh. After all, this wealth and privilege had shaped her in some way, maybe in all ways. One could argue she had become a doctor, found her calling because of her experiences. That included these walls and the people behind them, didn't it?

Smiling at the valet, she walked past the roses and the climbing vines and into the grand entryway. Her mother's voice filled the dining room before Ella had a chance to attempt an inhale. There it went, almost a total absence of air. Her entire body responded.

She set her gift on the round table by the five-story cake and paused to look past the glossy banister at the framed photos decorating the wall. She recognized most of them, but there was a new one just shy of the second-floor landing. It was the four of them, probably taken before Becca went to college. Ella was still in high school. God, it took her forever to grow out those bangs. It was a big picture, big and perfect in every way.

She braced her fingers on the gift table and pushed until her nail beds turned white. She hoped that would work, that pressure somewhere else would relieve the strain creeping up her back. She knew better. Nothing worked. The only way out from under her parents was through. She supposed the incessant need for perfection was bred into her too, but now that she'd come out on the other end of her childhood, she resented the new sheen of love and warmth her parents were attempting to apply.

"It's an old table that's been in the family for generations. We watched our babies grow up around this table," her mother's voice echoed through the large space.

Ella didn't turn around, but she was certain there was a cluster of bored-stiff guests following her mother around and patting her shoulder when she managed a tear for effect. *Now that was harsh, Ella.*

On the rare occasion she was home from school, she used to eat her dinner in her room or with friends. There were no family meals around that dining room table or any other. Ella never understood why her mother continued to insist on a legacy she couldn't have because she'd never bothered to work for one.

It was past time for a drink. Walking outside onto the patio, or terrace as her mother liked to call it, Ella noticed hundreds of people milling around on the grass. Tiny glass plates in hand and vibrant spring fashion everywhere. She made her way to the bar and ordered a club soda. She wanted a drink, but the need subsided at the thought of not being at her full wits to deal with the *Twilight Zone* episode that was guaranteed to unfold.

"E, I didn't even know you were here," she heard Becca's voice before her eyes adjusted to the sunlight and registered her figure gliding across the impeccable green of the lawn.

And... showtime.

Ella took her drink and squared her shoulders as her sister, in a pink linen dress and wedge sandals, stopped in front of her. Fingers and toes matching, the same Cartier diamond earrings she'd worn since her husband gave them to her as a "push present," and her hair pulled back from her once-beautiful face that was now barely on the right side of Botox and chemical peels. She was too thin. Even back when they were teenagers, Ella wanted to make her sister a sandwich. A big one, with cheese, because she was convinced the woman subsisted on little more than a heaping bowl of steam and a few Tic Tacs.

"Are you drinking already? It's barely noon and I need you steady today."

"Club soda," she held up her glass and leaned in for the double-cheek kiss that had become their adult greeting.

"You look tired." That was Becca speak for "you look awful."

"Thank you?"

"How are things at your new job?"

"Good. Great."

"Oh, honey. You don't need to lie to me. I'm your sister."

Thank you for the reminder.

"Becca, I'm good. I saw Mom when I came in, but where's Dad?"

She pivoted and scanned the yard. "Oh, I think they're both still in the library showing the new anniversary portrait to the Hirschfelds." Becca swayed just enough to confirm for Ella that her big sister was still mixing up the medication cocktails.

"Where do they find the wall space?" she responded with her best boarding school demeanor.

Her sister should have laughed but didn't. Instead, they stood shoulder to shoulder watching one more of their parents' parties. Christ, would there ever be room for their own lives out from under the giant clutches of Dr. and Mrs. Walters? At least they weren't in party dresses and patent leather shoes anymore.

Ella was given a horse for her eighth birthday. A warmblood named Good Vibes. He was fifteen hands and had a friendly face. She remembered wanting to jump right on, so excited and bewildered that an animal that size could be owned by anyone. She ran into her room to strip off her party dress and get her breeches on as quickly as she could.

"What are you doing, young lady?" her mother asked, standing in the doorway of her room.

Ella remembered running to her, wrapping arms around her legs, and squeezing as if she could generate enough love for them both.

"Thank you so much. I love him. I'm going to put on my breeches and I'll—"

"Don't be ridiculous. You're not getting on that animal right now. He's being brought to the stables and then in the morning he'll be driven to Exeter. You'll see him there during your lessons and free time."

Ella had protested, thrown a fit, and been made to stay in her room for the rest of the party. Except when her mother sent one of the maids up to wipe her eyes and bring her down to cut the cake.

After all, there were photographers, and all their friends would wonder where the birthday girl had gotten off to. Other than cutting into a chocolate almond birthday cake—Ella hated almonds—she spent the afternoon and early evening watching the party from her window.

Standing next to her sister now more than twenty-five years later, the festivities and characters still presented the same. Barely out of reach like a garden gathering scene trapped in one of those snow globes their grandparents used to bring home from their travels. Flawless and utterly cold at the same time. That way nothing got messed up, tantrums were contained behind closed doors, and no one ever actually touched. Ella suddenly felt sick at the difference between the life she used to know and the one of her own making. Even if it was only going to be one kiss with Boyd, there was more sensation in her times with Mason than she'd experienced in her whole life. Her friends, and the people she took care of in their community, stood in such contrast to the present chill. She wanted to run.

"How is it possible for a child to even survive in this?" she said, intending for it to be a thought.

Becca glanced over at her. "Are you talking about Margaret's children? I know. So rude, the invitation specifically said, 'an afternoon among adults.' Then again, I bet she didn't even read the invitation. She and her husband are constantly—"

"Not what I was talking about," Ella said as the crowd began to stir and her parents magically emerged from their ice castle and out onto the patio. Surrounded by enamored neighbors and acquaintances they'd known all their lives yet never knew at all, stood Dr. Langston Walters and his adoring wife Carolynn.

What felt like an eternity but was probably more like an hour passed and the guests gathered around so the happy couple could cut their cake. Her father's indifferent gaze skimmed the gift table to the left.

"Dear, I think I'd like to open our daughters' gifts before the cake," he said, kissing her mother on the neck.

Ella fought back the vomit and recognized the look in her father's face. This was a challenge in front of all their so-called friends. He was a master at putting people, especially his children, on the spot. She assumed he must have been tortured all those years ago in his residency, and since torturing countless sets of quivering residents was clearly not enough for a man of such self-imposed importance, he needed to bring that bravado home.

Their mother, demure and accommodating to the watchful eye, smiled and nodded in agreement. The photographer moved into place and Becca rushed to offer up her paper and ribbons first. Her gift was the size of a hat box. Somewhere deep inside Ella's adolescent mind, she told herself she would win this one easy. Books trumped everything else in the Walters home.

"Well, what can this be?" her father said with animated glee.

Ella sipped her champagne. She may or may not have started gulping at this point.

Her father lifted the lid on the box and gestured for his loving wife of forty-five years to do the honors. Her mother reached into the box and pulled out a silk envelope about the size of a... book. Ella glanced over at Becca, who smiled and looked right at her. Her sister clearly had no idea how screwed up this whole scene was. Only children opened gifts in front of guests. Scratch that, children and cruel parents.

"Oh my," her mother said as she pulled out a book and turned it to their captive audience. "A first edition of *Doctor Zhivago*. The first movie Lang took me to see our freshman year in college. It's lovely, Rebecca."

The crowd clapped, complete with oohs and ahhs while their father puffed his chest before the happy couple kissed, full on the mouth, likely an outward expression of their undying love. Ella resisted the urge to grab another flute of champagne. Anything more than one would result in things being said and more importantly, she'd make an ass of herself if she ended up drunk. She wasn't going let them do that to her, not this time.

Becca kissed both parents, and for some odd reason her husband stepped forward and shook their hands as if he were resecuring his place in the family.

"Which one is yours, E?" her mother asked.

"*Doctor Zhivago* is going to be hard to top," her father said, as if he were preparing to bet on a horse or a dog in Monte Carlo.

Her mother laughed and gave a halfhearted slap to his shoulder. "Stop it, Langston. This certainly isn't a competition."

Oh, but it is, dear Mother.

Ella pointed to her gift on the opposite edge of the gift table and sat back, waiting to take her place as a family misfit. Ella grabbed that other glass of champagne and drank half of it before the ribbon slid to the table. She had no way of knowing they were going to open their gifts in front of everyone, nor that her sister was going to pull out the big guns.

"Wow, well this is a different choice," her mother said, peeling back the wrapping paper. "Although Lang does love Truman Capote."

"Do I?" her father said, eyeing the cover and casually turning the book over in his hands like he was at the half-price cart outside Vroman's.

Her mother quickly flashed the book to their guests. "Another first edition. Thank you, E."

Ella grinned, the buzz of the bubbles kicking in. Her father's glare was meant to intimidate.

"Too bad that stopped working years ago." The second glass of champagne was gone and as predicted, thoughts were now leaking out of her mouth.

"I'm sorry?" her father released his wife's hand and stepped forward. The gathered crowd stood stoic and as if on a timer, they all turned to Ella.

"Okay, well, let's have cake," her mother said, reaching for Ella's father, who was now another step closer.

"Hang on a minute, dear. It seems our daughter has something she'd like to say."

Ella almost snorted as she stepped toward him. It was like an outtake from a *Dirty Harry* movie. Her mom reached for her father's arm, but he shrugged her away. Ella was his target now—someone was always the target. Under the champagne's sheen of bravery, she was positive the man had already said every hurtful thing imaginable.

She was wrong.

He acknowledged the crowd. "You all know my youngest, yes? She's a bit of a family... what would we call it, E?" He turned to Becca, who pretended to be occupied at the cake table. Her father feigned thinking and put his hand to his sharp jawline.

"Well, I guess Ella is a bit of a family stain. Huh, E? Horrible taste in men. She even quit her job over one. Christ." He pandered to his confined audience. "No one has even heard of the place she's working now. What is it, like a clinic, E?" He laughed in that way that sent frost straight up her spine. There were a few snickers from the guests who were no doubt indebted in some way to her parents. The rest of the group, to their credit, seemed noticeably uncomfortable. Ella would have felt bad for them, but she was busy trying to stay upright. She had stepped out of line, mumbled a few words of defiance, and Dr. Langston Walters was hitting back. The man had great aim.

She was surprised how quickly she absorbed the blow. It had been awhile since she'd allowed her father, her family, this close. She was out of practice. She turned in place. Ella purposely met the eyes of everyone in the room as they all but winced. This was exactly the way her father liked his guests, all people in fact, squirming. Ella did nothing to ease the tension. She stood right there in it. She looked right at her father as if to say—What else have you got?

"Lang, that's enough," her mother whispered in his ear. "Let's cut the cake."

"There you go, Mom. Redirect and distract." Ella moved behind her mother and patted her father on his shoulder, struck by how slight he felt. Not that she touched him much, but he had seemed larger back when she was small. Not so much anymore.

"Well, I'd better be going," she said, surprised how resilient and assured her voice sounded.

"Where are you going, E? We are having cake," her mother chirped as she corralled the guests toward the table.

Still glaring at Ella, her father took her arm. "You will not ruin this day for us. Get over there and eat some blasted cake," he said through clenched teeth.

He was absurd. Like something out of the comic books Mason tried to explain to her at one of their first meetings. The dark and evil villain, she thought. Ella remembered the last time some prick took her arm and realized, family or not, she didn't play this game anymore.

"Take care, Dad." She flicked her arm free of his grasp and spun toward the door.

Becca glowered and folded her arms. If her sister expected Ella to give a thought to her prissy attitude after that showdown, she was more clueless than Ella imagined.

Almost laughing, she pulled out her phone once she was away from glaring eyes and judgment. She had not wanted to come in the first place, but she'd arrived with gift in hand, watched the spectacle, and for maybe the first time ever, she was not left feeling small and powerless. Two years in the fresh air had done wonders.

"Happy Anniversary, Mom and Dad," Ella said as the Uber car arrived. She would love to say that her boldness was not aided by the champagne, but that would be a lie and above all else, she avoided lying, especially to herself. Her cheeks were warm and she was grateful for a quiet backseat.

Ella rolled down the window of the white Nissan as it got on the freeway toward her hotel, and checked her phone to see if she could still catch the late flight home. She needed to be back where she belonged. Bri had been right the other day. Human was better than the alternative. It didn't matter if Boyd called or not. Everyone she knew and had come to love in Petaluma opened something inside her. She could not wait to get home: the home of her own making to the family of her choosing. The driver turned on his music, and Ella rested her head back, imagining that the evening air could wash away the ugly.

Boyd and Mason took their kayaks out to the river early that morning. After loading everything back in the truck, they sat on the tailgate and ate bagel sandwiches. Boyd couldn't get Ella out of his mind, so he decided to try something new.

"Do you think these visits with Ella have anything to do with your mom?"

"No."

Boyd appreciated a simple answer most of the time, but not right now.

"I think since your mom isn't in your life and you have a bunch of uncles that maybe you're missing out on a woman's perspective."

"I have Aspen, and I like Sistine—she's super quiet, but I like her. I have Gram."

Boyd mocked a cringe. "Yeah, but who wants to talk to their grandma about girls?"

"Older women have some good advice. You'd be surprised."

He laughed. "Life is more than girls, Mase."

He rolled his eyes and let out a breath. "I know. I'm not saying life is all about girls. It's not even like I talk about them all the time," he said, crumpling up the wrapper from his bagel and stuffing it back into the paper bag.

Boyd raised a brow, giving his son a chance to reconsider his statement.

"Okay, fine. Maybe I have been talking about she a little more."

"Only a little." Boyd bumped him.

Mason lay back in the bed of the truck and stuck a beach towel under his head. "I don't know what I'm doing. I start to get excited about high school and then I get like this huge zit on my neck or something. I mean how does someone even get a zit on their neck?"

Boyd balled up the paper bag and leaned back, resting on his arms so he could see Mason, squinting as the sun teased through the canopy of leaves above them.

"I... guess there are pores there too. What does this have to do with high school?"

He shook his head. "I like talking to people, Dad. I want their opinion. It's not a big deal. I'm not going to freak out and start crying for my mommy."

"I'm not saying you are, but I'd like you to talk about these things, Mase. With me. I get that you're older and cooler, but some things don't have to change, ya know. We're still in this together."

Mason closed his eyes and Boyd knew he was getting nowhere.

"Aren't we?"

He sat up, legs dangling. "Not really. I mean you're my dad and there's that, but I'm the one going to high school. You've already done this part and you were probably some big badass. I'm... not that."

Boyd wanted to laugh because his son was comparing adult Boyd to freshman in high school Boyd who was anything but a badass, but laughter wasn't going to help his son right now.

"Badass takes time, Mase. Thanks for the compliment, but I likely had a zit on my neck in eighth grade too."

"No way."

Boyd nodded. "Way. I was as confused and twisted up as you are. I just channeled my stuff differently. It all works out. Believe me, someday all the pieces will fit together."

"Promise?"

Boyd bumped his shoulder. "Promise."

They sat for a moment, listening to the lapping of the river and watched a fishing boat coming into the marina.

"See, Ella isn't the only person who knows things."

"I know, but I've heard all of your things."

He laughed and when Mason joined in, he saw most of his teenage angst float away. Boyd knew it wasn't easy at his age, but he also knew there was no way to rush him through it. Growing up was a process.

"Maybe I need to start asking you what you need instead of telling you. You're old enough to control some conversations. I'll try that."

"Yeah? Okay, I need a GoPro."

"Yeah? You think that will help you with high school and girls?"

"Definitely."

Boyd nodded. "Nice try. I meant needs that don't involve my wallet."

"Ahh." He sat up.

"Do you need Ella?" Boyd said, as surprised by the question as Mason.

"That sounds a little creepy. I don't need her, but yeah, she's good to talk to. And she's funny in a sort of nerdy way. I like her."

Boyd resisted the urge to jump up and say, "Me too, me too."

"You do too, huh?" Mason said as if reading his mind and then flashed a devilish smile Boyd was certain came from his uncles.

"We're not talking about me."

"I know, but if we're in this thing together you and me, then maybe I can ask some questions too. Do you need Ella, Dad?"

"All right, smart-ass." Boyd hopped off the tailgate. "This bonding session is over. We need to get home. You have recycle to take out and weeds, so many weeds. Before that though, you need a shower." Boyd wrinkled his nose. "I don't know how to put this, but you stink, man."

Mason didn't move.

"I'm serious."

"About Ella?"

He nodded and jumped down.

"No. I don't need Ella. She's nice, you're right about that, but I'm fine. Happy with our life the way it is."

"She likes our life too. Why can't we like put our lives together?"

"Not sure it works that way."

"I don't get that. Look at Vienna and Thad. They're full-on kissing and holding hands now. And you should start thinking about what you're going to do when I go off to college. Brett, this guy in my history class, said his mom completely lost her mind when his older brother went to college."

Boyd laughed. "That's over four years away, and I'll probably move to Tahiti and party." They both climbed into the truck, and Boyd hoped Mason would pull out his phone as usual and get lost in showing him some new song or remix. He was willing to listen to anything if it meant the current conversation was over.

"Yeah? Cause you're such a partier."

"I'm fine, Mase. That's enough of the single-dad intervention. I'm glad Ella is your friend and I'll quit being a pain in the ass. Well, no I won't, but you know what I mean." He drew his son in and kissed him on the top of his head as they merged into traffic.

Boyd was a full-time dad by the time he was twenty-four. Claire had moved to Chicago and while she came to see Mason more back then than she did now, it was for weekend trips or vacations to visit her parents. He hadn't thought about her parents in years, save the birthday and Christmas gifts they sent Mason every year with a card that read "OXOX Mimi and Pop."

Glancing over at Mason now as he flipped through his phone looking for the perfect song, Boyd couldn't remember if they'd told him to use those names or if Mason had called them that the handful of times they were together. Like Claire, Mason's Mimi and Pop were far in the background by the time he was out of Pull-Ups and wielding a Spiderman toothbrush on his own. He supposed there was some "dysfunction," as the books liked to call it, in Mason's life, but it had never felt that way until recently. Boyd's mom started going to Mason's school for the Mother's Day Breakfast by first grade. A couple of other kids brought their grandmothers. Hell, half his classmates' parents were divorced.

Even though Boyd had grown up in a mom-and-dad family, he'd never seen that as the only way. In fact, it was probably his upbringing that led to Mason's situation. He'd tried to make things work with Claire. He wanted both of them in Mason's life full-time, but the day he showed her a couple of houses they could rent and she burst out crying, Boyd recognized there was only so much he could do. If she didn't want a full-time life with him, with their son, he needed to at least stop short of begging.

When it all fell apart, he was happy to take his son if the choice was losing him to Chicago and whatever nanny Claire decided to hire. It made perfect sense to him that if he was the parent who was eager for dentist appointments and framing school pictures, he should be the parent who raised him. Like most things, it had all seemed perfectly natural until they went out into a world dominated by the "traditional family." Boyd hated that phrase. Family for him was love and showing up. Those two things weren't mutually exclusive to any combination of parents. He learned quickly that not everyone saw it that way.

Mason didn't go to preschool. He spent most of his time strapped to Boyd's back or toddling around their backyard. Boyd worked from home during the day doing freelance engineering projects at first. Mostly for architectural firms started by a few of the guys in his college fraternity. Once he figured out he would never be happy as an engineer, he started bartending at nights. Those were tough years because he was a zombie. He'd catch a few hours while Mason was in school, but there was laundry to do, dinner to buy, and eventually homework. At night while he was working, Boyd paid Aspen to stay over. They'd all gone to school with her and on the nights she wasn't available, Boyd's mom was more than happy to play rubber ducky with her only grandson and read him a bedtime story. It wasn't perfect, he knew even back then, but it worked and eventually making a life for his son became a matter of routine.

"Here's what you need to do," Mason said, lowering the volume on a song that sounded like someone banging on a trash can. "Ask her on a date."

Boyd wanted to exclaim, "Who?" and play dumb, but his son was smarter than most adults. He'd see right through his game.

"Say exactly what I tell you and I guarantee she'll go out with you."

Boyd laughed. "How can you guarantee something like that?"

"Because she taught me everything I know."

"Everything?"

"About girls. Everything about girls. Peeing in the toilet and the rest of my life are yours, but she knows her stuff when it comes to girls."

Boyd nodded as they turned into their driveway. "Help me unload these and then the backyard weeds are calling you."

"I'm serious. It's a quick phone call."

"Maybe I don't have her number." Boyd released the straps on the kayaks.

"So, you *do* want to ask her out."

"I didn't say that." Boyd handed down the boat and Mason carried it overhead into the garage.

"Didn't have to," he said as Boyd passed, lifting the second one onto his shoulder.

"I have an idea. Let's crack open a couple of cold ones, go sit out on the porch, and I'll talk you through this."

Boyd shook his head and couldn't help but laugh again. "Crack open a couple of cold ones? What is this, 1985? Where did you even hear that?"

"Gramp."

"Figures."

"Except usually we're drinking root beer. I'd be up for a real beer if you're in the mood."

"Would you now?" Boyd nodded and once he saw the excitement in Mason's eyes, he said, "Not a chance. How about water bottles and weeds instead?"

Mason shrugged. "Are you going to ask her out?"

"I thought life wasn't all about girls."

"It's not. Ella is not a girl, Dad. She's a woman." He wiggled his eyebrows and Boyd cracked up.

He sat out on the patio and eventually helped Mason with the weeds. Ella Walters certainly was a woman. He could ask her out, but God that sounded so eighth grade.

Chapter Sixteen

Ella finished up a surprisingly exciting shift with a cup of hot coffee. She stepped outside the ER doors and watched the sun rise. Blue and peach, maybe purple too. It was lovely, and she wanted to hit pause and slow it down. Even though she was tired, it was Monday morning and once Dr. Campbell arrived, she would go home and ride the Freestone Loop. Driving into Petaluma on Saturday night, hearing the tinkling of the wind chime at her front door had done wonders to distance herself from the yuck of her family, but a bike ride was what she needed to fully gain perspective and wash away the feelings still churning in her stomach. The upside of the drama at the party and her late night return? She'd forgotten to think about Boyd until now.

Something about the wind on her face and the beauty of the sky reminded her of him. Was he up early? Looking at the same sky from his office or kitchen window? Did he have a window in his kitchen? Ella found if she loosened the reins on her heart, she craved him, which was silly. She hardly knew him. Maybe it was spending time with Mason or meeting the rest of his family that gave her an insight women rarely received outside the awkwardness of dating.

Finishing her coffee, she tossed the cup in the bin outside. The doors slid open and the air conditioning was particularly frigid after having the glow of the rising sun on her face.

Last night around midnight, a couple had rushed in and the woman, it turned out, was minutes away from delivering their first baby. After one or two questions, Ella had them whisked up to Labor and Delivery, where the woman gave birth to an eight-pound, six-ounce baby girl in the first fifteen minutes of a Monday morning. Lucky little girl, Ella told Bri when she arrived for her shift with her typical Monday blues.

"Poor kid is what you mean. Good thing birthdays fall on different days of the week. Saving grace there." She shivered. "Ugh, can you imagine every birthday being on a Monday?"

Ella laughed and handed Bri a wrapped box.

"What's this?" Her eyes were wide.

"Open it." Ella sat in the break room.

"I thought we were celebrating on Friday. You did this on purpose."

"I thought maybe I could turn you into a Monday lover."

"Knock, knock. I was told nonmedical people were allowed back here on birthdays." Vienna stood in the doorway with two of her famous boxes.

"No fair, you too?"

Vienna nodded and set the boxes in front of Bri.

"Two?" she asked.

"One for now and one for later. I don't think even you can handle cream cheese frosting before eight a.m."

"Carrot cake?" Bri peeked in the box.

"Your favorite." Vienna took the other chair at the table.

"That's totally a morning cake. What's in this one?" She opened the box. "Oh, sweet baby Jesus, can I get these every Monday?"

"Would that make Monday your favorite?"

"It would come pretty close." Bri tilted the box and showed Ella four giant, still-warm cinnamon rolls. "Thank you, my dear baking friend. I love you."

"Eh, it's the cinnamon and the sugar talking."

"Maybe a little."

They laughed.

Bri opened the now-unwrapped box and pulled out Ella's gift. It was a leather photo album embossed with *Annie's Auntie* on the front. Bri ran her fingers over the letters and went in for the biggest hug Ella had ever endured.

After stepping out to quickly bring Dr. Campbell up to speed on the one patient still in Exam 3, Ella rejoined her friends in the break room to split one of the cinnamon rolls. That was all the birthday girl was willing to share. Bri, prompted by the gift, passed her phone around with the latest pictures of her sweet and "growing like a weed already" niece. The whole birthday celebration, complete with plastic spoons and paper towels for napkins, took less than a half hour and was packed with enough friendship and kindness to almost undo her parents' extravagant anniversary. Almost.

After letting Bri get to work, Ella and Vienna walked to the parking lot together.

"You're sure you're all right checking on Pam while we're gone?"

"I am more than sure. You'll be gone a Tuesday and a Wednesday. Slower days, right?"

Vienna nodded, clicking her van open. She and Thad were taking a couple of days to visit his mom in Bodega Bay.

"Are you nervous?" Ella asked.

"About leaving my shop for the first time since I opened it, or meeting Thad's mom?"

"Both?"

"Yes, yes to both."

"Okay, well, what's the worst thing that could happen?"

"Oh, I have thought of them all. Sift could burn to the ground or Thad's mom could realize that their ginger son is dating a black woman."

Ella laughed. "Let's back up. I highly doubt that the guys who work for your ginger firefighter are going to let his girlfriend's bakery burn down while he is out of town. I'd be surprised if they're not circling the shop every couple of hours just in case."

Vienna smiled that warm, in-love smile, and Ella found she was a bit envious this time.

"And the last worry is absurd. His mother already knows the color of your skin. She has seen pictures and if she's half as smart as Thad and Aspen, she will recognize that your skin and your spirit are gorgeous. Her son is a lucky man."

"Aw." Vienna's eyes welled. She set her bag inside her van and touched Ella's hand. They both had cold hands. Too much washing, she decided.

"She does seem great. I guess it was cheap to say that. It will likely be my parents who will have the issue." She rolled her eyes. "My father, that man is something."

"That I can relate to."

"Oh, right, how did your parents' thing go?"

"Not talking about that. It's a perfectly pleasant Monday and I'm going home for a long ride."

"Over twenty miles?"

Ella nodded.

"All right, I will add your parents to the list of things we are not discussing."

"Thank you." Ella leaned forward and hugged her friend. It was a little hug, but Vienna noticed.

"To what do I owe the honor?"

"For being you. Have a safe trip, and I will see you Thursday."

After another round of promises that Ella would call at even the slightest problem, Vienna drove off in her delivery van. Climbing into her car, Ella realized she had a text from Mason.

Maybe she should have thought more about giving him her number, but Mason was her friend now and she didn't want him riding his bike to the hospital every time he had a question. This one was a good one. He wanted to ask Chloe out on a date and needed to know the best way to go about it. Ella was a little thrown that a thirteen-year-old would go on a date, but again, she knew nothing about teenagers. Maybe they were savvier now. She could call his father and let him know, but she wasn't going to do that. It had been over a week now. She'd moved on. She did mention to Aspen that Mason texted her every now and then, hoping somehow that would make it through the brewery grapevine. Boyd was obviously avoiding her, which was silly, but Ella wasn't exactly being an adult either.

She typed out three simple dating rules:

1. Write her a note to ask for the date. No texting or calling. Writing is romantic.

2. Offer to take her someplace that might not be your thing but someplace you know she'll like.

3. Make a plan. Don't tell her you want to hang out or you'll play it by ear. Have a plan.

Smiling, Ella put her phone back in her bag and drove home for her bike.

Boyd's phone vibrated on the seat next to him and when he saw Thad's name on the screen, his heart sank. Mason was at school, so that meant one of his brothers did something stupid, and he hoped like hell they hadn't burned down the brewery in the few hours he'd been gone. Why else would Thad be calling him?

"Hey, where are you?"

"On the 101 about twenty-five miles out. Why? What happened?" Boyd asked.

"Nothing. It's barely noon. What could have happened?"

"Okay, then why are you calling me? Almost gave me a heart attack."

"Ella was doing the Freestone Loop after her shift and some asshole knocked her into the shoulder. She fell off her bike. She's okay, but her knees are banged up and the bike is toast. She called Vienna."

"Why did Vienna call you?"

"Because we're on our way to Bodega to hang with my mom for a couple of days."

"Meeting Mrs. Pane. Wow, this is getting serious."

"It is. I love her."

Boyd couldn't believe the ease with which those words came out of Thad's mouth. Vienna had to be next to him in the truck. How the hell long could they have been dating, a couple months tops? He was already in love and happy as hell to blurt it out loud? Christ, Boyd couldn't even manage a phone call for a date.

"Wow. Who's going to be Cade's wingman now?"

"I am, but different. This isn't about me. I heard a rumor you were making a run to Clearlake for hops and I thought if you were out, you could get Ella?"

"That's probably not a good idea."

"Why not? You're like what, ten minutes from her?"

"Yeah, but she's not going to want to see me."

"What the hell did you do?"

Boyd didn't answer. He heard Vienna's voice and knew she was filling Thad in. That meant Ella had talked to her friends, which meant he was officially an idiot.

"Okay, so I guess you're a schmuck. I'll try Randy, he's the new young guy down at the station. He knocks out more pull-ups than the rest of us combined. I'll bet Ella would appreciate some alone time with him. Or you could quit tripping over your dick and hope playing hero will fix things."

Thad had a way with words.

"Where is she?"

"Roblar and Stony Point."

"Yeah, I'll get her. Say hi to your mom for me."

"Will do and thanks."

"Don't thank me yet. I'll let you know if I run into trouble."

"You won't. Enjoy."

Enjoy? Bastard.

Boyd checked the bench of his truck, then threw the trash from breakfast and a pair of Mason's cleats behind the seat. He lowered the radio and drove in silence for what felt like a crawl until he spotted Ella sitting on a rock right off Stony Point Road. She was in a tank top and bike shorts. Her skin glistened in the sunlight and she had not exaggerated, her knees were bloody and dirty. He pulled over.

"Thad said you needed a ride," Boyd said, walking toward her and knowing full well hero was not in his skill set.

"I do. What are you doing here?" She didn't seem happy to see him. Big shock.

"You called Vienna, Thad called me. Did you know he's taking her on vacation to Bodega with his mom?"

"She's one of my best friends. Of course I know. I thought they weren't leaving until two."

"I guess they left early." Boyd put her bike in the back of his truck and extended a hand to help her stand. She reluctantly took it. It was so good to see her.

"What happened?"

"I got too close to the shoulder because a car got too close to me. I hit gravel and now I'm being... rescued, I guess, by some man who wants nothing to do with me."

"I never said that."

"I'm paraphrasing then. Can we go, please? Thank you for picking me up."

Boyd helped her into his truck. Her elbow was scraped up pretty bad and while he pretended not to notice, her shorts were short.

"Why were you out here on a Monday? Doesn't Mason have school?" she asked.

"He's not homeschooled," Boyd joked.

She didn't laugh.

Clearing his throat, he realized this might be more difficult than he thought. "I dropped him off this morning."

"Where were you going?"

"Coming back from Clearlake. They have a new harvest of Chinook and I met Mo halfway. Today's brew day and I wanted wet hops."

"You honestly have no idea that you're speaking a language no one understands, do you?"

"Sorry. I guess I don't." He stumbled over his words trying to explain. "I mean what part of that doesn't make sense? I use hops for beer. Usually they're dried, but Mo, the guy who grows most of our hops, lives in Clearlake. He has a fresh harvest. That means wet hops instead of dried hops, which is special. I want some for a recipe I'm trying out today."

"Got it. Thank you. Well, you better get back and start cooking up the hops."

Boyd turned in the opposite direction from home.

"Where are you going?"

"There's this place that makes loaded hot dogs in Tomales and since you're already angry, I thought we'd have one."

"I am"—she held up her hands and stretched her legs long, somehow making the shorts tinier—"literally covered in dust, dirt, and blood, and you thought now would be the perfect time for a date? You know, it's a mystery you're single."

He tossed her some wipes from the console of his truck that he used to use for Mason's messes when he was little. He still kept them in the truck because he wasn't ready to admit Mason was too old for messes, at least the ones that could be cleaned up with a disposable wipe. "Use these. You don't look that bad, and this isn't our first date. We need to talk."

She opened the package and gently started cleaning her knees. Boyd remembered the first time she touched him to clean and repair his hand. That seemed like a lifetime ago now. She was much nicer then, probably because she wasn't expecting much from him at the time. Since looking at her knees somehow made his mind wander to other forms of touching, and not in a clinical way, Boyd kept his eyes on the road.

Oh, how he longed for that simpler day in the emergency room when all he had to worry about was bleeding to death.

Chapter Seventeen

By the time they pulled onto the gravel parking lot at Big Dogs, Ella had managed to get most of the blood and dirt off her knees. She was still a wreck, but a cleaner one thanks to the baby wipes. Boyd turned off the truck.

"You still carry baby wipes?"

"Habit."

Ella smelled them one more time and handed the package back to him. She wasn't sure what that was about. Did she like the smell of babies or simply the thought of a younger Mason with dirt or chocolate on his hands? Before she allowed more analysis than was necessary, she redirected her attention to being annoyed that now, of all times, Boyd decided he needed to talk.

The night after they'd kissed, which could go down as one of her most romantic memories ever, Ella had imagined things. Since none of those things came to fruition and she'd moved on, mostly, she could admit there had been a cafe table, a long walk by the river, and a new black date dress similar, but much longer than the one Bri had decided on. The kiss and the expression on his face that followed had even rendered her stupid enough to wonder what his house was like, even imagine a shared newspaper the next morning. One by one over the past week, she'd popped those silly "this could happen now" bubbles. Never had she imagined being skinned up on the side of the road and having hot dogs with Boyd. There was no way a logical mind could conjure that up. Real life had a way of turning everything around. Whatever she'd thought would happen next didn't and now here they were sitting silently in the cab of his truck.

"I didn't know you rode bikes," Boyd said, clearing his throat.

"I told Mason that first day at the hospital that I had a bike."

"Having a bike and what you've got going on here are two completely different things." His hands gestured up and down her body, and Ella had to remind herself that he had kissed her and not called her since. She had to remember the unpurchased date dress, the popped bubbles. If she didn't keep the obvious brush-off fresh in her mind and the wasted anxiety that followed, she was going to climb into his lap right there in broad daylight and kiss the crap out of him all over again.

What was it about trucks? She had no idea because she could count on one hand how many times she'd been in a truck.

It was an all-encompassing vehicle. This simple truck took on every part of the man sitting next to her. It was warm and smelled like plants and whatever the oil was he used on his beard. Vienna clued her in that that's what kept his beard so soft. He smelled delicious all the time. Like a great forest or some camping trip Ella had never been on. The last time she went camping, she was at Exeter and they did a survival weekend. The staff came out to their campsite and made dinner. Ella guessed that was not legitimate camping. Boyd was legit and so was his truck, right down to the baby wipes.

He didn't call, she reminded herself again.

"Well, there are a lot of things you don't know about me. It's not like we're friends."

"Like what?" Of course, he skipped the dig and went right for the information. Ella understood where Mason got his investigative skills.

"Like... I learned to crochet last year."

"With Vienna?"

"And Bri and Aspen too. Weird how you and I run in similar circles but are only recently... acquainted, right?" She needed to get out of his truck before she blathered on about feelings she'd vowed never to entertain again.

"What else?" Boyd asked.

The man was impossible. Was this a conversation or an interview?

"I have... always wanted to have a brew master kiss me and then blow me off like nothing happened. Oh, wait..."

Without looking at her, Boyd got out of the truck and walked around, but Ella had opened her door before he got to her. They went into Big Dogs in silence and ordered. When they were seated with their laminated number, he finally met her eyes.

"I wanted to kiss you. I'd like to do other things with you."

Oh wow, a man of few words, but they were good words.

"But?"

"But I don't know how to do this. I've lived my life with one purpose for a long time and—"

"Number forty-four," a woman with dyed red hair and a brown uniform that looked like a mash-up of a fifties diner and a UPS driver said, placing a tray between them and taking the number without another word. Boyd placed Ella's hot dog in front of her, took his, and put the tray behind them.

"And?" Ella said after taking a sip of her Coke.

"I guess that's it. I've spent thirteen years raising a son. I don't think I've ever thought about having a relationship before and if I did for a second or more it was, without a doubt, squashed by diapers or not wanting to screw him up."

"It was a kiss, Boyd."

He bit into his hot dog; Ella did the same.

"That was not just a kiss and you're not some hookup. I knew that. I felt it the first or second time I saw you."

"Knew what?"

"Knew that I'd go up in flames if I kissed you and sure enough, I went ahead and did it anyway."

"And that was a bad idea. The flames being a metaphor, of course."

"It wasn't a bad idea. A complicated one, no doubt. The flames are not the point."

Oh, but they were, Ella thought. Men did not blurt out that they went up in flames after kissing a woman, at least not any of the ones Ella knew. Of course, she'd never met a man who was raising a son. She had never known a man with baby wipes.

"So, now I don't know the next step." Boyd continued. "That's why I've been avoiding you until I figured something out." He took another bite and washed it down with his Coke. Christ, the man was even a sexy eater. Ella guessed it was again because he was unstudied.

She wondered if having a child did that to a person. It certainly hadn't made her parents any more genuine, nor had it her sister, but her parents didn't raise two daughters. They weren't up in the middle of the night with a teething baby or helping a young person navigate his first crush. They delegated those responsibilities to a team of nannies and boarding schools.

Boyd was sleeves-rolled-up raising his son, and what grabbed her around the heart and squeezed was that there didn't appear to be an ounce of burden. He seemed perfectly content being a dad and was now struggling to tell Ella he didn't have room for more than a kiss. Something in her wanted to slowly back away and leave him exactly where he was, but the other part wanted to love him with an intensity she'd never felt in her life.

"Well, we are eating hot dogs while your hops dry up in the back of your truck. That's a start. Kind of a next move," she said. "Technically you rescued me from the side of the road. Points there."

Boyd smiled. He needed to stop doing that if he wasn't going to kiss her again.

"Thad said that would help."

"Did he?"

Boyd nodded, and she could tell she'd taken some of the weight off their conversation. There was satisfaction in that, in getting out of her own way and being concerned, connecting with someone else.

"Thirteen years. Wow, that's a long time to go without sex, Boyd. Was that right? You said you haven't had a relationship since Mase was born? Long time." She grinned because he nearly choked on the last bite of his hot dog.

"I didn't say anything about sex."

"Yeah, men never do, do they?" She cleared their trash.

Moments later, Boyd held open the door of his truck, helped her in, and just like that they were heading home. *Would spending time with him always float right to the edge of something real?*

At least she was joking and appeared to be having a good time. Boyd was reminded of his first junior high dance. He'd gone with Sophia Blanch. His dad had dropped them off. "Show her a fun time," he'd said. Boyd had no real memories of the dance, or whether Sophia had fun, but he remembered the advice. God, he hadn't thought about being a kid, the one on the receiving end of advice instead of the one straining to come up with it, in a while. He let out a slow breath and thought of Mason's advice. It was funny how roles switched throughout a life. One minute he was explaining the fine art of fly fishing knots to his wide-eyed son and the next he was recalling dating advice from the teenage version. Boyd certainly wasn't going to go through with Mason's plan, but damned if he didn't feel like a novice.

"How are your knees?" he asked after they'd been back on the road for a while.

She touched the sides of her legs. "I'll survive. My poor bike on the other hand..." Ella glanced over her shoulder at the mangled mess.

"Did you go down hard?"

"Kind of. It's a race bike, which you'd think would be strong, but it's surprisingly light. It doesn't handle being thrown into the shoulder well. I don't either," she said, and Boyd wondered if she caught the metaphor there too. Of course she did. He hadn't been out of the game that long. Women were Yoda when it came to things meaning something else. Ella glanced out the window.

"Why did you move to Petaluma?" he asked.

Her gaze returned to him and he thought she might not answer.

"I wanted something different from what I had."

"Makes sense." Boyd turned left. "Did you lose a patient or become addicted to narcotics you were supposed to be giving to your patients?" He felt confident it wasn't either of those, although she had to have lost patients in her career. Didn't that happen to all doctors eventually?

She laughed and the sound sang right across the dash and enclosed him. She was stunning and had no idea, or maybe she did and it got in the way of her work. He guessed that was a problem for a lot of women in general but especially women who fell into some stereotype. Guys had labels too, but it seemed trickier to be a woman.

"Watch a lot of *Grey's Anatomy*, do you?"

Boyd kept his eyes on the road. Beautiful and funny. He was in so much trouble.

"Reruns of *ER*. I used to watch them when Claire and I... I mean when I was up feeding Mason every three hours. He was like clockwork."

Boyd knew the next question.

"Is that Mason's mom, Claire?"

He nodded.

"Huh. And they're not close? Did something happen or..."

"She's in Chicago."

He prepared for a million more questions to follow and knew he'd have to drag out the same old story that seemed to define him. Instead, she sat quietly as if she sensed that was all he wanted to share.

"Are you going to the Art Walk?" she asked.

"I... wasn't planning on it, but is that something you're interested in?" They entered downtown and turned at the street Ella indicated.

Boyd tried to remind himself it was brew day. He had wet hops and he still didn't have a next step, but maybe there was no plan, no recipe. Maybe this was how it was going to be. He wasn't ready to let her go yet. He knew that for certain.

"I would like to go. Do you think Mason will want to come?"

"If you're going. Are you kidding? Of course."

Ella smiled. "He's so great."

"Agreed."

"My house is there on the corner."

Boyd pulled over and was surprised. He had not imagined her house yet, but he wouldn't have guessed it would be a redone historic. Navy blue and white, a phenomenal porch with potted plants along the edges. He would have thought she'd live in something more modern. That made no sense, but it struck him how little he knew about Ella. Did she want to share more and he'd not asked the right questions?

It was odd how sitting out in front of her house could feel intimate. Once again, he felt like a sweaty-palmed kid. Christ, maybe he was the girl among his brothers after all. Stumped for something to say, he went with a modified version of Mason's plan.

"Cade got some new wine in at the Tap House."

"Sorry?" Ella said, her hand on the truck door handle.

"You like wine. Maybe we could stop by the Tap House after the Art Walk. Art and wine. Both things you like, I'd imagine."

"I do." She appeared to hesitate. "But, I also like your beer."

"Yeah, okay good. So, the plan is I'll pick you up on Saturday at noon. We'll spend some time at the Art Walk and have an early dinner at the Tap House. Are you off on Saturday?"

What the hell was coming out of his mouth? He sounded like he was confirming a reservation. *Thank you, Dr. Walters. Enjoy your trip.* Mason in his head was a bad idea.

Ella nodded, presumably that she wasn't working on Saturday. Then she climbed out of his truck. He walked around to her side and she was pressed up against the door and laughing. Not an amused giggle, this was hand-on-stomach laughing.

"Sorry. I'm sorry." She held up her hand and seemed to pull it together. "Yes, that sounds like two things I would enjoy and a well-thought-out plan."

Ella was still smiling like someone with a secret, and Boyd knew his thirteen-year-old dating coach had been exposed. Was there a maximum amount of awkwardness a man could endure?

He stopped her before she could get her bike.

"Let me hang on to that. I know a guy."

"You don't have to. It was my stupid mistake."

"No, it was some asshole's mistake. I'll call in a favor."

Her eyes softened. "Thank you."

"You're welcome."

"Can I kiss you, Boyd?"

He nodded, surprised by the question but happy to be moving on to something he knew he wasn't going to screw up. Ella pulled him down by the front of his shirt to the heat of her lips. She kissed him gently, teased him with her tongue, and left him wanting so much more.

Her eyes opened, still glinting with laughter.

"What?"

"How can a man like you, a man who looks like you." She touched his beard, kissed his neck. "Someone who is so good at loving his family and making a life possibly need dating advice from me?"

And there it was, he was busted.

"I have it on good authority that you're the expert when it comes to winning over women."

"Is that so?" She ran her hands over the front of his shirt as if that would somehow help him let her go—it had the opposite effect.

Boyd nodded. "I meant to call. I should have called, but the truth is it's difficult making sense when I'm around you, Ella."

"I'm familiar with that feeling," she said. "I'm looking forward to our date, Boyd."

He turned and popped open his glove box. Might as well go all in if he'd reached the embarrassment threshold already.

"Step one," he said, handing her an envelope.

Ella took the envelope and held it to her chest. Her eyes went a little glossy and Boyd hoped that was a good sign. Hoped she didn't have some weirdo in her past who wrote her a note or some jerk who broke her heart with a poem.

She opened the envelope, read the four lines he'd written, and pulled him back into her. The crush of her mouth was still new. *Holy hell, would kissing her ever get old?* She shifted and wove her hands into his hair, giving him the answer. He was already drunk on the feel of her, the taste of her mouth. And right then he knew. Knew like he knew whether to use wheat or barley, that nothing would ever be the same again.

"I am good at this female dating advice stuff," Ella said after she eased away and walked up the three steps in front of her home.

"Mason's a smart kid."

She turned outside her front door. "Thank you."

"For?"

"Everything. Rescuing me and my bike, the hot dog, the kiss, and the note." She held it to her chest again. "Connection, Boyd. It turns out you are a master at connection."

Their eyes held for a moment. Standing in place for a few beats, uncertain he could move, Boyd had never been so glad he agreed to meet Mo for wet hops in his entire life.

He had a date tomorrow. A day date that included his son, but a date was a date. Climbing back into his truck, Boyd felt closer to his son than he had in months. All guys, young and old, were made of the same stuff, he supposed. Wanting something more, faster, better never went away. He'd simply been on hold for a few years.

Chapter Eighteen

*E*lla knew there was a reason she hated Fridays. She was in the hospital cafeteria telling Bri about her roadside assistance and the note. She sighed as friends do and for the first time, she was comfortable letting someone into her feelings.

"I'm so happy for you," Bri said right as Ella glanced up, and it was as if someone had rolled over onto the remote control of her life.

Mask pulled around his neck. Familiar dark stubble and eyes made for both intimidation and seduction in equal measure. *What man pulled off a scrubs cap like that?* He did, and Ella cursed herself again as Dr. Marc Pierce walked toward them.

Did his wife still see the man she met in college when she looked at him? Ella wondered. Or did she only recognize him the way he was now: expensive shoes and sparkling smile? There must be memories packed into their relationship somewhere: a tired resident she loved a lifetime ago before he became a cheating prick. No man started off as the self-absorbed narcissist smiling at her now, did he? Surely there was a time when Marc had been genuine.

His greeting was one of long-lost friends. Ella stood quickly, her entire body on alert and prepared for a blow she thought she'd taken for the last time. She glanced at Bri, who now stood at her side as if she too knew what was coming. That was impossible. She didn't know Marc. In over two years of solid and honest friendship, Ella had never shared that part of her life with anyone. Which somehow made the entire moment even more constricting, as if she was still trapped in a secret she'd never asked for but now needed to keep. Bri was her friend, but also her colleague, as were all the people in this hospital. Ella couldn't jeopardize that. Above all else, she couldn't taint what she'd built for herself.

She'd left him behind along with her career. She was happy now, connected, and it was as if some beacon went off once she and Boyd figured out their next step. Like Marc was in his asshole cave and received the message, "Time to shut this shit down now."

His eyes sparkled with mischief, and Ella knew some sick part of him found this romantic. That he'd played this exact moment through his mind. She was going to be sick, but not right now.

"Ella? Wow, I did not expect to see you here."

She was once again flooded with the "how" and "why" she'd ever let him into her heart.

"Sure you did." She stepped back when he went in for the standard longtime-no-screw hug. The one that was supposed to render her speechless, captivated by his expensive cologne or his aura of excellence.

Mother of God, he was standing in her hospital cafeteria. She nearly forgot Bri was there until she cleared her throat. Ella turned, expecting to find Bri salivating on herself. Marc had that effect on women. But that was not the expression at all. Bri was chin held high, eyes serious and ready for a battle there was no way she even understood. She was a much better judge of character, or it was simply years of experience spotting jerks.

Ella wanted to turn and walk away without a word, but she knew Marc. He'd find that even more of a challenge. *Son of a bitch.*

"Dr. Marc Pierce." He extended his hand to Bri, and Ella thought she might puke right there on the floor.

Bri nodded. No hand.

"Dr. Pierce, this is Bri. Bri, Dr. Pierce. His is one of the top cardiothoracic surgeons in the country. Right here in little ole Petaluma. Shame though—we were leaving."

Bri didn't say a word. She simply held Ella's arm, and somehow that made her feel better, stronger.

"I finished the first part of my lecture on thoracoabdominal aortic aneurysm repair. Such a small world, right?" His attention flickered between Ella and Bri as if they were all colleagues.

"Not really. We're not a trauma center."

"Well, your medical director wanted an expert and I volunteered. Since my wife and I have separated, I've had some extra time on my hands."

Ella laughed. It was a blurt of laughter, like the kind kids couldn't hold back across the dinner table after a crass joke. It was a milk through the nose laugh but without the milk. This one had a heavy layer of disgust. Was he telling her and a total stranger that he'd separated from his wife? Was that supposed to matter after close to two years and a tangle of lies she'd been incapable of unraveling?

"Maybe you should volunteer with Doctors Without Borders."

His jaw twitched, barely there, but she knew she'd made contact. He flashed his dazzling grin. Sick bastard.

"Yeah, well, this has been fun." Ella turned to Bri, who'd still said nothing. Her eyes softened and she pulled Ella in the direction of the ER.

"Are you okay?" she asked as they walked down the white hall, clogs squeaking on the slick floor.

Ella nodded and glanced over at her. "How did you—"

"I've never seen that look on your face. Since you've been here, never. I remember about a year ago telling myself someday I'd understand what happened to you, why you didn't want anyone close. Today was that day." Bri pushed them through the doors and into the back hall of the ER.

She led Ella into the on-call room. "I need to know you're okay."

"I'm okay."

"I doubt that, but I'll take it for now. Stay in here. I will come and get you if they need you. I know you want to charge out there and push whatever the hell that douche bag was to you behind your job, but please stay here and let it hit you. I won't hug you, but don't crawl back into that isolation, honey."

Bri's eyes watered as she turned and left Ella alone with her secret.

She stood with her back against the wall and commanded herself to not cry. She would not shed one more tear for a man who cheated on his wife, on his daughters. What he'd done to her, to her heart was collateral damage, but the main point of impact was that woman, the one he'd promised. The thought that Ella had been a party to destroying another woman was almost more than she could take two years ago. The shame had dulled now. She was moving on, and there he was, snake in the grass, still slithering around.

Ella sat in the chair and glanced at the yellow piece of paper tacked to the bulletin board across from her—I attract only good things to my life—it read. Closing her eyes, she struggled to remember a time when she'd attracted anything more than chaos outside of work. The one thing she knew how to do was be a doctor. She was so well suited for her job she sometimes questioned if that was why nothing else fit into place. Most people hated their jobs—and Mondays, she reminded herself.

She met Marc her first year of residency. He was approachable and outgoing for a cardiologist. He wore a backpack to work and often forgot to shave. Ella would never know if any of that was genuine or an act he put on for unloved residents looking for their first mistake, but from the minute she laid eyes on him, she was intrigued. What followed were months of romantic dinners, extravagant gifts, and eventually an apartment they shared near the hospital. After about a year, things had settled into a routine. Marc was gone for two or three weeks at a time. She would text him and he'd call her when he could. He was off doing good in the world, so she thought. He even created a schedule for her so she would know where he was and the time zones.

Ella rested her head back on the chair and did exactly what Bri had advised, she let the whole thing crash around her.

They'd met for coffee the night Marc ended things. The one right across the street from the hospital. He was smart to choose a place in public, but they kept getting interrupted by colleagues standing in line for one last dose of late-night caffeine. Ella remembered glancing at her phone at 9:53 p.m. and wondering if the shop closed at ten or eleven.

"How was Bangladesh?" she'd asked him once the crowd had shrunk and all she could hear was the tapping of laptop keys nearby.

"I didn't go." He'd taken her hand across the table.

She almost laughed now as she recalled the look on his face, all sad eyes and feigned hopelessness. She would learn later that Marc had never been hopeless a day in his life.

"Why not? Is everything okay? Did they send you somewhere else?" she'd asked. Christ, she must have sounded so naïve.

"I can't keep doing this, babe. It's not fair to you and it's not healthy for me."

"What are we talking about?"

"I don't work for DWB. I'm married." That part had hit like one of those sequences in the martial arts films her roommate in medical watched to "unwind before bed." They were poorly dubbed so the words and the mouth movement didn't match. Ella had stared at Marc's lips that night, bewildered.

"I live in San Diego. I'm only up here for certain surgeries."

She didn't remember most of what happened after that, but she knew she stood up at some point because the scratch of the chair along the hard floor made a noise not suitable for a mellow coffee spot so near closing time.

She didn't say anything that she remembered. There was no "you bastard" or a drink in the face. All she could recall, even years later with distance behind her now, was the ice-cold chill of numb. Dead like a corpse on a classroom table.

Marc stood at some point and took her wrist. "I'm sorry, El. I love you, but things got so twisted and I've got kids I need to worry about."

She'd grabbed her coat off the back of the chair and snapped her arm from his grasp. During the hundreds of times she had replayed the scene, one moment stood out: when she pulled her arm free. Every time she beat herself up over not smacking him or making the scene he was so careful to avoid, she hung on the fact that at least she'd pulled away.

Marc had followed her out to the parking lot. "El, let's not end like this." Holding his arms open under the fog-splintered light, he said the words that would haunt her every minute that followed.

"Can I at least get a hug?" He moved closer and wrapped his arms around her.

Ella had allowed it. She'd allowed him a goodbye and while it took her months before she fully understood the tableau, she remembered the tears on her cheeks. Not for her broken heart or what he'd done to his family, but because she was going to miss him. In the middle of a parking lot, wrapped in the arms of a man who had lied to her for the better part of two years, she was still sad for the loss.

She had never been able to forgive herself for that moment. She knew she had not consciously stopped hugging after that, but something broke her that night and until recently, she'd never bothered to repair the damage.

Opening her eyes now, Ella thought of Mason. Thirteen-year-old Mason, and she recalled the day he told her to "hug it out." Smiling, she realized that was exactly what she was going to do. That was her way forward through whatever new game Marc was playing. She may have skulked away with her heart dragging behind her the first time, but he was messing with the wrong woman now. She was no longer distracted by ambition or approval. She was fueled by simple joy this time around and strengthened by friendship.

Sitting in an old chair that could give out at any minute, things were so clear. She was able to recognize the wisdom of a teenage boy. Maybe Marc circling back around was the final push she needed because Ella felt awake again, alive for the first time maybe in her whole life. The heart working away in her chest wanted a man because he made her knees weak and he was good. She didn't yet know what he ate for breakfast or the things that made him tick, but she knew she deserved every "could be" Boyd managed to stir in her. That knowledge was more powerful than anything Marc had left in his arsenal.

"Hug it out," Mason had said. Ella would hug until she was brimming with so much that the ugliness of her past had no choice but to let go and drown.

"I think I've held them off as long as I can unless you want me to come up with some elaborate lie, which I'm down for but we may need props and—"

Bri was silenced when Ella grabbed her and pulled her into her arms.

"Oh, well okay." She didn't even tense or pull back. Her friend was a natural hugger and Ella was happy to finally return the favor.

"Thank you," Ella said, squeezing her a little tighter.

"Breathe, honey."

Ella found she was trembling and, still holding on to her friend, she cried.

Chapter Nineteen

Boyd had no idea what he was doing. He was thirty-seven years old and still had superglue on his hands from fixing Mason's science fair car. He'd won third in his class and seventh overall. Not bad. He told Boyd he wanted to keep the car, so they'd cleaned off the Big Red and fixed the wheel properly. It was on the top shelf of Mason's bookcase next to the alien made of bottle caps Boyd bought him at Everything Old is New Again a couple of years ago. The comic books were still in the closet, but now there was something.

Standing in the fogged mirror of his bathroom, he closed his eyes. He didn't want this date to feel like a mistake. He wanted to plan it all out in his mind, kind of like a new recipe and have it work, but even he knew the perfect brew took time, trial, and error.

This was a trial, he told himself as he opened his eyes and wiped the steam from the mirror. Nothing had been set in stone. He was going to the Art Walk with his son and his... friend. That's how West had put it opening night at the Tap House, and maybe that's what it was. Ella and Mason were friends, and there was no reason Boyd couldn't be her friend too. He lathered up his shaving soap. A couple of wrinkles with that theory, he'd never had a friend he wanted to know more about and kiss in equal measure. A friend who made his pulse charge forward while his heart, suddenly alive and well, started tapping on his rib cage asking to be heard.

She wasn't his friend. There wasn't enough beer or denial in the world to stop what was happening between them, and his determination was overwhelmed by want. That was the problem. He'd grown so accustomed to managing his want. He worried that if he satisfied some of it, let himself like Ella or imagine how she could fit into their world, he might let it all out and screw things up royally. He hadn't had a relationship since Mason was born, and Claire had left six months after that. He knew some headshrinker would have a party with that, try to paint him as some abandoned heartbreak, but the truth was he'd been so busy securing a life for Mason—both financial and fun—that it had been easy to keep his own wants at bay.

Until now, he thought and immediately remembered the first time she'd said those exact words to him in the emergency room. He'd told her he had never cut his hand on the keggle. "Until now," she said, and given him a glimpse into something that, if he were completely honest, he wasn't sure he knew how to have. His relationship with Claire had tanked and in the end, he'd made a fool of himself. What had started as "What should we paint the baby's room?" had quickly spiraled down to him practically begging, "Please don't do this to him—he needs two parents."

Claire had left shortly after and Boyd shoved everything that didn't pertain to Mason or the brewery to the back of his heart. It was the only way he knew how to give his son the childhood he deserved.

There was another problem, he thought, wiping the excess shaving soap off his neck. He knew how to be a dad, knew how to be a son and a brother. He had no clue how to be a partner, a lover, someone Ella could count on.

Boyd pulled on his shirt and buttoned the front. It was a date, one date in the middle of the afternoon. His son would likely be there handling all the conversation. Why was he letting himself get so far ahead?

The answer stared right back at him in the now-clear mirror. He wanted something, someone, and the last time that happened he was turned away and left scared out of his mind. Boyd didn't have the strength to go through anything like that ever again. But like a fool, there he was holding up a different shirt and wondering which one looked better. He hadn't second-guessed anything he had worn for years. He sat on the edge of his bed to tie his shoes.

"You ready yet?" Mason called from the living room.

Not even close, kid, Boyd thought, grabbing his keys and wallet off the dresser.

"Did you like high school, Ella?" Mason asked as they shared a hot pretzel and made their way through everything from oil paintings to macramé plant hangers.

She didn't know what to say. Was there a good, better, best response to help a young man on the edge of high school? She glanced at Boyd and he shrugged, indicating there was no right answer. Huh, so honesty, she thought, that was how this parenting thing worked.

"I did not," she said, pulling another piece off the pretzel Mason held between them.

They stopped to look at the glass-tile elephants and Mason slurped the last of his soda. He handed the pretzel to Boyd and searched for the last drops of soda, his straw making that groaning sound.

Right as Ella thought answering his question had been easy, Mason said, "Why not?"

"I... it took me a while to figure out who I was and what I wanted. High school can be a confusing place for a girl trying to sort things out."

"Like what? What were you trying to figure out?"

Boyd snickered and she bumped him.

"Where my parents left off and I began."

"Huh. Are your parents nice?"

"No." Ella reached for the last of the pretzel. Mason grabbed it like he was going to beat her to it and then pulled the last piece in half. It was nuts how much she enjoyed this kid.

"Are they jerks or do they drink too much?" He stopped walking. "Do they knock you around?"

Boyd laughed. "Sorry, not funny. Funny delivery, but not funny."

Ella tried to find the right words. "They're troubled."

"You're not giving me anything good here, Doc."

"I thought we were talking about high school." She ran her hands along a handwoven tapestry, thinking it might look good over her couch, but decided against it.

"Right. Were you in any clubs or did you play any sports?"

"I was in the medical careers club and I was on the cycling team."

"Your school had a cycling team? That's awesome."

"What about the medical careers club?"

Mason shook his head. "Not so much."

The three of them laughed and stepped aside to let a woman pass with a cart on wheels filled with colorful canvases.

"Did you like high school?" she asked Boyd.

Mason smirked.

"What was that for?" he asked.

"Nothing. Go ahead, answer, Dad."

"I guess you think you know what I'm going to say?" Boyd took Mason's cup and chewed on the ice.

"Ah, yeah. You played football. Of course you liked high school."

"Maybe you could let me answer?"

Mason gestured an exaggerated "go ahead" with his hand. Ella liked watching the two of them together. There was an ease and mutual respect that she found fascinating.

"I was good at fitting in during high school. Unlike Ella, I wasn't thinking about much. It wasn't until after high school, a while into college, before I realized how screwed up things were in high school."

Mason appeared genuinely stunned. "I kind of assumed—"

Boyd raised his eyebrows.

"Yeah, yeah, assuming makes an ass out of you and me. Whatever."

"High school is like this time we all have to serve and survive. It has its awkward moments for all kids. I don't care what clubs you're in or sports you play."

Ella nodded. "Agreed."

"Wow, guys. I can't wait to get started."

Boyd ruffled his hair and pulled him closer as they turned toward the larger painting booths.

It smelled like rain, Ella thought. She hoped the sun would win out for at least another hour. She was having a great time. After being at her parents' house and the unexpected Marc visit, perhaps everything was heightened, but she didn't think so. Boyd and Mason were rare under any circumstances. She knew that like she knew she could eat a chocolate croissant every morning for the rest of her life. It was obvious, clear to anyone who was paying attention.

For not the first time, she pondered if all their magic, the perfect cadence of their relationship, came from being a pair. If Mason's mom had been in the picture more, would they be different? Ella had no way of knowing, but lately she hoped there was room for her, that their life wasn't like the art they were walking among and she was supposed to keep her distance and not touch.

She'd meant what she said to Boyd, she understood his reluctance. It wasn't fear or selfishness—he had a good thing. He'd managed to navigate a path of love and sheer joy in raising his son. Maybe he had no idea how he managed it all and kind of like crossing fingers or avoiding a black cat, he simply didn't want to push his luck.

"Let's talk about something more important now," Mason said, tossing their pretzel bag and his empty cup into the trash. "Pop Rocks. Do they kill you if you eat them with soda?"

Ella shook her head and allowed the thunder of their laughter to roll right through her. Yeah, if she were Boyd, she'd try her damnedest to stay right where things were too.

No one was more surprised than he was when Boyd took Ella's hand as they walked toward the Tap House entrance. Mason ran ahead, no doubt making a beeline for Galaga to see if he still had the high score. Her eyes found his, easy and warm. The whole afternoon had been that way. Normal and so off-the-cuff that Boyd caught himself a couple of times forgetting he was on a date. He'd never seen anything like the way she was with Mason outside of his family. Watching his son with her was enjoyable, and that nagging feeling that he should keep his distance was all but gone. She wasn't Claire. Ella wanted to be with Mason, be with both of them it seemed.

Before he dealt with the imminent teasing and sarcasm guaranteed from his brothers as soon as they walked into the Tap House, he wanted her all to himself.

"Do you want to see something?"

Ella wiggled her brows. "What exactly did you have in mind?"

He laughed and pulled her toward the brewery.

"Oh, wow, are you taking me to your happy place?"

He nodded and was swept up in the playfulness. He tugged her hand one more time and she jumped on his back as if they were on a playground. Boyd hoisted her high onto his back and his chest expanded. He wondered if she knew what she did to him or how long it had been since he'd felt like a man without a care in the world. He couldn't know how long this was going to last, but if it ended, he was certain whatever she left him with would be enough to carry him through the rest of his days.

He set her down inside the door of his brewery.

Ella pushed her hair off her face, smiling in that glorious flushed way that seemed to come naturally these days.

"Wow." She walked around his space, touched the sides of the copper tanks. "This is gorgeous. I had no idea beer making was so..." She turned to face him and Boyd kissed her. Heat twisted between them, and the need once again could have swallowed him whole.

He eased back, rested his forehead against hers.

"Was it something I said?"

He shook his head. "I can't let go of you."

She smiled and held him tighter. "No rush. I'm still mastering my connection skills, remember?" She gently kissed him.

"I was going to tell you that I've seen real improvement, Doc."

"Have you?"

"Oh, yeah. You're an incredibly fast learner." He kissed her again, held the sides of her face and let his thumbs relish in the thrumming of her pulse. He'd meant what he said—nothing mattered in that moment but staying close to her. The thought scared him, and then as if by default his next thought was—Where is Mason?

As if not ready to return to reality, he shut down his mind and kissed her again. His son was no dummy and they were surrounded by family.

Had he and Mase been surrounded all along? Had there been room for Boyd to have needs of his own and he'd never taken them? Maybe he had the support all this time, but the thing with Claire had made him feel like he was on his own. It was true the two of them weren't "in love" by the time Mason was born, but they'd loved each other and that seemed enough for Boyd at the time. Mutual respect and a common goal, that's what he'd argued and lost. Maybe all of that had taken its toll on him, on his ability to let someone else have the controls.

Their mouths eased apart and Ella met his gaze, the expression on her face searching not for answers, but for a place among his thoughts. She must have sensed he was about to drop to the floor, because she grinned in that calm way she had the first time he'd met her and instantly put him at ease.

"So, since we're here in the happy place, I'd like to see that infamous keggle."

"I'm sorry, I can't show you behind the scenes on that level. I mean that would be like you showing me how to do that thing doctors do when someone can't breathe." He pointed to his neck.

"A tracheotomy?"

He nodded. "I think you doctors call it a 'trach.'"

Ella laughed. "We do, but in real life, there's no soundtrack and no one wants to see a trach unless they have to. Give it up, beer man. Show me the keggle."

Boyd gave her the tour and wasn't surprised when she was drawn to the back wall. The brewing process was impressive, but everything human was on that back wall. He had a hunch Ella couldn't get enough of the human side of things now that she was mastering connection.

After looking through pictures and sharing a few stories, they made their way back to the Tap House, which was filling up. After the success of opening night, they'd decided to host a live band Friday and Saturday nights. He held the door for Ella and two guys carrying in instruments. Boyd checked that Mason was in the back room playing Galaga and then found Ella at the bar talking with Cade.

As he approached, he steeled himself for some smart-ass comment, but his brother greeted him as though it was the most normal thing in the world that he was there with a beautiful doctor.

"How was the Art Walk?"

Boyd leaned on the bar. "The rainbow elephants are still kicking ass."

Cade laughed and poured him a beer.

"Ella, can I get you a glass of wine?"

She was holding a menu. "I heard from your nephew that you can match beer to any kind of food."

"I do have that reputation."

She pursed her lips and Boyd waited for some healthy doctor meal. He'd seen her eat pretzels and monkey bread, so there was no reason to assume all doctors ate leafy greens, but he did.

"I'll have the pulled pork sandwich."

Like he told his son, assuming made him an ass.

Cade glanced at him and smiled. "Excellent choice. I'd suggest Naked Neck. It's a porter and one of your date's masterpieces."

Ella glanced at Boyd.

"It's a good beer."

"Is there a chicken called naked neck?" She gestured to the board. "These are all chicken names, right?"

Boyd nodded as Mason joined them, reaching behind the bar for a Coke Cade had no doubt agreed to save for him.

"Did you order something?" he asked.

"Buffalo chicken wrap. What are you guys getting?" Mason said.

"Pulled pork and a Naked Neck." Ella handed her menu back to Cade.

"So good. I mean the sandwich. I'm not allowed to have the beer."

"What are you having?" Cade asked, returning from helping two couples at the end of the bar.

"Cheeseburger. We're going sit over there. You all right bringing our food?" Boyd asked, looking around as the place started to fill up.

He scoffed. "I'll deliver it personally," he said as Ella and Mason made their way to the table near where the band was setting up.

"Don't," Boyd said, leveling a stare he hoped convinced his brother to behave.

"Oh, but I want to." They'd reached the teasing portion of the evening. "Pulled pork, huh? It's like she was made for you."

"Let's not get crazy."

"What? That's your order and your beer. You went nuts over that beer, remember? Like you were da Vinci or something."

"Da Vinci?"

He finished entering their order into the computer. "Yeah, did you know he went for twenty-four-hour cycles without sleep?"

Boyd shook his head, glancing back at Mason and Ella.

"Or that Virginia Woolf wrote standing up?"

"Is this one of your random late-night internet searches?"

"It started after I watched this thing on PBS about the deepest part of the ocean and shit. Before I knew it, I was on to artists, some weird crap about cubism, and when I put my iPad down, it was two in the morning. I've got like chronic curiosity or something."

Boyd laughed.

"Anyway, back to you. Who would have thought a doctor would order something so—"

"I get it. She's cool. Mason's already told me a thousand times. Can I get a glass of water too?"

"She's more than cool, she's your match."

He laughed again to cover up the punch of his brother's words.

"Laugh all you want. Dozens of people can't be wrong, I'm a master at the match." Cade slid a glass of ice water to him.

"With beer and sandwiches maybe."

"No, with all things. I can spot a match, and she's yours. Now get over there and don't screw it up."

"You're crazy."

"I am." Cade went back to work and Boyd joined Ella and Mason. He'd never thought about having a match. There'd been a time when he thought Claire was the person he'd spend his life with, but even then, he would have never called it a match. For a guy with such jacked-up hair, his brother was full of insight.

If Ella was his match, if it was as simple as pulled pork and a perfect beer, maybe Boyd had all the skills he needed to keep from screwing this up. He doubted it was that easy, but the band was playing, his son was smiling, and an amazing woman seemed to enjoy kissing him. He sure as hell wasn't going to waste any of that worrying about tomorrow.

"Dad, since Ella's here, can you show me how to dance with an actual woman? That way I can watch."

"Can I get some clarification on 'actual woman'? Who is your dad normally dancing with?" Ella asked, trying to remember when she'd ever laughed so much.

"Once with Uncle Cade and once with me, but since you're here and you're a girl, I think it would be better. Dad has moves."

"Is that so?"

Boyd did a shake-nod combo, took another sip of his beer, and grabbed her hand. It was as if there was no point arguing. Ella guessed Mason had been persuasive from birth. Right as she was about to stand and follow him to the dance floor, he let go of her hand.

"Sorry. I forgot I was giving a lesson." He stepped back, extended his hand. "Ella, would you like to dance?"

She had no idea if it was the evening air or the sparkle in his eyes, but she felt young. Like a girl at a bonfire hoping the boy she liked would sit next to her. He stood, waiting for her answer as she took in the sight of him. Dark hair—left a little over his collar on purpose. She wondered what he told his hairstylist or barber. Where did he get his hair cut? There she went again with the questions. Suddenly the simplest of appointments struck her as intimate. Ella imagined water and a woman's hands threading through all that thick hair like hers had only moments ago.

Mason cleared his throat and Boyd dropped his hand to his side. "Mase, maybe Ella is tired and she's not interested in—"

She stood, grabbed him by the front of his flannel, and pulled him the rest of the way to the dance floor. The band switched to a slow one as if on cue and when his arms wrapped around her waist, that young legs-too-long girl she was in high school returned. Taking in a slow and steady breath, she noticed Mason out of the corner of her eyes. He was sitting backward on a chair as if he were watching an important documentary.

"All right, that's one way to get a girl, er... woman to the dance floor," Boyd said, playfulness rumbling through his chest and traveling to the tips of her fingers.

"I got you to the dance floor," she corrected, already moved by the pounding rhythm of her heart.

"Right. And that's an important lesson, Mase. The woman can lead, she can make the first move."

Ella nodded and relished the heat of his body and the sheer size of him as she placed her hands on his shoulders.

"Where do the hands go?" Boyd asked.

"Waist," Mason said. "I'll probably pass out right there, so we don't need to go any further."

"You'll be fine," Ella said. "She'll be nervous too and won't notice you're nervous. The first time dancing, being close"—she caught Boyd's eyes as they fell to her mouth and then her collarbone—"is special. You want to try to remember it as best you can."

"Okay, Dad. Show her your moves."

"Let's see what you've got," she said, feeling ready for anything.

The song picked up at the chorus and Boyd moved her across the dance floor. It was classic country music. Ella didn't listen to country, but the singer's low twang made her think she might need to add some to her playlists. She was grateful she'd learned the two-step in ballroom class. Boyd did have moves. Strong, confident hands that placed her body around his in a series of steps and turns that would put any guy in a tux to shame.

"You with me?" he asked into the back of her neck before spinning her around to face him.

"Does it feel like I'm with you?" She was always good at faking brave until her courage kicked in, but with every turn she felt herself fall for him a little more.

He held her gaze and nodded, right before he spun her under his arm and returned her to the original position. Her hands landed on his chest this time. By way of moving back into position, her hands slowly traced across his chest before resting on his shoulders. Boyd pulled her close and touched the bare skin right at the back edge of her blouse. For a second Ella forgot how to dance. The song changed and she remembered Mason was watching them. Boyd smiled as if confirming he felt everything too and then they were back into the shuffles and steps.

"Does Mason dance like this?" she asked once she caught her breath.

"He's learning."

"Well done, you. Young girls all over Petaluma will be grateful. This is fun."

"Did you hear that, Mase?" he said as they moved to the front again. "Ella said this is fun. That's the key. You want her to have fun. Don't worry about being cool."

Mason nodded, tapping his foot and grinning as his dad twirled her one more time past the band and around to the center of the floor. The music stopped and they stood for a moment, blurry and suspended among the now-crowded dance floor.

"Food's here," Cade said.

They turned and even though Ella didn't have a brother, she had a feeling all sorts of things were passing from the oldest to the almost youngest.

Chapter Twenty

"I'm not sure this is for me," Ella said the following week as she hung upside down in a silk hammock suspended from the ceiling. The instructor asked that they now extend their legs, and Ella had no idea how to even get her legs out of the thing. *Had anyone ever gotten tangled in this class and had to be rescued?* "Actually" — she managed to pull one leg free — "it's my professional opinion this might be life-threatening."

Vienna, who released both legs at the same time and was now like a floating starfish in the floor-to-ceiling mirror's reflection, laughed. Their instructor, Rain, glanced over in that way that made Ella feel even taller and more awkward than she already did.

"Set your intention first, Ella. Don't forget to drop your shoulders back into the pockets," Rain said, touching her leg gently. The woman was shiny, and Ella wondered how much water she drank. She guessed she didn't eat monkey bread. As her thoughts turned to whether Rain was her given name, Ella's foot scooted one more inch closer to the edge of the fabric and sprang free. She looked like a giraffe emerging from the womb, she'd later tell Vienna over lunch, but in the moment, she focused on keeping a straight face so she didn't pee her yoga pants.

"You need to give it more than one class," Vienna said, still a perfect starfish, once Rain returned to the front of the class and guided them through the last pose.

"Uh-huh," Ella murmured as her feet finally hit the floor. They'd done some strange stuff together, but this was a contender for the strangest.

"Can we have your bakery for lunch? I think I've earned monkey bread," Ella said after Namaste and as they walked to the car.

Vienna laughed. "You did kind of look like a monkey toward the end there."

"Yes, I did. This monkey needs her bread."

"Fine. I'll feed you."

Ella rested her head on her friend's shoulder and put her seat belt on. She was learning to love days like this. Days where joy was front and center. She'd spent so much time anticipating doors busting open or the other shoe dropping. So much time observing that moments with her friends where she was allowed to sit in joy, relish time without fear of falling behind was truly a gift. One she didn't intend to waste.

"Have you told him yet?" Vienna asked.

"Told who what?"

"Told Boyd that you are in love with him."

Ella snorted. "I have done no such thing. Look at you feeling all bold and poking around in my heart."

Vienna grinned as she drove them toward downtown. "You should. Love looks good on you, sis."

Ella was taken aback by so many things that she could not tell which needed her attention first. Sis, Vienna had used this endearment before, but after spending time with her biological sister, the love behind it softened Ella. Probably melted more of her ice heart, as Bri was so fond of saying. Sis was human, real, and a connection that suddenly felt important.

When Ella tried to think about what she felt for Boyd, or sharing those feelings with him, her mind shut down, so she focused instead on being a good sis.

"We will not be discussing my feelings. You have not said one word about your time with Thad and his mom. Spill it, sis."

Vienna pulled up to the second light in town, one shy of her bakery, and glanced at over. "You are my sister, Ella Walters. In every way that counts."

The women in her life never failed to erase the past, who she thought she was when she arrived. A tear traveled down her face and Ella quickly wiped it away.

"You will never know what that means to me. Thank you." The light turned and she leaned over to kiss Vienna on the cheek. Vienna patted her hand and pulled around the back of the bakery.

"His mom still listens to records."

"Seriously?"

She nodded. "Easy listening. Lots of Barry Manilow."

Ella didn't know if that was a good thing or not.

"And..."

They got out of the car and she waited while Vienna ducked back in for her bag.

"Motown," she said, her smile bursting with what seemed like relief.

"Is Motown important?" Ella asked.

"Oh, you have no idea. It's my father's credo. He trusts no one black, white, purple, or green who doesn't like Motown. 'Something wrong with a person who can't see that genius,'" Vienna mocked in an older man's voice.

Her parents lived in Los Angeles too, but Ella had not met them yet. After that impression, she was looking forward to it.

"Motown is everything if our families are going to get along. Motown might be the glue that holds every Thanksgiving and Christmas together. Our marriage could hinge on Motown."

"Marriage?"

"Well, not yet, but we're heading that way."

Ella didn't know what to say. She'd thought of herself as a confident woman, at least behind the walls of her job, but she had nothing on Vienna.

"What?"

"Nothing. I love that you are so comfortable with your feelings."

"Sis, I'm thirty-five. Up until that wall of delicious man walked into my shop, I was certain I was happy alone. I'd made it through my first year of owning my own place. I wanted for nothing until Thad. Now, I don't want anything without him." She set her things down in the back kitchen. "If that's not ready for four-tiered wedding cake, I don't know what is. Nothing to hide."

"I'm happy for you."

"I'm happy for me too. I'd like to be ecstatic for both of us, but since you've managed to derail my fact-finding mission for Bri, Aspen, and even Sistine, I suppose there's nothing left to do but feed you."

"Fact-finding? They asked you to take advantage of me while I was trapped in that class?"

She nodded, gesturing for Ella to take her seat out front.

"Yeah? Well, tell them they underestimated the power of my... Namaste."

She rolled her eyes. "Not the right use of the word. Go sit."

Ella walked to her favorite table. She had not brought a book this time and it was odd at first to sit alone at a table without a distraction or a place to bury her face. But then she noticed the people milling through the line, the smiles and animated conversations. All those people had been there before, but Ella was too wrapped up in her own stuff to notice. She scooted her chair into the table a bit more and tried to roll the kinks out of her neck. She stopped mid-roll when she noticed Boyd and Mason a few tables over.

Boyd heard Ella's laugh before he saw her. Mason did too because he turned from his Social Studies homework in the direction of the counter at Sift right as she and Vienna appeared behind the counter.

The bell on the door jangled, and Thad joined the line that ran past their table. Boyd tipped his head and the same confident "We know everyone in this town" nod was returned.

"Little late for breakfast," Boyd said.

"Just got off work."

"I can see that. Two days off now?"

Thad confirmed. A woman and her daughter let him go in front of them after a soft "Thank you for your service."

"My pleasure," he said, stepping forward. "Catch you guys later." He waved a hand.

Mason had flipped through a couple more pages of homework by the time Thad made his way to the counter. They both looked up in time to see Petaluma's fire chief walk around the counter, wrap Vienna in his arms, and kiss the hell out of her.

"Wow, maybe I should be getting advice from Thad," Mason said.

The line, almost eight people deep, clapped. He set her back down on her feet and kissed the top of her head. Vienna kissed him one last time softly and handed him a box. After adjusting her apron, she apologized to the next customers in line, who of course couldn't have cared less because they had front-row seats to that kiss.

Thad walked past them on his way out and patted Mason on the back. "The National Bank, huh?" He scanned the open book. "Nice. You know they made a musical about that guy." He leaned on the back of Mason's chair as if he hadn't easily put every other guy to shame. Boyd wondered if the chair would snap in two.

"Alexander Hamilton," Mason said, looking up. "Yeah, I know. He was awesome."

"He was. Okay, well I'm heading home to fill my gut with sugar and fall asleep."

"That kiss was awesome too," Mason said. "What's the secret?"

Thad blushed. Boyd double-checked, and there it was on his six-foot-whatever frame—pink cheeks.

"It's love, man. She's easy to kiss."

Mason gave him a high five and looked at Boyd. There was a strange beat where he wanted to reach forward and somehow keep the next words he knew were coming out of his son's mouth firmly behind his lips.

"See, Dad? You need to let it fly."

Thad's eyes went wide and his chest rumbled with laughter. He reminded Boyd of Mr. Clean but with hair.

"Gotta love this kid." He bumped fists with Mason. "Take care, guys."

"You too," Boyd said. "Hey, thanks for that PDA."

"Anytime, my man. Anytime." Thad left, making the slight jingle of the door seem even smaller.

Boyd braced himself for the inevitable pep talk.

"Did you see that?" Mason went to close his book, but Boyd held it open.

"Ah, ah. No Social Studies, no movie."

He slouched back down in his chair. "Fine, but are you at least going to talk to Ella?" he asked, now waving to her from the round table in the corner and rolling his eyes while he went back to his book.

Boyd had been so struck by Thad's entrance and what followed that he'd forgotten Ella was over there sipping coffee. As soon as their eyes met, he questioned how he'd ever forgotten she was in the same room.

"Be right back," he said. "*Alien: Covenant* is at one o'clock. Get to work. No homework, no popcorn."

"You're like a, like a…"

"Dad?"

"Yeah. So annoying." Mason shifted in his chair, as if that might help him get through the last ten pages of reading.

"That's the job."

"Go over there and don't mess it up. No way you're as cool as Thad, but let's try to at least hold up the McNaughton name, okay?"

Boyd laughed. "I'll do my best."

By the time he got to Ella's table, his stupid heart was at it again. The thing was like a new puppy lately. She smiled and gestured for him to sit. He tried to find his big boy words because all he wanted to do was kiss her. Haul her into his arms and do his own version of Thad and Vienna, but Boyd's life was as far from a bakery romance as possible.

For starters, his son a few tables down probably skimming over his reading all the while debating if he should get an Icee or a Dr. Pepper when they got to the movie theater. The dishwasher decided to dump water all over their kitchen floor last night. Boyd had a meeting with his brothers and Aspen tomorrow to go over how in debt they were now, and the timeline for the autumn beers.

He clearly wasn't Thad, or any lead in a romantic story, but he wanted to be more than he'd ever bothered with before if it meant spending time with her. He hoped that was enough.

"They're something, right?" Ella said, taking her glasses off and setting them on the table. Her eyes pulled him under in any light, anywhere.

Boyd grinned. "I'm telling you if you knew Thad in high school, you would have enjoyed that show even more."

"Really?"

He nodded and filled Ella in on some of their history.

"That's fantastic." She glanced over at Mason. "No school?"

"Teacher in-service day."

"On a Monday. Nice. But he still has homework?"

"Seems like he always has Social Studies."

She grimaced. "Can't say I was a fan of that subject."

"Me neither." He tapped the spoon on the table, searching for something to say. He decided the last time he'd followed Mason's lead, he went on the best date ever, so he relied on another favorite—twenty questions—without the big intro. No sense making an ass out of himself.

"What was your favorite subject in school?" He knew it was a dumb question the moment it left, but there was no going back.

Ella smiled. "Science."

"Right. That makes sense. Mine too."

"Yeah?"

"Science and math. I majored in engineering."

"Huh. What kind?"

"Civil. I worked in structural for a while."

She nodded, and he tried to ignore the interest in her eyes that somehow validated all those years of homework.

"When did you know you wanted to be a doctor?" he asked next after confirming Mason's book was still open and his eyes were on it.

"My sister is allergic to shrimp." She finished another bite of monkey bread, moved the plate over, and leaned in on her forearms. "I don't know how she made it all the way to ten without trying it—especially in my parents' household—but she had her first shrimp at one of my mother's luncheons. She had an allergic reaction and her throat started to swell. I'll never forget it. My dad was out of town, so my mom called 911. The paramedics came and saved her life. She was screaming and carrying on. Becca's not all that likable when she's not coming out of anaphylactic shock. She's a handful when she's distressed."

"Even at ten?" Boyd asked.

"She's two years older than me so I wasn't witness to those years, but I'm guessing since birth."

He laughed and accepted an offered piece of her bread.

"I stood in the hallway and watched them work on her. I was eight maybe and I was hooked. She was lifeless and they brought her back, knew what to do while my mom was on the verge of passing out. Up until that point, all I knew about medicine was that my father was rarely home and when he was, he and my mother were entertaining. But these paramedics were none of that. They were the calm in my crazy household, and I wanted to be that. Wanted that control, that power."

"You knew you wanted to be a doctor when you were eight? That's dedication."

"Well, I wanted to be a paramedic first, but my father is a doctor." He noticed her jaw clench and sensed she wasn't close with her father. He certainly wasn't going to push. That's where he and Mason were different.

"When I got older, I researched emergency medicine, hence a trauma doctor." She held out her hands in an animated ta-da.

"Car accidents and gunshots?"

"Oh, you're speaking my language." She ate another piece of bread and washed it down with coffee.

"So, you're an adrenaline junkie."

"Not exactly. I mean I know doctors who are, but I'm more of a calm junkie. I like to bring order to chaos. That's my addiction. Is it my turn now?"

Boyd was busted again.

"Twenty questions, right?"

He shook his head. Was there any dignity left, damn it? "Your turn, sure."

"How did you meet Mason's mom?"

"Wow! I go for career and you head right for the big prize."

Ella laughed. "What? You are a single father, Boyd. What's with the mystery?"

"I met her in college. Fraternity and sorority. Boring story. Was your sister all right?"

Ella nodded. "You're avoiding my questions. We can check with Mason, but I think that's against the rules."

"I am not. I get tired of talking about that event in my life. Sometimes it seems that one moment defines me. People see me with Mason and it's like I don't exist, or my life doesn't exist outside of being his father. That didn't sound right." Boyd checked on Mason, who gave him a thumbs up and made a big deal of closing his book. "I love being his dad."

"I can tell."

"Good, that's good."

Mason was packing up his stuff. Boyd was running out of alone time.

"Do you work tonight?"

"I go on in a couple of hours."

"What about tomorrow?"

"I'm off," she said, twisting a piece of napkin.

Boyd stood. He could sense his son's approach and for whatever reason, that made him jumpy. "Do you like chili?"

"I do."

"Great. Let's have chili at our house tomorrow night."

"I'd like that."

"Like what?" Mason asked.

Boyd closed his eyes. It was like the timer had gone off a few seconds early.

"Chili," Ella said. "What movie are you going to see?" she asked, navigating right past Mason's questions. Now he really wanted to kiss her.

They discussed the movie and how he hoped the new *Alien* was as good as the original because the last one was "a little weak." The kid's vocabulary bordered on adult most of the time, but when he talked about movies or comic books, he was practically a prodigy.

"The original had Sigourney Weaver, right?"

Mason nodded. "She's not in this one. But Katherine Waterston is, and she was in *Fantastic Beasts*."

"Oh, I loved that movie," Ella said, sweeping crumbs into her hand and depositing them onto the plate. She put her glasses on and like a kid himself, Boyd almost lost his mind.

"You've seen it? Awesome, right?" Mason was all but jumping in place.

"So good." Ella flung her bag over her shoulder and set her plate in the dish bin by the garbage. She waved to Vienna and followed them out as Mason continued to jabber away about movies and comparisons.

Boyd was barely paying attention. He wanted her alone. In his bed, or hers, it didn't matter. His entire body flushed with need and he could not seem to control it. She was talking to his son about which Batman was the best for crying out loud. It was hardly the time to be thinking about her beneath him, on top of him, and everywhere in between. Boyd stopped on the sidewalk and ran a hand across his face.

"We're going to be late," Mason said.

"Are you okay?" Ella touched his arm.

He wondered if his face showed exactly how screwed he was. Maybe the beard hid some of the insane need. He sure as hell hoped so or he might scare the crap out of her, or maybe not. Maybe she was wild in — *What the hell is wrong with me? Don't go there.*

His brain finally made its way through the fog of lust. "Thank God." He blinked in the sunlight when he realized he'd spoken out loud. "Yeah, no. I'm good. Are you two finished? Putting me to sleep, that's what that was." He grabbed Mason under his arm.

Ella laughed.

"Say goodbye to the good doctor."

Mason squirmed free and fixed his hair. "So weird." He flipped his bangs. "Bye, Ella. Have fun at work."

"Bye, Mase. I'll expect a full report on the movie. I hope it's good."

"Me too."

She leaned in, put a hand on his chest, and kissed him. Only her lips, completely rated G, but his entire body snapped. He pulled her closer and stopped right at PG when Mason cleared his throat.

"We are going to be late. You two can be all mushy later. I don't want to miss the previews."

Ella beamed and stepped back. She stumbled a little and waved, leaning against her car. Boyd felt like he was finally getting it right. The expression on her face and the backward stumble felt like that moment when a beer recipe comes together, and despite trying to make something extraordinary out of water and plants, it's perfect. His feelings for Ella, the way she made him feel, all of it was complicated. But in that moment he'd managed to stun her, and it felt good. He was still smiling when they said goodbye.

When they got into the truck, Mason lifted Boyd's hand and bumped his fist.

"What was that for?" he asked.

"Unexpected. I didn't think you had that in you. I mean it wasn't fireman level, but it was close, Dad. Nice execution."

Chapter Twenty-One

*E*lla settled on jeans after deciding her favorite wraparound dress was too fancy for chili, and the new skirt she'd bought while shopping with Bri and Vienna was god-awful. She didn't know why she kept thinking she could wear stripes without looking like she was getting on a yacht. Other women pulled it off. Maybe it was her height. Whatever it was, that skirt was going back.

She pulled on her favorite light sweater, the blue one Sistine made her for her birthday last year. Ella's mother had what she termed "the cashmere closet" in her bedroom. It was full of luxury in every color. When Ella came home from school and her parents were out, she used to sneak into that closet and put her face to the folded sweaters. They were soft and smelled like Chanel No. 5, but none of them ever made her feel like the one Sistine made with her two hands. Ella supposed kindness changed everything.

Dropping her hair out of its clip, she put on some mascara and lip gloss. It was chili, she told herself. Chili by its very nature was casual, wasn't it? She had never seen Boyd dressed in anything other than jeans and she certainly didn't want to show up overdressed. Was Mason going to be there? It was a school night. She assumed he would be and while she loved seeing him, something in that kiss yesterday had her hoping for time alone. Maybe that was selfish. Did Boyd ever have alone time? If he didn't, was she fine with that?

Ella shook her head to silence the endless game of twenty questions. She grabbed the Sift box off the kitchen counter and her keys before she thought everything into the ground. She knew it was collateral damage from Marc that caused her to put anything that came close to her heart under a microscope. She'd seen him at work again yesterday, only a couple of hours after she'd been talking movies with Mason and his father kissed her until she practically fell over. Marc had attempted to rub her shoulders in the nurses' station and when she'd backed up, she rolled the chair over his foot.

"What the hell are you doing?"

"Jesus, Ella. You seemed tense and I was only—"

She'd stood up. "I'm not tense. I'm perfect. Why are you still here? Isn't your lecture over?"

"A few more days." He'd gestured for her to follow him around the corner.

Ella stayed put, amazed at the balls on the man. If she didn't want to scratch his eyes out, she honestly had to give it to him. The gall was right up there with her father.

"Have dinner with me," he'd said quietly.

Ella laughed. It was loud enough for Trudy to turn around. She knew people often laughed hysterically during times of trauma and she supposed that's what she was experiencing, only less important. She'd learned over the last two years that making Marc as unimportant as possible was the key to her sanity. He wasn't a trauma, he was a joke. That's why she laughed, she'd realized. Without another word, she had turned her back to him and asked Trudy if the patient in Exam 3 had indicated any allergies. She'd ignored him and at some point, he must have slithered away.

Ella sat outside Boyd's house now. She could hear the cicadas in the trees above.

Her phone vibrated and she answered.

"Why are you on your mobile at work, Nurse B?"

"What are you doing?" Bri asked.

"Sitting outside Boyd's house. Why?"

"I heard Dr. Sith Lord tried to ask you out to dinner yesterday."

"Trudy has a big mouth."

"I love that about her."

"Me too, I guess. Yes, Marc made an ass out of himself again. Why is he there?"

"I don't know. Maybe it's to show contrast, you know? Like an MRI."

"Wow, and I work too much? How was your date last night?" Ella asked.

"Not bad. He's a touch obsessed with golf, but the man has all the right equipment and he's not afraid to use it."

Her eyes widened. "You slept with him? On the first date?"

"You sound like my mother. Yes, I slept with him. He has a great body, we had a nice night. Why the hell wouldn't I sleep with him?"

"All good points."

"Speaking of good and sex. Why are you sitting outside Boyd's house?"

"I don't know. I'm taking a minute. Did you know cicadas only come around every thirteen to seventeen years?"

"What the hell are cicadas?"

"They're locusts. They make that zapping sound in the trees."

"Christ, I hate those things. I always think they're going to drop into my hair."

Ella laughed. "Boyd liked science in school too. Did you know he has an engineering background?" She sat in the stillness of her car, picking at the side of her nail polish. She was searching for something to order all the feelings she had for him, but nothing seemed to work. They were all free floating and messy.

"You know, there are so many comments I can make about science and that engineers know how to erect things, but I'll keep those gems to myself. Is Mason going to be there for the chili date?"

"I don't know."

"Well, get in there and find out. If he's over at a friend's house or somewhere with his hot uncles and you don't... I need you to listen to me. If Mason is not in that house and you come to work unable to tell me exactly what Boyd's headboard looks like, I swear to God I'm disowning you."

"You wouldn't do that."

"I would. First the Monday thing and now this endless crawl to the inevitable hot sex story. I can't take much more of this. Do you hear me?"

"I do. Can I hang up now?"

"Yes. Go get your man."

Ella hung up before Bri launched into actual suggestions on how to "get" Boyd.

Cade picked Mason up at six to stay the night at his place. After Boyd reminded both of them one more time that school drop-off at 7:15 meant exactly 7:15, he checked to be sure Mason had his books and money for his yearbook before hugging him and messing up the hair that had entirely too much crap in it these days. He would need to thank his brother for that the next time they were alone.

"We're going to swing by work first and confirm everything is running nicely and then we're hitting the town, right little man?"

"Can I drive?" Mason asked.

"No, you can't drive. Cade?"

"Not this time. Maybe we can take the bike out for a few minutes after dinner."

Boyd shook his head.

"Or not. Let's get out of here before Mother Hen has us tucked under our blankies by seven."

"It's a school night, Mase."

"I know."

He did know. He was a good kid, Boyd reminded himself. He knew he sounded like a prude and couldn't help it if there was some weird guilt thing gnawing at him because he was sending his son off so he could... hell, he had no idea what he was going to do when Ella knocked at the door. Whatever it was required some privacy. Cade, always subtle, waggled his eyebrows, told him to "have a good night," and they were gone.

Boyd paced around, feeling so out of his element he thought he might need to get drunk. This was insane. After he stirred the chili for what felt like the hundredth time, the doorbell rang. He forgot he had a doorbell. No one ever used it. Before he had a chance to punch himself for thinking that might be a sign, he opened the door.

"Did you know cicadas—"

"Come around every thirteen or so years, yeah."

Taking the box out of Ella's hands and tossing it on the half wall between the entryway and the living room, Boyd kissed her before he lost his damn mind.

He knew it wasn't gentlemanly to want sex before dinner, but when her hands slid under his shirt and pulled it over his head, he rightly could have pled the Fifth. There was not a man alive, let alone one who couldn't remember the last time he'd had average sex, who was going to stop what they'd started, politely escort Ella to the dining room, and make sure she had enough butter for her cornbread. She was devouring him in the best way and if he didn't figure out how to turn off the chili now, they'd be ordering pizza.

Her purse dropped to the floor as he lifted her, and she wrapped her legs around him. "Chili," he said, carrying her into the kitchen.

"Later," she breathed into his ear.

He bumped into the kitchen doorjamb when she pulled his bottom lip between her teeth and moaned into his mouth. He had no idea how he found the burner knob on the stove, but he did and managed to make it back to the living room. Holy Christ, he thought as he dropped onto the couch with her straddled across his lap. Pulling her sweater over her head, Boyd felt like he was going up in flames, and then for an instant he felt self-conscious.

The worst possible thing happened next— his mind kicked on. First with the brilliant suggestion that he needed to hike more, or at least stop taste testing everything Cade put in front of him. And then second with the question of whether or not he remembered how to love a woman.

What the hell? Shut that shit off and let's go.

His body was begging for silence but his brain stayed on. He was confident he knew how to please most women, but loving her was different. That required all sorts of things he'd packed away years ago.

Ella looked down at him, willing and wanting. Boyd knew he would need to dust those skills off if he was going to do this right. She'd need the pleasure right now, but she would want more eventually.

"Boyd?"

Every time she said his name, it was like hearing a song he thought he knew but realizing the new version was better. He needed to just feel his way through this. When had he gotten so up in his head?

"It's been a while," he said.

What. In. The. Hell?

"Me too." She ran her hands over his chest, and he remembered exactly what he was supposed to do next.

He'd need a bed.

As he stood them both up, Ella slid down his body. Before he could make his next move, her hands snaked around and she grabbed his ass. A smile stretched across his face. She made him feel hot. Like a guy any woman would ditch her date for. It sounded nuts, but Boyd had been a dad for so long he forgot what it was like to have a woman look at him like she wanted him to climb inside her.

Most of the women in Boyd's life wanted to make him brownies or help him with the carpool schedule. There were even the occasional women who wanted to be Mason's replacement mom, but Ella was none of them. She saw him outside the context of his life while somehow managing to respect everything he held dear. He was a man to her first, and that did something to him, brought him back from somewhere he hadn't realized he'd gone. For that, for those feelings alone, he needed to get this right. Ella woke him up and now he would make damn sure neither of them fell asleep, at least for tonight.

When he undid her bra, Ella's eyes drifted closed. The minute his lips gently touched her shoulder, her mouth almost fell open and she bit the side of her cheek to keep from moaning. They fell into bed and she was wrapped in his arms, their legs tangling. Her body was pulsing with need but somewhere in the middle of their shifting kisses and wandering hands, she sensed a change. She tried not to sound clinical for fear Bri would disown her, but his breathing was labored, his shoulders tensed, and when Ella arched up, her hands gripping at the waistband of his jeans, Boyd pulled back and fell onto his back.

She glanced over at him and even in the darkness lit only by the full moon, she recognized the look of disappointment. It squashed every sensation in her body. She was never one to question her appeal, but something was wrong.

Boyd touched her hand, ran his fingers up her arm, but stared at the ceiling. It took Ella longer than it should have to understand why instead of being washed away in the throes of what had been building between them for months. They were side-by-side, breathless and, save their shirts, fully clothed. What had started as barely-in-the-door passion had somehow grown complicated, for him at least, and well, there was no easy way to put it—he was no longer hard. She couldn't recall if this had ever happened to her before. Most of her sexual experiences were heated, intense—a lot like her life was back then.

She knew there were moments her last partner was distracted by a case or, she now knew, thinking about his daughter's braces, but now was not the time to dissect those experiences. She could practically feel Boyd's mind spinning, his hand still aimlessly touching her skin as if he needed to confirm that she was still there. Ella touched him back, twining her fingers in his and leaning over to kiss his shoulder.

Sweet Lord, those shoulders.

His eyes were closed now as if he wanted to somehow transport himself to a place where every man's worst nightmare had not happened to him. Ella kept her gaze to the ceiling, knew she should say something, but wasn't sure anything would help. She tried anyway.

"You know studies show that men are a lot more in their head when it comes to sex than originally—"

"Not helping." His voice was a low growl.

This was crazy. It's not like they were in some romance novel.

"Boyd." Ella rolled on her side and put her hand on his chest. The man turned her on by breathing. She was trying to stay removed from the situation, but doubt crept in. Maybe she didn't do it for him, maybe that was why—

"It's not you." He turned to her. "Please, dear God, don't turn this into you."

"Oh, I... I know. It's not a big deal."

"I think it is. I had one shot at the heart-pounding first time or even the hot and sweaty screw that left you panting, and I blew both."

"I was panting there for a while."

"Yeah, that's because I was wearing you out trying to get it—" He cut himself off, shaking his head. The back of his hand trailed along her bare side and Ella's entire body was ready again. "I mean, this right here has been keeping me up for weeks. I've wanted you for so long. Now you're right here and—" He kissed her shoulder again and Ella tried to breathe.

"Maybe we started too fast." She touched his face. Searched for something to stay connected to him. "Did I tell you my skinned knees are finally healed?"

Boyd laughed, deep and sexy.

She swatted his shoulder. "That was not a hint. Although, if that's working for you, I could keep making awkward sexual references."

He dipped his head and brushed his lips along her neck.

"Everything about you works for me, Ella. I'm sorry. I wanted this to be—"

And there was the problem. Ella knew all about pressure to perform and expectation. Anxiety to be something someone else imagined was practically in her DNA. She didn't want him to feel any of that with her. Turning his face to her, she met his beautiful hooded eyes.

"I'm not looking for anything other than you. I want you. If that means I get you"—she moved closer to him, trailed kisses up his chest and spoke into his ear—"slow and easy or rough and a little dirty." She pulled his earlobe between her teeth and bit down gently. "I'm ready. I want all of you, Boyd." She climbed across his body, kissed the other side of his neck as the pounding in her chest matched his. His arms closed around her. "Please don't waste your energy figuring out how to turn me on. Breathing—you turn me on by breathing," she whispered.

He rolled her onto her back, his expression more hunger than nerves now. Ghosting his hands along her sides, he stopped at her waistband.

"Do you remember the first time I kissed you?"

Ella couldn't speak as he moved the jeans off her body. She nodded.

"You asked me if there was something between us and about a dozen other questions." He was braced over her, bare chested, arms flexed, and achingly patient. "Do you remember what I said after we kissed?"

She could barely remember her address, but she managed to say, "Yes, to all the above?"

Boyd slid off the bed long enough to remove the rest of his clothes and returned to her, gorgeous and managing to shatter any of her earlier attempts at seduction. She reached for him, and he rested over her on his forearms. He kissed her face, brushed the hair off her neck.

"Yes, to all the above is my answer again, Ella. Since I blew the last one."

It was Ella's turn to laugh. "There's no way around the innuendos."

He smiled and she stopped laughing. Gloriously naked and suspended over her, he spoke into her neck. "Let's start with slow and easy." He kissed her, deep and unhurried. "I'm going to try this again. Are you with me?"

A soft smile spread across her lips. She loved this man. Deep down in her presently liquid bones, she knew he was her person. The one she was meant to love. Despite all the other crappy stuff, he was a gift.

"I'm with you," she managed to say as her hands moved up his back.

"Good. If slow and easy goes well, maybe you could show me your idea of rough and a little dirty?" He kissed down her neck and by the time he made it to her breasts, Ella lost all conscious thought. She was flooded with sensation and the unbridled need to bring him closer to her than she had ever allowed another human being.

See, studies were right. Some men were more in their minds. Ella appreciated a thinker and sweet Lord, was there anything better than a man who took his time?

Chapter Twenty-Two

"Why don't you get along with your family?" Boyd asked and immediately wanted to smack himself upside the head. He could have said, "That was the hottest sex of my life," or "You're unbelievable," or even better, nothing at all. Nope, after they'd both enjoyed slow and dirty twice, Boyd decided to lead with her family. Because every woman glistening in the aftermath of amazing sex wanted to talk about her family, right? Jesus, he was an idiot.

She surprised him by rolling closer and answering. "I don't exactly have a family."

He couldn't tell if she was joking, but there'd been no amusement in her voice.

"You don't have family?"

Her head was resting on his chest. "Not by your definition of family."

"What kind of family do you have?"

"Disjointed, dysfunctional, sometimes disturbing." She laughed. There she went letting him in, and Boyd wasn't about to waste the opportunity.

"My family was never a selling point. Does that sound strange? Ella Walters comes with a prestigious degree, a noble profession, assorted gym wear, a great little house in Petaluma, and a penchant for scary novels. Maybe that's how I used to view things. I don't know."

"You're impressive without the packaging. Don't you think?"

She rolled on her stomach and met his eyes. He had been worried before she'd arrived that what they had only existed among their friends, or Mason. Looking at her now, lips raw and hair dancing, he knew once again he'd been worrying about nothing. The draw was between the two of them despite the joy and noise around them.

"I think so, I think I know that now. To answer your question, I have a 'dis' family. Is that a thing?"

He ran his hand along her jaw and wanted to believe everything his heart was spinning.

"We all have some 'dis.'"

"Is that so? Where are you hiding yours because from my seat, your family seems genuine. Not perfect, but real and kind."

"We've grown into the kind part."

"Then what? I haven't met your dad yet. Is he a drug dealer?"

He laughed and shook his head. "My mom, as you probably know, is a bookkeeper, and my dad is a contractor."

"See, solid, honorable professions."

He kissed her because she seemed to need his mouth on hers, or maybe it was the other way around.

"Are your parents drug dealers?" he asked when they eased apart.

Grinning, she toyed with his beard. "Why? Is that a problem?"

"I just want to hire enough security."

"Ah."

"You do that a lot. Move the conversation off you," Boyd said.

"Do I?"

"You do."

Ella took what looked like a deep breath of reluctance. "Well, you know my dad is a doctor. But not only a GP"—she paused at what must have been his look of confusion—"general practitioner. My father is not *just* a doctor, as he likes to say. He's a neurosurgeon. The recently retired Chief of Neurosurgery at Cedars-Sinai, if you want all the bells and whistles."

"And your mom?"

"She's a design editor."

He held back, knowing there must be more, something to match or at least complement her father.

"For the *LA Times*."

Boyd nodded. "So, your parents are losers. I can understand the shame."

She laughed in a way that seemed more glorious, because she seemed to be holding her breath from the moment he'd brought up her parents. He wondered what had to happen in a family for that level of pain.

"Neurosurgeon, huh? In common terms, that means your father is a brain surgeon. So, when he's at work and some other guy says, 'Dude, this isn't brain surgery,' he gets to look at them and say, 'It sure as hell is'?"

"I have never thought about it that way, but yes."

"Does he like what he does?"

"I have no idea."

"Do you like what you do?"

"I love it."

Boyd was once again struck stupid by her as she lay wrapped in his sheets. Had she slept with many men who did their own laundry, knew which fabric softeners worked? He was making a judgment, but Boyd guessed most of the men allowed to touch a woman like Dr. Ella Walters had a service for things like laundry and grocery shopping. The thought didn't stop him from wanting to climb a little more under her surface.

"I'm going to give your own words back to you." He cleared his throat for effect. "Dr. Walters, I'm worn out. I'd like to see if there is anything left of the chili I made and then lure you back to bed. A professional such as yourself can understand that, can't you?"

Ella smiled.

"Great. I can't do any of that unless you're a little more forthcoming. Can you help me out?"

"I don't know what you're talking about. I'm answering your questions. I might not like the answers, but I'm responding. You were practically grunting the first time I met you. I'm sharing."

213

"Yeah? You think so. Maybe we should move off your parents."

"That is the best idea you've had all night." She ran her finger along his chest. "Well, second-best idea."

"You have a sister."

She nodded.

"Do you two get along?"

"No."

"No? That's it?"

"Let me see if I can answer a lot of questions at once and be more forthcoming, Mr. McNaughton."

Christ, he loved it when she called him that. Ridiculous, but still true.

"My father is a doctor, as we've covered. My sister is an interior designer married to a doctor. My mother is second in command in the design department at the *LA Times*. They all wear shoes that cost thousands of dollars. I stepped in gum yesterday walking from the ER to my car. I soaked it off the bottom of my clogs because they're my favorite pair."

"Thousands as in three zeros? Are they made by actual elves?"

"Italian elves no doubt."

"So, what does all of this mean? You're not like your family?"

Ella exhaled.

"Hey, there are steps. We don't have to like them, but we—"

"Oh, shush. My life was never my own growing up, and my parents are cruel. There's no other way to put it. When I graduated college, the summer before med school, there was this great place called Lucy's right off campus. I bought my first pair of cutoff jean shorts, had ice cream for dinner, and cried."

"Wow, you're screwed up."

"Told you."

"Who cries while they're eating ice cream? Don't tell Mase that story or he may reconsider the friendship." It was the first time he'd mentioned his son since she rang the doorbell, since he'd taken her to his bed. The earth didn't shake. Somehow his happiness and his son coexisted, at least for now.

She threw a pillow at his face as he snaked an arm around her waist and pulled her back into him. They were spooning now. Boyd kissed the top of her head. "My turn," he said, searching for something from his past that would help the world she came from sound less alarming, which was going to be hard because her childhood sounded downright miserable. He wondered if her dad drank beer. Probably not.

"Thank God."

"Okay, let's see. Before I had Mason, I had no idea what I was going to do with my life."

Ella laughed.

"What? I'm trying to share here."

"Nothing. I'm sorry, but I think I've won this round."

"Eh, maybe. But I didn't go to Harvard and I don't have the talent to save people's lives every day when I go to work." He gently pushed the hair off her face and already wanted to climb back inside her eyes. "There has to be a decent amount of bad to go with all the good that you are, Ella."

She twisted to face him again, kissed him, and pulled his bottom lip into her mouth as if she didn't want to waste one moment of them. Christ, the woman made him feel like there was nothing he couldn't give her.

"What does that mean? Why does there have to be bad?"

"There's bad and good in everything. It's like beer."

"Of course, it is."

"You have malt, which can be wheat or barley. I'll always choose barley, but that's not the point. The malt is the sweet. It's usually a pretty color and it smells good when it's milled. But no one makes a beer with only malt. If they do, they're idiots because it's so syrupy it has no right to be called beer. Any brew master will tell you the key to a good beer is balance, so you add hops. Hops are funky looking, sticky to touch when it's wet, and bitter. It takes down the sweetness of anything. There's all kinds of other crap that needs to be adjusted too, but you get the point."

"Balance?"

"Yeah, I think life is like that. Good and bad. You have a lot of good. Seems only fitting that you'd have parents who spend too much money on shoes and aren't fun."

Ella exhaled and her breath drifted across his chest. He could feel the weight of her thoughts.

"Are you hungry?" he asked because he had not intended to put that weight on her.

"Starving." She stood, taking the sheet with her and wrapping it around her body as she walked out to his living room. She looked good in his home, their home, his mind corrected as if it was some-how wrong not to include Mason in the picture. He hadn't meant to exclude him, but he was able to admit he was enjoying being with Ella, only the two of them, for what seemed like a night suspended above both of their realities.

Boyd pulled on his jeans and willed himself to think only about salvaging the chili. *Chili and more sex*, he heard Cade's voice in his head. Turned out Cade may be the smartest brother of them all.

"Okay, I need to stop laughing or I'm going to choke on this surprisingly delicious reheated chili," Ella said.

"Why is that surprising? Chili is a go-to dinner option here in the McNaughton house. That and chicken kebabs. We like those too." Boyd wiped his mouth and his eyes were filled with fun and flirtation. Ella couldn't take her eyes off him. She didn't want to look away or miss one minute.

Still wrapped in his sheets, she no longer felt completely ex-posed—chili and excellent beer had all but extinguished talk of her family. She hadn't been prepared for another round of twenty ques-tions and at the same time, there was something liberating about getting all her mess out in the open. Most of it anyway. There were some things she might never be able to explain, but that was a worry for another day. Right now, all she needed to do was make sure Boyd knew what he was getting into because she wanted to be with him, wanted to be a part of his life. There it was, plain as day, pulsing through her heart as he shared a couple of stories from his childhood, including the time his mother made them all dress as chicks for Butter and Egg Days.

In addition to loving every bit of who Boyd was when his clothes were on, getting naked with him had been the best sex she'd ever had. Ella knew that sounded stupid romantic, but it was the God's truth. The best. Not because he was a ripped stallion who liked to talk dirty and had magic fingers. Nothing wrong with that, of course, but Boyd was not that guy. He was better because while Ella was no stranger to the ecstasy of an orgasm, she was sadly unfamiliar with being cherished.

He touched every inch of her body as if she were the only woman he'd ever touched, ever wanted to touch again. She had no idea if they could make a relationship work, but in and outside of the bed, he made her feel things she never knew were possible. It could be that he had this effect on every woman. Maybe it was his style, his technique. Boyd was a skin worshiper, that's all there was to it.

Once they'd finished off the last of the cornbread that went with the McNaughton chili dinner, they got dressed and lay outside on a hammock under the stars. She rested under his arm and wondered if anyone had ever been on the hammock except for him and Mason. How many things in their house had been untouched by a woman who loved them? Ella caught herself and remembered assuming was dangerous.

"You know there are a lot of health benefits to drinking beer," Boyd said, turning the now-empty bottle in his hand.

"Is that so. I guess I'm used to the other side of what alcohol does to the body."

"I didn't say alcohol, I said beer."

She laughed and he pulled her closer as the hammock swayed. "Now I'm curious. Do tell."

"Okay, well, drinking a moderate amount of beer can reduce your chance of heart attacks by something like thirty percent."

She rolled to face him, her hands perched under her chin and resting on his chest. She felt small next to him, but in a way that didn't make her feel less than.

"And there's the key word—moderation," she said.

"True. Lots of B vitamins and zinc."

"Things also found in vegetables and a healthy diet."

"Yeah, but nothing tastes like a good beer. Oh, and there are two things I'm not even going to try to pronounce, but they are important for a good night's sleep."

"Well, you'd better put that bottle down then." She braced one arm on each side of his chest and slid up his body, which was no easy feat on a hammock. The bottle teetered in his hand.

"Why? I can still hold it."

She leaned into his ear. "I'm not finished with you, beer man. The night is still young and I'm going to need your full attention."

Boyd dropped the bottle onto the grass. "Done." He held her hips.

Ella rested her hands on his chest and sat up. "That's all it takes?"

He nodded.

She pulled on the ropes of the hammock. "Do you think this thing will hold us once we start, you know, moving?"

Before she could say another word, Boyd stood with her in his arms. She laughed again—that had to be some kind of record, she thought.

"Aw, I was hoping to experiment. Where are you taking me?"

"To bed. I have nosy neighbors."

Sometime later, his hand trailed down the dip of her spine and rested flat on her lower back. He was warm and his chest moved silently in and out at her side as she fell off to sleep.

Chapter Twenty-Three

Ella arrived in the ER the next morning to silence. There were no patients, no voices. Nothing but the faint sound of the television in the waiting area. It was as if the universe was acknowledging that Ella Walters had phenomenal sex and it wanted to ease her back into reality. Thanking the universe, she put her things down and prepared to relieve the evening doctor. Who was... she checked the board. Dr. Campbell. All was right with the world because he was organized, albeit sometimes late getting back from vacation, but he was an outstanding doctor and succinct with his rounds. Ella sat at the nurses' station, opened the latte she'd picked up from Vienna, and breathed in the fresh smell of yummy caffeine.

"Good morning, sunshine," Bri said, coming around the corner with a box of four-by-fours and two scissors dangling from her fingers.

"Morning. Hot pink nails today."

She set her stuff down on the counter and splayed her hands so they could be admired. "It's summer."

"That it is. Ghost town in here."

"According to Wilma, last patient left over an hour ago. Sinus infection."

Ella stretched and checked that her phone ringer was silenced. Bri restocked Exam 3 and returned, arms folded as she leaned on the front admit counter.

"What?" Ella said, looking up to find her assessing.

"You seem happy," Bri said. Work or no work, she was waiting for the details.

"Aren't I always happy?"

Bri raised a brow.

"When I'm not working a double and I've gotten some sleep."

"I guess, but you look peppier this morning. New... face cream?"

"Actually, yes, I am using a new face cream. Thank you for noticing." She sipped her latte and licked the foam off her lips.

The door zipped open and Boyd stood in the entrance. Jeans and a T-shirt, simply jeans and a T-shirt she told herself, but damn he looked good.

"Boyd," Bri said, stepping back from the counter. "What brings you in here bright and early? Did you know Ella is using a new face cream?"

"I... no. Should I know that?"

He moved closer, and all Ella could do was sit there and smile.

"I need to speak with El... Dr. Walters," Boyd said in a jumbled mess that Bri was obviously enjoying.

She glanced between them. "Okay, well, you're in luck because she's right here." Bri circled behind the nurses' station on her way out, but not before leaning past Ella to grab her magazine. "Face cream, my ass. Looks like I will not have to disown you after all." She chuckled and then jolted in surprise. Ella knew Marc was standing behind her even before Bri started humming the Darth Vader entrance theme. She could see it on Boyd's face, so she turned to confirm.

Yes, yes, there he was. Freshly shaven, sporting a dress shirt and lab coat today like he was playing small-town physician. She'd had about enough of this.

"Dr. Pierce, can I help you?" she said.

Bri ducked out and Ella wished she could join her, but Boyd was now walking closer.

Marc put his hand on her shoulder. "Can I see you for a minute?" he asked softly enough to sound intimate.

Ella shrugged from his touch. "What do you need?"

"Oh, are you busy with a patient?" He homed in on Boyd, who was now at the counter, a curious expression on his face.

How many times would she have to introduce her biggest mistake?

"No. Boyd is not my patient. Boyd McNaughton, this is Dr. Marc Pierce."

"Pleasure." Marc extended his hand.

"Sure. Good to meet you." Boyd shook his hand.

The greetings were followed by what felt like an endless pause as each man tried to figure out where the other fit. Ella stood, hoping the awkwardness would fall away.

"Marc... Dr. Pierce. I will need to talk with you later. I'll bet you have something to do in the meantime."

She grabbed Boyd by the arm and brought him to the on-call room.

When they were alone, she kissed him and instantly felt like she'd been plugged back in. Familiar heat coursed right under the surface with a promise that it could erase a past she no longer wanted to own.

"Who's the doctor, Ella?" he asked, moving her hair aside and gently kissing her neck.

"A doctor. This is a hospital. There are lots of us."

He met her eyes. "You sticking with that story? He sure seemed like he wanted to take you into the break room and, well, do this."

She laughed, which was absurd.

"Yeah, well, that's not going to happen. I can't control the desires of other people."

"True." He took her mouth again and everything melted this time. Her past, her present—all Ella felt was the moment.

"You need to go. I can't breathe when you touch me."

His lips met the curve of her ear. "Is breathing important in your line of work?"

All she could do was nod.

"I'll go, but we should talk about the movie-star guy in the lab coat out there."

"Do we have to do that now? I'm working and things are—"

"Busy?" He lifted a brow, and suddenly his impromptu visit went from fun to complicated.

Once again, thank you, Marc Pierce.

Ella cleared her throat.

"Fine." She locked the door and crossed her arms, as if Boyd had already judged her. "I dated Marc for two years."

"I figured."

"He told me he worked for Doctors Without Borders. You know, they go all over the world helping people."

Boyd leaned against the wall. "Noble."

"I saw him once every few weeks. We had an apartment near the hospital. We went on a couple of vacations together."

"Okay. I really don't need the details, Ella. Let's get to the part where you tell me you've never stopped loving him and now he's back and you're confused."

"What?"

His expression indicated he knew the ending to a story Ella hadn't even read yet.

"Let's get on with it."

"Okay. Marc doesn't work for Doctors Without Borders."

Boyd met her eyes, not even bothering to hide the surprise. She had a hunch he somehow expected rejection or an admission that sleeping with him had been a lapse in judgment and she was now going to run back into the arms of the chiseled doctor. Stupid *ER* reruns.

"He was married," she continued. "He is married. Seven years, two children married."

Full shock now registered on Boyd's face as he stepped away from the wall. Ella couldn't tell if there was judgment in his eyes.

"How did I not know, is that what you're thinking?"

He shook his head.

"How did I spend two years with him, sleeping with him right next to me?"

"Details, Ella. No need for details."

"I'm serious. What kind of a woman doesn't know?"

"Okay." Boyd let out a deep breath. "You get back to work and I'm relieved as hell to not be living in an episode of *ER*, so I'll be quick. The guy must have been a good liar."

"Or I'm a fool."

"Were a fool, if that's how you need to look at it. I'm guessing he's the reason you moved?"

Ella nodded. "I should have noticed things. I should have known."

"Yeah, and I should have made sure Claire and I were using protection every time so I wasn't trying to raise a teenager on my own when what he needs are two sane parents. We could sit here in this... what is this place?"

"On-call room."

"Right, this on-call room and 'should have' ourselves to death. That serves no purpose. Claire and I created a surprise that changed my life for the better. You made a mistake."

Ella knew he was offering her part of his past, a piece of understanding to help steady her own history.

"It doesn't feel that simple."

"But it is. Well, maybe not for the asshat who's circling for one more shot at you, but for you, it's simple... unless you still love him."

"I don't. What we had was never..." Ella should have said after thirty-six years that she finally knew what love felt like, finally found a connection not wrapped in lies or ugliness, but she was at work and now wasn't the best time to spill what remained of her heart right there at Boyd's feet.

"Okay then, that wasn't so bad. I told you every woman had a secret. Yours obviously is more complex than monkey bread."

Ella smiled. "I like you, beer man." She kissed him.

"Go save some lives, Doc." He turned to leave. "You could stop by the brewery after work, watch Mason try to win back his high score from one of the waiters."

"I'd like that." She was in so much trouble. Ugly secret out of the bag and the man was still looking at her like she was the best thing in clogs and glasses.

Boyd tried not to draw comparisons as he drove to the brewery. Ella wasn't Claire and even though Mason's Social Studies teacher espoused that history often repeats itself, that's not what was happening.

Less than twenty-four hours ago he'd been in bed with Ella, drifting into her eyes while she told him about her family and he told her about growing up. He'd shared his home, his bed. The fact that Claire started living with a guy who looked almost as sleek and shiny as the doctor back there less than a year after leaving him and Mason to fend for themselves was irrelevant. That she married said guy another year later was unimportant too. Boyd had spent years learning how to manage thoughts that did no one any good. That's why he listened when she shared another piece of her past.

He and Ella had a great night. No matter what happened, nothing changed that. He could sense himself backing up, not quite changing his mind, but needing the tempo of his normal in case Ella decided to return to the big city, discovered she'd made a mistake. Somewhere along the way, Boyd had become fine with any and all scenarios. Knowing what was up ahead, expecting it, proved a hell of a lot less painful than the kick of surprise.

So, even if the shiny doctor returned newly divorced and begged her to come back. Even if she somehow morphed into stupid and believed him. Even if she returned to her bigger hospital and started buying shoes made by Italian elves too, Boyd would be fine. It was part of his makeup now, his "metal" as his dad phrased it. No matter what happened, Boyd and his son would always be fine.

Chapter Twenty-Four

*E*lla received the lab work back that confirmed the girl in Exam 2 did have mono. She was preparing her discharge notes when Mrs. Graham approached the admit counter pulling Mr. Graham from behind. He was holding his stomach.

Trudy gestured for them to sit and began asking questions. Mr. Graham was gray and could barely answer. Ella tried not to play the game, but something felt dangerously off. She sensed a buzz, a tingling at the base of her neck.

"He's been this way since this morning. He hasn't eaten anything, but his stomach is kind of hard. I searched on WebMD," Mrs. Graham continued as Trudy took his blood pressure and glanced over her shoulder.

Ella checked the digital display. His pressure was low, crazy low. Trudy continued with her questions as Ella moved closer.

"Mr. Graham," she said, putting her hand on Trudy's shoulder. "Pain on a scale of one to ten?"

He held up both hands to indicate ten and then wrapped his arms back around his midsection.

"Do you think it's the flu, Doc? Maybe something he ate?"

"I do not think it is the flu, Mrs. Graham." Ella tried not to sound too stern, but she truly hated WebMD. "Trudy is going to take your husband into Exam 3 and we're going to take a closer look. Things will move quickly for a little bit, but I promise to explain as soon as we know more."

Mrs. Graham's eyes went wide and then pooled with tears Ella didn't have time to tend to because she needed to save this man's life. She needed blood and a way to get him somewhere other than Petaluma Valley, and she needed all of it fast.

"Bri," she called, eyes still on the friendly face of the hardware store man she'd first met in line at Sift with his granddaughter. He had a granddaughter and two grandsons if she remembered correctly.

"Did you call me?" Her friend and best nurse was at her back. Ella had been out of the game for a while, but this was something.

"I need you to find Dr. Pierce."

"The ass—"

"Bri, please. I know he's in the hospital today because I saw the sign for one of his keynotes when I came in this morning. Find him, now."

She was gone without another word.

Ella went into Exam 3, where Trudy and two other nurses already had an IV going and one unit of blood was nearly gone. They were waiting for Ella to give them further instructions.

"Get him something for pain." Ella took his blood pressure again herself.

"On the way." Trudy noted his pressure in the computer.

"Mr. Graham, we're going to try to make you more comfortable."

"Good luck. I feel like my insides are ripping."

She tried not to flinch. She knew the pain he was describing, not personally, but she'd had patients with this and worse before. A flush of calm she had not experienced in years ran through her.

"Mr. Graham, do you have a history of aneurysms that you are aware of? Family maybe?"

He grunted a response Ella didn't understand.

It didn't matter that Trudy hung another unit, which would make it three in the last fifteen minutes—his pressure was still low. Ella knew what was wrong and she'd almost figured out the best way to proceed.

"Trudy, call down to radiology now and get Mr. Graham in for a C-scan."

"Excuse me, Doctor. Can I come in and sit with George?" Mrs. Graham appeared in the door. "Is that blood?"

Ella wanted to grab the man, wheel him into radiology, and do the scan herself. She didn't have time for chitchat or the limitations of this hospital.

Instead, she explained to Mrs. Graham what was going to happen next. The small elderly woman held her white pocketbook with both hands. Ella wanted to put her at ease, but the truth was her husband was in trouble and as luck would have it, the answer to his prayers was somewhere in the building speaking way over everyone's head in that self-absorbed way he'd mastered.

"They can take him now," Trudy said.

Ella's eyes briefly left Mr. Graham and found the nurse's nervous but determined face.

"They'll be here in two minutes," she added.

Ella thanked her just as the radiology tech arrived with a wheelchair. Marc was right behind him.

After settling Mrs. Graham back in the waiting area, Ella turned and walked to the back of the nurses' station.

"He has an aneurysm. Triple A, I'm sure of it."

"The guy in the wheelchair?"

She nodded, recapped the symptoms, and then watched in amazement as the polished facade of Marc Pierce melted away and the brilliant doctor emerged. Engaged and more than a little curious, he asked where they were taking him and with little more information, he was gone.

If Ella was right, and she knew she was, Mr. Graham would not be staying at Petaluma Valley for longer than it took to find him transport. She would wait to hear from Marc first, but she was certain they'd Air Evac him out as soon as possible and Mr. Graham would be in surgery soon after.

Marc returned less than an hour later and finished coordinating efforts to have Mr. Graham sent to Zuckerberg Memorial. The aneurysm was close to three inches. Unstable, but not ruptured. Air Evac would arrive within thirty minutes.

"I've called ahead. They're ready for him."

"You're not going with him?"

"El, Hamm just got out of surgery and if he can't take it, Anderson will. He'll be in good hands."

"I want him in your hands. He's lived here his whole life, raised kids and grandkids. Do you see the woman in the waiting area? They've been married for almost fifty years. He owns the hardware store right around the corner from my house." Ella knew she sounded insane, but she was suddenly filled with such a rush of connection that it was spilling out of her. "You are the best, Marc, and Mr. Graham deserves nothing less."

He sighed, ego firmly aglow, and she knew she'd secured arguably one of the best surgeons in the country for what should be an uneventful procedure now that the aneurysm had been found. She also knew that this world-class medical care came because of Marc's sick need to win her back. To make the grand gesture in a bid to rekindle the enamored glow she'd once had around him. Before it all went to hell, and like her parents and the bad necklace, he turned her neck green.

Ella knew all of these things as she squeezed Mrs. Graham's hand and explained that the helicopter was more noise than anything else. As she watched them fly off toward San Francisco, she didn't care. It didn't matter why he was going to save Mr. Graham's life. All that mattered was that come next year's Butter and Egg Days, Mr. Graham was outside his shop handing out those egg-shaped measuring tapes.

"Where is he?" Ella asked as her eyes adjusted to the shaded light of the Tap House.

Patrick raised a brow, and Cade pointed to the back like a kid used to tattling.

"He's coming up with his autumn recipe. It's commune with nature week. He's out back. Probably not a good idea to bother him."

"Thanks." Walking past them, she didn't care if it was a good time or not. She had something to say. After she got the call that Mr. Graham was resting comfortably in recovery, Ella decided she'd held back long enough.

Pushing through the creak of the large metal back door, she didn't see him at first. Nothing but a couple of storage sheds, a huge overarching tree, and the river's edge. Her eyes followed a rusted railing that separated the back of the brewery from a railroad track long out of use, and off in the far corner on a tree stump sat Boyd with a notebook open on another stump in front of him. He was smelling something in his left hand and tapping a pencil with the other.

Cade was right, he appeared to be in full contemplation. She was about to blow that Zen wide open when Boyd started walking away toward what she now knew was his office. Her feet wouldn't move. The love and fear that propelled her to that spot somehow ran dry at the sight of him solitary and deep in thought. He didn't see her before disappearing into the maze of buildings that was Foghorn Brewery.

Ella turned to leave right as Patrick opened the door.

"You're leaving?"

"He seems busy."

"He's not. He is like a Boy Scout working toward his next badge. Come into my office and I'll show you busy."

She laughed.

"I came out here hoping for a front-row seat. From your entrance, I thought we'd be able to hear the fight from inside."

She sat on the bench outside the door and was surprised when Patrick pulled at the legs of his crisp khakis and joined her.

"I get it now," he said. She looked at him and recognized pieces of Boyd. She knew all about genetics, but as with most things learned in a book, it was different when it sat living and real right next to her.

"Get what?" she asked.

"You're not mad at him. You love him."

She would not have been more shocked if Patrick had stood up and dropped his pants. Well, maybe that was an exaggeration, but she had not expected someone so seemingly together and smooth to be a mind reader too. The wind blew across her face and she felt a strange sense of relief that someone had uttered the words at last.

"You're good."

"I know."

She laughed.

"So, why are you sitting here? He's in his office making a big deal out of something that should take him half the day. It's what he does. Christ, I hate nature week almost as much as deadline week. Believe me, you're not bothering him."

"He seems fine on his own. Happy."

"First, there's a big difference between fine and happy. As I'm sure you already know, Boyd makes do with what he's given. It's really one of the noble things about him. He pushes through and pushes on. Mason makes his life joyful, fulfilling, but you, Dr. Ella Walters, you are his happy."

"You don't know that."

"I think we've already established that I'm good."

She wondered how any woman or man for that matter was safe around the McNaughton brothers. They were each an element on their own, but good God, together they were a force. No wonder Foghorn Brewery beat the odds and was thriving. They were unstoppable.

"I'm fairly new at connecting."

It was Patrick's turn to laugh.

"Now that I've calmed down, I think I'll wait for him to say it first," she said.

"Bad idea?" He leaned forward. "He loves deeper than anyone I know, but words are not exactly his strong suit."

She closed her eyes. It should feel awkward talking to a man she barely knew about a man she loved, but it didn't. Nothing had gone as expected since Boyd walked into the ER, and there was no indication things were going to change.

Ella stood and brushed off her scrubs. She should have changed before she left. She used to hate it when doctors went to the grocery store or some school event for their kids in their scrubs. Germs, hello? She wanted to scream and now here she was, an emotional germ spreader.

"My nephew tells me you are the 'girl expert.'"

Ella laughed. "If only I were the man expert, huh?"

"You're a doctor. You'll figure it out. The heart seems pretty important."

"That's almost poetic, Patrick."

He stood holding up his finger to his lips in a childlike "shh" and then slipped back into the Tap House.

After a deep breath, Ella took in the beauty of the river, and for the second time in a few months, went to tell Boyd she had a feeling.

Boyd decided to fix the lid on one of his tanks. It wasn't sealing right, and he needed a break from coming up with the autumn recipe. He was thinking of turning on some music when Ella walked onto the brewery floor in her scrubs. Her hair was wild, barely a ponytail at the back of her head, and Boyd remembered the first time she walked into that hospital room and into his life. His chest warmed, but as she came closer, she seemed determined or pissed. From a distance, he couldn't tell the difference. Closing the lid on the tank, he braced himself as he walked down the metal stairs.

"Why do I feel like I'm in trouble?"

She marched right in front of him, clogs squeaking, and put her arms around his neck. "Because you are. We both are," she said, a little out of breath, and then she kissed him.

When she'd kissed him within an inch of his life there in broad daylight, Boyd questioned if they worked too much because it felt like some great times went down at the brewery or the hospital. Opposites, he thought at first, but then realized both places healed in a way. The mass of ingredients and worries swirling through his mind came to a screeching halt when she pulled back from the kiss and said, "Are you in love with me?"

His grip tightened at the back of her shirt, as if he could somehow hold her and not answer at the same time. "I'm trying," came out of his mouth before his brain engaged.

"Trying to love me?" Ella went to step back, but he held her in place.

He needed her to understand and at the same time had no words to explain.

He shook his head. "Trying not to. I'm trying not to love you."

"Why?"

"Because I don't want to feel all of this. I don't want to fall in love."

"Okay. Well, good luck with that because I'm already there and I'm not chickening out."

"Nice chicken reference." He raised his brow, hoping to redirect a conversation he was trying desperately not to have.

She took her face in his hands, and Boyd felt like he was falling. Out of a plane, a moving car, it didn't matter. He was going down.

"I love you, Boyd." Ella let out a breath that whispered across his face, and he closed his eyes as if he could capture her. "That inopportune smiling and thinking about you thing has already set in for me."

"See? Who the hell wants to feel like that?"

Her face lit up with warmth and a serenity he'd never seen in her before. "I do. I'll take it all if it means I get you. Get to wake up every morning next to you. If it means making a life and being around Mase more. If saying I love you leads me anywhere close to a family with you and Mase, then I'm done holding back."

Boyd's eyes welled with tears that he promptly wiped away. "I… Christ, what do I say to that. I'm sorry."

"Don't be. I was beginning to wonder if I would ever love someone. It's nice to be alive."

He shook his head as she smiled up at him. No agenda, no need for the perfect response from him. She was just bursting with love and needed to tell him. Boyd was officially the luckiest man on the planet and the biggest idiot all rolled into one.

"You're insane."

"Oh, now you're tuning in."

"So, you love me." He was trying to catch a full breath and formulate something that wasn't asinine.

She nodded. "I do."

"How are you so comfortable with this? Aren't you supposed to be all angsty and in denial? I thought you had a hard time connecting with people?"

"Practice and patience." She smiled and stepped back from his arms. "Mr. Graham has an aneurysm. Well, doesn't anymore because Marc took him to San Francisco, but he had one earlier today."

"Marc, Marc? He's still here?" Boyd leaned against his work table and crossed his arms.

"No. He just got out of surgery in the city."

Ella filled him in on the details, which made for an unbelievable story, but he kept circling back to the three words she said before Mr. Graham came into the conversation. And why he was unable to say them back to her.

"I used to see people struggle and lose all the time in my job, but now the whole connection thing is in full force. I can't be sure what's changed, but I feel everything these days. My heart is in charge. I want to kiss you right through breakfast every time I see you. I'm happy. I think I'm your happy too. That's why I'm here... in my clogs." She tapped her shoes and blew a stray hair from her face.

Boyd had never seen anyone so free, so open and armor down. It was stunning.

"Holy shit."

She smiled, slow and deliberate. Maybe she wasn't exactly enjoying watching him squirm, but she knew she had the upper hand. Did she also know he loved her back? Did he need to say it right then or were her words enough for both of them?

"I need to go. Book club meeting tonight." She kissed him one more time, and Boyd wanted to give her the answer written in every romance. He wanted to tell her she'd saved him and he'd imagined all the things she'd said and more. He wanted so much it felt like his chest was going to cave in, but as his father often said, "Wanting isn't enough. You have to put in the work." In that moment, Boyd couldn't find the words.

"Okay." He cleared his throat. "Did you just walk right out of saving a man's life to blow me away?"

"Is that what I did?"

He nodded and felt the lump firmly back in his throat.

"Then yes, yes I did. I'll see you later?"

"You will."

She spun like a child at Christmas, and Boyd knew it was a privilege to see this side of Ella. She was almost to the door when his brain started to kick in.

"Ella?"

"Yeah?"

"Thank you."

"For what?"

"Loving me."

"Anytime. In fact, it's my pleasure."

"Mason's at my parents' house tonight. You could stop by after book club."

"The meeting is at their house. I'll get to see him."

"And then you could come and see me."

She walked back and leaned into him. "What exactly are you offering, beer man? I've had a long day and"—she stepped away and rolled her shoulders slowly, her eyes never leaving him—"I might not have the energy."

"You need to get out of here now before I haul you into that closet." Boyd laughed and felt them return to a familiar space.

"Promises, promises." She huffed. "I'll text you when I'm on my way."

She kissed him quickly and then she was gone.

Boyd sat at his work table and ran a hand over his face. She deserved to be loved in return and he'd blown it. Again.

He was still unsure how to be that guy. He was thirty-seven and he'd been raising a son most of his adult life. The fantasy where he meets the love of his life, like his parents had, wasn't his reality. While he loved Mason more than anything in the world, he had given things up. Every choice left something behind. Boyd didn't know how to be the guy who sweeps a woman like Ella off her feet *and* the guy with reusable grocery bags in the back of his truck. He doubted they could exist together in the same person.

His phone vibrated. Certain it was Ella with one last word, he ran his thumb across the screen and nearly dropped the phone when he saw Claire's name.

I've moved some things around and I'll be at Mason's graduation. Can you pick me up at the airport next week?

Boyd closed his eyes. Happy for Mason that his mom would see him graduate eighth grade and confused as hell by what this meant for him. Was it another sign? A beautiful, brilliant woman capable of telling if a man was going to bleed to death simply because he had stomach pain had all but danced over to him and declared her love. Expecting nothing in return. She adored his son and Mason worshipped her right back, so why was he suddenly struggling to find a place for all these pieces?

For now, he needed to keep things simple and focus on what was most important. He texted Claire back, and minutes later, she sent her flight information.

Chapter Twenty-Five

Ella hugged Mason when he answered the door at the McNaughton house. For the first time, she held on longer.

"Wow, you're becoming a master Jedi," he said. "Gram said I'm
supposed to ask if you would like something to drink."

"I would love some water."

He wrinkled his face.

"Or a glass of wine?"

"Better answer." He took her hand and pulled her into the kitchen
where Bri and Sistine were sitting at the round kitchen table talking
with Sara, Boyd's mom.

After greetings, Ella told them Vienna was running late.

"Something about finally getting a guy in to repair the lighting in
her front pastry case. Is Aspen coming?"

"On her way," Sara said.

Her eyes were the same color as Boyd's. A sort of fairy-tale green.
Ella had met Sara a few times now and she'd never noticed that
before, but as she had with Patrick, she spotted pieces of Boyd
everywhere now. Mason stood next to his grandmother, and the
warmth in Ella's chest grew.

"Do you have any updates for me?" she asked Mason.

He shook his head. "The friend thing is working, but I'm kind of moving on. Besides, I'm too psyched about graduation. Are you coming?"

She glanced up at everyone around the table, their expressions as if they knew something she didn't.

"When is your graduation?"

"This Wednesday."

"I... wow, that is so soon. I don't think I'm going to be able to make it." Her eyes met Bri's and sent out a call for help.

"She tried to get it off when your dad invited her, sweetie, but we're short-staffed."

Mason huffed. "That sucks."

Sara cleared her throat.

"I mean that is a shame. That's what I meant to say. I guess saving people's lives is important though."

Ella was dumbfounded as her mind tried to order what exactly was happening. Mason was graduating in three days, and Boyd had not invited her. It seemed everyone at her book club meeting knew how screwed up the situation was, but that didn't explain why.

"Sorry I'm late." Aspen stopped short at the silence. Mason ran past her when his grandfather called from the other room. "What'd I miss?"

"Nothing." Sara offered drinks.

Aspen put her stuff down and Vienna arrived with boxes of goodness. Before Ella could think much more about why the man she'd poured her heart out to had not seen fit to invite her to her favorite eighth grader's graduation, the book club meeting was underway.

She tried to concentrate on the questions Sistine found online, but it was no use. Maybe there were only so many tickets, she thought. By the time they got to whether Leland Gaunt was supposed to represent the devil, thus bringing in a religious theme, or if he was simply evil, Ella had convinced herself she was being silly. There could be a dozen reasons why Boyd had not invited her to Mason's graduation or even mentioned it. At all.

"I'll admit I may have slept with the lights on for a couple of nights, but it was a great read," Sistine said. "I'd like to ask the group though, what do you think King is trying to say? It's bad to want something or it's bad to want too much? I know there's a message that greed is evil, but that seems too simple."

Ella heard bits and pieces of the discussion that followed. She nodded politely and even managed to pour her wine down the sink and get a glass of water now that Mason was inside watching a movie with his grandfather. She was no longer in the mood to sip wine with friends. She was suspended in her mind, trapped amid a running list of reasons. She should not have assumed she was important to Boyd, that he loved her back. What had Mason said when they were at the Art Walk? Assuming makes an ass out of you and me. It was funny then, not so much now. Boyd had looked dumbfounded when she told him she loved him. It had not mattered because she felt loved by him, it encircled her every time they were together. He was never much for words and she assumed he would... there she went again assuming. *Oh, God!*

"Ella," Bri said. "Do you agree?"

"With what?"

"That King is saying perceived need brought on by consumerism and propaganda is the real downfall?"

"I have no idea."

"Are you okay?" Vienna looked up from the notes on her Kindle.

Ella nodded. "Yes, sorry. I'm good, fine. I think he's trying to say it's all a load of crap. That people get along and think they're happy, but all it takes is a little pressure and everything falls apart. It's best not to need anything. It's best to keep your damn hand up and your heart on ice. That seems to be the overall arch, don't you think?"

Several mouths were hanging open by the time Ella was finished with her literary rant. The whole table knew she'd been set aside, left in the dark. As hard as she tried, she could not escape slipping on the cloak of embarrassment. The last time she'd felt this way, it had been the result of private whispers. This time, the fact that she was among friends, made being in the dark somehow worse. Not that she could compare withholding an invitation to an eighth-grade graduation to screwing someone for two years behind his wife's back. They were certainly not the same things or themes since they were discussing books.

And yet they were, Ella realized as she politely explained she had a headache and went home.

Marc never offered her any of his life, none of his real life anyway. Boyd, while certainly not a scumbag, was giving her the pieces he wanted to give her. He wanted her at the brewery, in his bed, and among his friends. She was even allowed to have a relationship with his son, but there was a limit, a door she was not allowed through.

On the drive home, something changed. Her instinct was to crawl back into herself, as Bri so aptly put it. But this time she wasn't cowering, she was accepting certain things about her life so far. She was tired of half, sick of being grateful for the crumbs her parents sprinkled and less than everything from the men in her life. Being in Petaluma, doing the work on herself, and letting people in wasn't something she was going to run from. It had taught her to want it all. She'd expected excellence in her education, her work. And now, no matter how much it hurt, she was ready to hold the rest of her life to the same standard.

Boyd's mom called him when Ella left the book club meeting early. She wasn't much for lecturing her adult sons, but he recognized the edge in her voice. The edge that said he was screwing up. Ella had not stopped by after the meeting as planned and was not returning any of his calls.

He sat in the cell phone lot, blindly staring at the list of flights and waiting for Delta 455 to read "ready for pick up."

He couldn't think about it right now. Patrick claimed Boyd was a master at putting things in buckets and shutting off any stresses while he was making beer. Boyd was grateful for those skills at the moment. He knew he was screwed, but he also knew his son was graduating and a woman he hardly remembered anymore would be sitting next to him in—the sign flashed ready—a few minutes.

He focused on the most pressing buckets and did his best to ignore his heart screaming that he was a moron, at least for the time being.

He thought about calling Claire to confirm she was on the curb and then realized he rarely called her. They sent text messages and pictures of Mason occasionally, yet they rarely spoke anymore. Mason was getting older now and with his frequent visits with Ella and the other females of Petaluma, Boyd didn't know if he was supposed to tell Claire what was going on. She'd never been all that interested in being a parent before, but she was older now and maybe he was supposed to include her? For some reason, the thought made him angry. What the hell, was she allowed to check back in now?

For the first time, maybe ever, Boyd wondered what went through Claire's mind. Did she think of herself as a mom? Did she feel even a moment of what Ella said she felt around Mason? Did she think about Mason or what he was doing all the time and if not, how did she turn it on and off?

He supposed he could ask her, but there seemed no way to do that without sounding like he was judging her. They had a good relationship, and this was the best situation for Mason. Boyd didn't want to jeopardize that with his own curiosity. Besides, it didn't matter what was going through her mind. All that mattered was she was going to be there for his son, their son.

Pulling up to the yellow curb, he saw Claire part through the crowd of arrivals. She was in a white coat, her long brown hair fastened somehow at the back of her neck. She appeared the same, maybe a little shinier, and there was no ignoring the huge rock on her left finger.

He had met Claire Danner their sophomore year in college. She was studying design and he'd settled on general business, his third major change since arriving at UC Berkeley. He would change two more times before getting a degree in engineering. Boyd was in a frat; Claire was in a sorority. They met at a party and were inseparable. She was everything he was supposed to want and he was everything that drove her parents crazy. They were a match made in college, but as parties and dreaming of "what if" faded into a shared past, he and Claire began to grow apart. She wanted to be one-half of a power couple and Boyd wanted more time to figure things out.

They'd started spending less and less time together, but they did go to their last formal, and that's when she told him she was pregnant. Punched him right in the stomach with the news as they were getting on some stupid party bus. She wasn't crying or scared—it was a simple matter of fact that he was going to be a father.

Claire moved into his apartment, and a month later, she moved out. She received a job offer in Chicago the same week Mason was born. By January of the following year, she was in Chicago and Boyd had moved back to Petaluma with a six-month-old baby.

"I'll keep him with me. I have family to help, and it will be fine," he had told her, having no idea what he was getting into but knowing he needed to be near his son.

"Are you sure you want to take this on? My mom has a list of nannies and we'll be great."

"I don't want to live in Chicago, Claire."

"You don't have to. We'll come visit, or you can visit."

"I'd like to be a full-time father."

"Okay, well, if you know what you're getting into. I'd appreciate the help and I should focus on my new job anyway. It will be nice knowing he's with you."

Boyd knew what people thought. That she was a heartless bitch only concerned with her career and money. Over the years, when people learned their story, he'd heard the grumbling about how a woman could abandon her son, but he ignored it. It might not be typical for a mother to leave her son with his dad in lieu of a career, but men did it all the time. Men chose career over parenting, and the truth was Claire wasn't interested in being a mom. She tried, but it wasn't enough for her. Boyd saw raising Mason as the greatest adventure of his life, so why wouldn't he take him? Why stand by and watch nannies raise him to maintain some social order that made everyone else feel more comfortable?

Looking at her now through the windshield of his truck, Boyd noticed how Claire's heels stood in stark contrast to the all-white of her outfit. She was one of those women who seemed comfortable in heels, even when they were younger. Her sandals had all been heels too now that he thought about it. Her hair was a lighter shade and her lipstick brighter. Mason had her nose, Boyd thought, and her full-face smile. Claire took off her coat and draped it over her arm as she wheeled her bag to the curb. The emotions and questions swirling in Boyd were quickly silenced as he opened the door to the noise of arrival traffic and helped the mother of his child with her luggage.

Chapter Twenty-Six

Mason Danner McNaughton graduated from the eighth grade on what turned out to be one of Boyd's favorite kind of days. Blue sky speckled with big clouds and enough breeze to keep things comfortable. The ceremony certainly wasn't the same flash as high school, but the junior high band played a few songs. The athletics department sold cookies and refreshments at a table off to the side of the seating. It did strike Boyd as odd that the athletics department would be pushing sugar, but his head didn't have much time for superficial thoughts today. He needed all of his brain power to keep his heart from bursting as he approached his brothers, his parents, and his... Claire, who were all kissing and high-fiving his son.

His son. Boyd stayed back a minute, sipping watered-down lemonade, and realized he was still dumbstruck that the human being standing there in new tan dress pants because the other ones were too short, and a tie with roses and skulls his Uncle Cade bought him, was his flesh and blood. That years down the road when Mason talked about his childhood with friends or a girlfriend, when he referred to "his dad," that was Boyd. The memories he had already made with his son and the ones they would cram in before he had to let him out into the world would fuse together as his childhood.

Boyd's eyes filled behind his sunglasses. He turned and quickly wiped them away. Christ, he needed to get a grip or he would never make it to college.

Whoa, let's take it one step at a time.

"Dad, what's the name of that hike we went on?" Mason asked from a few feet away.

Boyd raised a brow, hoping he was going to give him more of a hint than—a hike. They'd been hiking since he was six months old.

"Super tall walls," Mason added. "Oh, and we walked through water most of the time. Remember when your feet got all wrinkly because you bought the wrong socks and we forgot the canned sardines?"

Boyd took in a breath and commanded his heart to cut it out. Be a man for crying out loud. He nodded, giving himself a minute to swallow the lump that seemed permanently in his throat these days.

"Pariah Canyon."

"Yeah," Mason said, putting his fist in the air as if they'd finished the four-day hike. "Pariah," he told his friend Trevor. "It's in... Utah?"

Boyd nodded.

At the confirmation, Mason walked toward the cookie table with his friends explaining with animated hands the massiveness of Pariah Canyon. It had been a terrific trip. Boyd had forgotten about the socks and the sardines they left on the kitchen counter. Crazy, the things kids remembered. Mason was stumped on where they'd hiked, but he remembered pruned feet and the canned fish. All of it made Boyd smile—that trip, this day. The handful Mason had been as a toddler and the man he was becoming. All of it somehow brought comfort. Move it forward, he told himself.

"Wow, is that lemonade?" Patrick asked, parking next to him, hands in pockets. "You're so old." He bumped his shoulder, something he would never have done when they were younger. Boyd was twice his size back then.

He took another sip and nodded. "It's a family event, Trick. There are no promotion opportunities here."

"Don't let anyone hear you saying that. Beer goes with family."

Boyd laughed. "Yeah? Is that our summer slogan?"

He took a pull of his water bottle. "Shows what you know, our summer artwork was done in February."

They stood, watching as the crowd of graduates slowly morphed back into the kids they would only be for a few more years. Sleeves rolled up, most of the ties pulled loose or off altogether.

"Congratulations, big brother."

Boyd didn't look at Patrick. There was simply no way to keep it all inside.

"For what? Mase did it all."

"Oh, come on. We don't have much time. See that group of girls over there?"

"Yeah."

"In about five minutes Mase and his friends are going to run out of things to say and they'll want to hightail it out of here and start the party. So you're only getting a few minutes of praise. Don't go all humble on me." His brother faced him, took his shoulder. "I'm serious. You're raising a person. None of us can top that." Patrick pulled him into a hug.

"Even you, super brother? You can't top that? Can I get that on the record?" Boyd tried to joke his way out of the emotion.

"Proud of you." Patrick patted him on the back and when Boyd did the same, his eyes welled up again.

What the hell? He lifted his sunglasses just enough to wipe them quickly away. He waited for his brother's smart-ass remark but noticed his eyes were a little glossy too. Patrick wore those fashion lens Boyd never understood. Tinted meant they barely protected his eyes. Both of them shook their heads and smiled.

"Um, I'm sorry. Is this the Girl Scout meeting?" Cade, who had surely noticed them and came in for the kill, asked. "We have a reputation to uphold, losers. Why are you drinking punch and hugging it out?"

"Lemonade," Patrick said.

"What?"

"He's drinking lemonade."

"Oh, well that's better. What little secrets are you two girls sharing?" Cade batted his eyes and pressed his hands together.

Boyd finished his lemonade and crunched down on the ice cube for effect.

"Nothing. Just telling Boyd I'm proud of him."

Cade was poised for his next response when his expression went all mushy. It took a lot for their younger brother to look soft. The guy had spent one too many nights at the tattoo parlor for Boyd's liking and lately had a totally screwed haircut, but his face warmed nonetheless.

"That's a given. Me too, big bro." He glanced over his shoulder as Patrick's prediction came to fruition and Mason walked toward them. "He's the best. Handsome like me, well-dressed like string bean here and—"

Hell, Cade was sappy today too?

He swallowed. "A good man like his dad," his brother finished.

"Man in training," Boyd said.

Cade nodded and pulled him in for a hug. By the time the sun set, they'd probably be back at one another's throats, but for now, Boyd allowed the love to fill him up as it had for so many years.

"Couldn't have done it without you guys."

Patrick and Cade shrugged. "Yeah, that's true."

They all laughed as Mason pulled Claire and his grandparents over and announced it was time for the party.

"Hell, yeah it is." Cade took his nephew in a neck hold as they all made their way to the school parking lot.

"Hey, where's Ella?" Patrick asked as he and Boyd got into his truck.

"I... I'm sure she's working or with Vienna. Why?"

His brother looked confused, and Boyd wasn't in the mood to discuss why he'd thought about inviting Ella at least a dozen times and like those stupid jigsaw puzzles their dad made them do every summer, he couldn't figure out how to put her and Claire and Mason in a room at the same time. He couldn't make it work, so he left her out.

"Rumor is that you didn't invite her?"

"So you already know where Ella is, asshat."

"Why the hell didn't you tell her? This is a big day for Mase."

Boyd clenched his jaw and turned onto Bodega Avenue. When he glanced over, his brother was still staring at him.

"What? Let it go, Trick. I didn't invite her."

"It's fucked up, man. I mean all this time I thought you were the healthy one."

"We only recently started... whatever it is and I don't know, I thought she might be uncomfortable."

"You thought she'd be uncomfortable, or you would?"

"Both."

They drove in silence.

"Remember when we used to lock each other out of our rooms? You know, we'd get all pissed, slam the door, and leave the other one pounding on the door in the hallway?"

Boyd kept driving. He had no idea where this was going, but Patrick was the introspective brother and there was bound to be symbolism in there somewhere.

Christ, I do not need a life lesson today.

"Mom would get mad and she'd make us open the door." His brother looked out the window. "God, now that we're older I realize what shits we were sometimes."

They both chuckled, and Boyd thought maybe Patrick was only sharing a memory. Yeah, he should have known better.

"Remember what Mom used to say when she finally got us all by the arms and in the same room?"

Boyd remembered, but he said nothing.

"You don't lock people you love out. You can be mad or frustrated, but you don't lock them out."

Boyd let out an exhale it felt like he'd been holding since Patrick started the story.

"Then she followed it up with—"

"Understood?" they said together and laughed.

"You love her. What's the problem?"

He tried to concentrate on the road, the lines separating the lanes, the signs, or the brake lights in front of him.

"I don't know what I'm feeling. She's great, but that's not—"

"Oh, Jesus. You should go back to drinking the lemonade if you're going to be a chickenshit."

"Okay, said the man who's had how many successful relationships?"

"None. I'm holding out for my soul mate."

"Yeah? What's she, late?"

Patrick shrugged. "You should have invited her. Mase is important to her and you love her. You can't keep doing this."

They pulled into the parking lot of the brewery. The lunch crowd was going strong at the Tap House and everyone else was already inside. They'd sectioned off a whole area for Mason's celebration.

"Doing what?" Boyd turned off his truck.

"Living alone."

"I'm not alone. Christ, I've never been alone. I have Mason. I don't need anyone."

"And now it's time for the bullshit. We've all raised Mason. You two aren't an island."

"Oh, yeah? Great, can you take him to the pediatrician week after next to get his sports physical? He's in summer league, did you put that on your calendar?"

"You know there's more to him than appointments and schedules. Cade taught him how to skateboard. I took him to the bank to open a high school checking account. Dad went hunting with him the first time. He watches old black-and-white movies with Mom and never complains. Aspen plays those damn arcade games with him. He's all those pieces, Boyd. The kid would be totally screwed up if you raised him on an island, and you know it. You're his dad and I meant what I said, endless respect for that, but Mason reached out to Ella. It's kind of like he pulled her into your life because you needed her."

"Okay, you think my thirteen-year-old son is orchestrating my love life now?"

Patrick shrugged. "He's a smart kid and she's great with him—and with you. Why the hell would you let that get away?"

"I'm not. Jesus, I didn't invite her to an eighth-grade graduation. Will you get a grip?"

Boyd practically jumped out of the truck because suddenly he was having trouble breathing.

"Mom said Ella looked pissed," Patrick said. "Or maybe it was hurt. Did she say hurt? I can't remember." They walked into the glorious noise of the party. Finally, something to shut him up.

Boyd needed a beer. Maybe two.

Ella was off in fifteen minutes and once again dreaming of food. A burger and fries from the Tap Room, her stomach was specific. Vienna had texted her that she and Thad were grabbing dinner and they were hoping she'd join them. It was Wednesday, Mason's graduation, and while she knew from Boyd's mom that they were going to the brewery after graduation, it was almost nine o'clock. Celebrations for kids didn't last into the night, did they?

She didn't want to show up for a party she wasn't invited to, but she'd also become addicted to the fries at the Tap House. Bri agreed via text that there was no way Ella would be crashing an afternoon graduation party at night. On that advice, she would grab her dinner and be home before anyone even noticed. That was the plan.

Boyd had not tried calling again since the night of the book club meeting. He'd obviously shifted gears and was back focusing on his son, which was how things were supposed to be, she decided. Her initial instincts were right when she saw Boyd contemplating his autumn recipe. She should have left well enough alone.

"Dr. Walters, can I have a minute?"

The air was immediately sucked from the empty ER. *Is this karma?* Why the hell else would this man be back again to torture her more than he already had? Hadn't she put his brilliant ass on a helicopter? What did it take to get rid of her past once and for all?

Ella didn't even look up from her end of shift paperwork. "I'm busy, Marc. What is it?"

He sat next to her, and the familiar smell of him spun a web of confusion as his hands reached for hers. She stood up so fast she almost fell over. "What the hell is your problem?"

Marc put his hands up. "Sorry. I'm... I am going back to the city tonight. I wanted to tell you how good we were the other day, with your hardware guy. I'm certain you already know he's doing well."

"I've seen him. Thank you."

"You bet. So, I came back here to finish my last lecture, and then I'm going home."

Ella met his eyes. It was so much easier now, and he took a big breath like a kid about to blow out his birthday candles.

"I want you to come with me."

She should have laughed, but his face was so sincere she was left bewildered. How could someone so accomplished be so clueless? Was it possible he didn't understand that the entire world wasn't waiting for his command? Her heart steadied in the same way it did when she had to deliver troubling or even disastrous news to a loved one in a waiting room. The calm in the storm.

"Have a safe trip home."

"I love you, El. I screwed up, I know, but we have something. And now that I'm available I thought—"

She held up her hand, and this time it worked. He stopped speaking, and she had no idea how to explain the obvious. "You don't love me. You have never loved me. People don't lie when they love. They don't hide and deceive. It's not part of the love thing, Marc." She grabbed her bag because this wasn't going to end well and she was off shift anyway. Marc held her arm gently.

"Didn't the hardware guy bring back how great we are? Don't you miss us? What we used to be?" he said quietly near her ear.

"His name is Mr. Graham. Stop calling him the hardware guy. And no. Not for one minute. I have erased you from my heart because what you did to your wife was the worst kind of ugly. I used to blame myself, but recently I've learned that it had nothing to do with me. I could have been anyone."

She jerked her shoulder and he let her go. "Go home, Marc. Be a father to your daughters. Be a better man."

It felt as if her heart was beating behind her ears rather than safely in her chest by the time Ella reached her car. In the darkness, she put her hands to her face and prepared for tears. Instead, she smiled. She'd meant what she said. What had happened with Marc wasn't about her. She hadn't made vows and broken them. She'd simply been a fool for believing him. Somehow, allowing that in, admitting the mistake was more about Marc's issues than anything else allowed for a freedom she'd waited over two years to experience. Boyd had been right—she was only responsible for her own actions.

Ella loved Boyd in so many ways that the mere thought of him wrapped around her chest and squeezed, but she had a feeling that once again her love alone was not going to be enough.

Walking into the Foghorn Brewery Tap House, she heard Mason's laughter before she knew where it was coming from. The music overhead filled the space and by the time she figured out where Mason was, it was too late to turn around. She stood there somehow trapped in that sad movie moment when the protagonist is splashed by a passing car or trips and falls at the feet of the man she's loved forever. Ella was mere feet from Boyd, Mason, and a woman she knew instantly was Mason's mom. Claire, Ella remembered her name.

There was a lull in the music as the playlist shifted to a slower song, and Mason let out that booming laugh she now knew well. Ella's gaze snapped back to the door she'd just walked through, but it was too late to pretend she had not seen them sitting like any other family out for dinner after a long day. Mason saw her and hopped to his feet.

"Ella," he called out.

If ever there was a testament to her love for the child, it was then because she somehow managed a smile. She would probably smile at him if she were trapped in a pit full of snakes. Maybe not then, but she cared so deeply for him that though she could cut the awkward with a knife, she walked over and met his hug.

"Congratulations, graduate. How was it?"

His hands were moving even before the words came out. "You know, most of it was boring speeches, but it was still cool. I'm officially a freshman in high school."

"Yes, you are. So proud of you." She leaned in and kissed his cheek. Mason blushed.

"We missed you. How was work?"

Ella was prepared with a token answer, and then Boyd finally looked up from the glass he'd been staring at and all her words were gone.

Chapter Twenty-Seven

Ella stepped closer to the table and extended her hand to Claire with such purpose Boyd almost fell back in his chair. "I'm Ella. You must be Mason's mom."

"I am." Claire stood in a waft of perfume and sophistication to take Ella's hand. "I've heard so much about you from Mason."

Her gaze cut to Boyd as if to say, "I wish I could say the same," but she quickly returned to small talk with Claire all while fielding questions from their overly caffeinated son. Boyd sat there like he was watching a movie and he was clueless about the ending. It never occurred to him in that moment that he had the ability to affect the outcome, to stand up and kiss the woman he was in love with and tell her right there in front of everyone he'd been a complete ass to cut her out of an important day.

"I'm picking Mason up for our week together. Start of summer. I thought I was going to miss his graduation, but I had some things fall off my schedule and voilà. I'm here."

"Voilà." Ella's eyes went wide, and Boyd continued to feel like a world-class idiot. "That is... so great. I'll bet Mason is thrilled to have you early and... Boyd too."

"That may be an overstatement. Does Boyd do thrilled?"

Ella let out a strangled laugh that sounded more like a bark. The whole thing was painful and yet he did nothing to stop it.

"Mason and I are leaving in the morning for Los Angeles," Claire said. "I've rented a convertible and everything."

"I had no idea you were going to LA for a week." Ella directed her attention back to Mason. "That's awesome. Take lots of pictures."

"I'll text you."

"Sounds good."

Claire gestured for her to sit.

"Oh, no thank you." She glared at Boyd this time. "It was great to meet you, Claire, but I'm only here to pick up dinner after a long shift and then I'm off to bed. Have a great rest of your night."

"Pleasure meeting you too, Ella." Claire reached over and touched Mason's hand as Ella stepped back.

Boyd wondered how many shades of screwed up this was. Was Claire threatened? Was that possible?

"Mase, say hello to LA for me," Ella said.

He stood to say goodbye, and Boyd finally pushed back from the table and stood too. He couldn't remember feeling more ridiculous, and that included high school. Mason gave her a hug while Boyd stood silent. She squeezed Mase back and then pulled away as if she was in pain. He'd caused that pain. By doing nothing, he'd hurt her, and that weight sat squarely on his chest.

"Boyd," she said with a quick nod in his direction before grabbing the bag on the bar, waving to Cade, and leaving through the side door.

Mason flopped back in his chair and chewed a mouthful of fries, oblivious to what had just gone on.

"She seems nice," Claire said.

"She's awesome." Mason scrunched his brow. "Dad, was she acting a little weird?"

Boyd nodded and looked toward the bar as if Cade could somehow rescue him. Yeah, he was on his own for this one.

"Oh, God. Are you two dating?" Claire rarely missed these kinds of things. "That's why it felt weird. You're... together."

Boyd started to shake his head and then got tired of feeling like an asshole.

"They're friends," Mason said. "Friends who like each other a lot, but Dad is only admitting the friend part."

"That is not true. Yes, we are together. New, it's new and none of your business. Either of you. So, what were we talking about?"

"Did you need to go after her?" Claire asked.

"No. I need to finish this dinner without discussing my private life. That's what I need to do."

"Jeez, sorry," Mason said.

Ella had finished the double cheeseburger, most of the Cajun fries, and was solidly into episode three of *The Gilmore Girls* reunion when the knock hit her front door. She knew who it was but wanted to stay with Rory and Lorelai in Star's Hollow. The knock came again. She hit pause and shuffled to the door. After turning the knob, she returned to the couch, unable to face him. She heard the door close behind her and the warmth of him at her back. Boyd sat on the couch beside her.

"How are the fries?"

"So good." She picked up another one.

"I'm not sure which screw-up I should apologize for first."

Ella said nothing and kept chewing.

"Right, well let's start with I'm sorry I didn't invite you to Mason's graduation. I'm... I guess finding my way with all of this and by the time I thought to invite you, things got complicated with Claire. I wasn't expecting her to show up."

"You don't owe me an explanation. She's Mason's mom and your ex... whatever. Seems weird to call her an ex-girlfriend since you share a child. I don't know. I didn't think you were going to be at the brewery so late. Your mom mentioned at book club that the ceremony was early. I assumed. I've never been good at surprises."

He touched her leg and she pulled away.

"She's Mason's mom. That's it. We do not have a relationship outside of parenting our son, and I do most of that on my own anyway."

"You said she was 'not in the picture a lot.'" Ella shook her head. "Not that it matters because it doesn't. She can be in the picture all she wants. She's first." She pulled her legs closer to her body as if that would somehow keep everything from spilling out of her.

"Mason is thirteen. Things stopped working with us a long time ago."

"Let me guess, she was a massive manipulator and never understood you. She spent all your money too and you've grown in different directions. I think I've heard this story."

"I... um, wow. I didn't think I needed to explain this." Boyd shifted away from her on the couch.

"Why not? Why didn't you think you'd need to fill me in on certain things in your life? Is it that our relationship, if you want to call it that, is new? Is that why? You keep saying that. What is your usual wait time for full disclosure?"

Ella felt her control slip, and she wanted more than anything to get through this with her dignity intact.

"She is Mason's mom. We were never married. She's complicated, not all that hands-on as a mom, but that doesn't make her a bad person. I love raising Mase, so our arrangement works."

Ella nodded. She'd come to Petaluma for a new start. She didn't want to be anyone's curiosity or surprise ever again.

"This must be some kind of karma. No, it's not that. I don't believe in karma," she said.

"No?"

She shook her head, trying to control what now felt like anger. "It's flawed. Shitty people don't always get what they deserve. Karma is something the loser tells herself when things turn to crap and she hopes it's better the next go around."

"Wow."

"What?"

"Nothing. Not to be too technical here, but karma is the way you respond to the crap in your life. That's what creates karma. It's not what happens to you, it's how you react."

"Oh, well I'm screwed then too."

"Looks like it." Boyd laughed.

At the sound, her heart softened and she had no idea what she was feeling anymore.

"How do you know about karma anyway?"

"Cade."

She nodded and offered one of her last fries to him. He took it and they sat in silence. Neither of them seemed to know a way past the surface, so she jumped in.

"I need more, Boyd. This isn't going to work for me."

He turned to face her. "I love you. I should have said it before. I'm sorry I didn't handle graduation the best. I know I keep saying it's new, and that's not an excuse. I love you, Ella."

She would admit she'd imagined him saying those three words, but now that they were out, it felt organic. Like she'd known all along and the declaration was more of a technicality.

"Love me more. Harder," she said.

He smirked.

"You know what I mean."

He nodded, smirk spreading to a full smile.

"Do not make me laugh right now. You didn't invite me to Mason's graduation. I know I sound ridiculous, but walking in there and seeing the three of you was... Look, this is probably me, in fact I know it's me and how I'm coming into the relationship, but I can't do partway again."

"Are you seriously comparing me to Marc?"

She felt like she'd been punched. Somehow hearing him throw a name up she'd barely whispered to herself for the past couple of years seemed like he was calling her out.

"No. I am not comparing you. I'm trying to explain why with my past, I cannot settle for half."

"Settle? I can't control Mason's mom or that my life has... stuff. This is all I have right now, Ella. It seemed like it was enough before you walked in on what you've imagined is some little family. Mason is my first—"

"Oh no. Don't you dare do that." She stood. "I adore Mason and I would never ask for his space in your heart. But you're not even giving me what's left. You're not adjusting or working to include me. You left me out and then barely acknowledge I was standing in front of you because you don't know what to do with me?" She stood. "I'm loving you with my whole heart and that is scary when you're still hanging on just in case." She shook her head as if she were one of those Etch-a-Sketch things and she could erase what she'd recently revealed.

"I'm not saying you have a problem with Mason. I said I was sorry. What the hell do you want, me on my knees?"

This wasn't going to work. She was never going to explain something she barely understood herself. She wanted more and he had no idea what that looked like.

"I'm tired. You should go."

Boyd stood. "It's fine. I'll let you get some sleep."

"Honestly, I'm tired of other women's men," She blurted out as he walked toward the door. "What you have going seems great and completely adult, but I can't... correction, I won't do this again. Or anything remotely resembling this."

"This meaning something like Marc?"

She was flailing now, but as he moved closer to the door, it seemed essential to her sanity that he understand. "I don't want to be the extra woman, the piece on the side, the second choice. I can't be that person. I know you have your 'stuff' as you put it. I respect that, but you need to respect mine. I need to be the only woman, my person's only woman. Now if you want to say I'm comparing you to my past, so be it. That's how I come to this relationship."

Boyd seemed confused. Guys usually were when a woman presented needing any more than they were willing to give. The problem with this one, she knew, even through her fuzzy sleep-deprived brain, was that he wasn't married. That didn't matter. She still wasn't going any further with someone who had slept with anyone else. Wait, that would mean she'd be looking for a thirty-something virgin. Not that. And she wasn't looking. Jesus, she needed him to leave before she proved herself certifiable.

"For the last time, I'm not her man." She could see his jaw tighten.

"Well, you're sure as hell not mine."

"I can't do anything about my past," he said, sounding defeated.

"I'm not asking you to. I'm saying I'm not the right person for you."

"Okay." Boyd raised his voice and then his shoulders slumped. "Fine. It's not right, not going to work. Got it loud and clear, Doc." Boyd wasn't the type to beg or "oh, please baby let's talk this out." Ella knew that. On some level, she appreciated the space.

"I'll see you later." She started to walk past him to open the front door, but he gently held her elbow.

"I don't know what's going on. I'm sorry. I get that there's a lot in my life to... take in."

She whipped around and held his face. Her eyes welled up. "You need to hear me. Mason has a mother, a woman you certainly loved at some point and shared a connection with. You two have a beautiful son and there are so many women out there who would love what you've built and the fact that you seem to have a healthy relationship with your ex. Lots of women, Boyd. I'm not one of them. I have... baggage. God, I hate that word, but it's true. I have stuff that I can't erase. I don't expect you to understand, but I won't live my life wondering what will happen if I pop in unannounced. I need to know I'm wanted and expected." She gently kissed him, took in the glorious outdoor smell of him, and opened her front door.

Boyd hesitated for a moment and then as if he was stumped on the answer to some riddle, he turned and left without another word.

Chapter Twenty-Eight

Mason was showing his mom the food trucks before her flight back to Chicago. Ella had all but told Boyd to disappear. For the first time in a long time, he was alone and unsure. The brewery was quiet and he'd wasted two test batches because suddenly he'd forgotten the basics of making beer. Forgot the yeast entirely for two rounds. He'd lost his mind. He loved Ella. He'd survived the balancing out on a cliff moment and said the words, but maybe that would never be enough — maybe he would never be enough. Boyd had been there and done that before. If she wasn't the right woman for him, then he'd be fine.

"Heard you screwed things up." Cade walked in eating again.

Is that a gyro?

"Not now." Boyd pulled up his grain inventory and started a new order on his computer.

"I'm only saying that she's your match. You're crazy about her. How could you jack this up?"

"It didn't work out. She thinks she's sharing me or I'm not letting her in. Blame it on me if you want. Leave."

"Nah, this is good." He sat on a stool next to the work table. "Why does she think you're not letting her in?"

"Because I didn't invite her to his graduation and then she stopped by and we were having dinner with Claire. She's on this kick that we looked like a big happy family."

Cade took his last bite, balled up the napkin, and checked his breath.

"Does she know Claire is... strange?"

"She's not strange. She's Mason's mom."

"True. But she's strange." He circled his finger to the side of his head in the universal sign for crazy.

Boyd was not amused.

"Anyway. The general consensus is that you should have invited the love of your life to your son's graduation, but I get how that could be weird with Claire deciding to show up in the last inning."

"Yeah, well it's over. Claire is going back to Chicago tonight, Ella is moving on, and I'm fine."

Cade stood and shook his head.

"What? No funny comeback? What the hell does that head shake mean?"

"Quit saying that. You're not fine. Fine is such a screwed-up word. It's like... neat or nice. It says nothing. Being fine is like being barely alive. You know when you catch a fish and it does that flappy gill thing as it's dying on the—"

"I'm fine. Now, get out of here. I've got work to do."

Cade stayed put and Boyd met his eyes.

"What the fuck do you want to hear?" He threw his clipboard on the worktable and faced off with his brother. "You want me to tell you that I'm afraid if I screw up my kid that it's all on me? That when I was younger, I had no idea if I could do it on my own and now he needs something I can't give him? Do you want me to rest my head on your shoulder and tell you I love her so much that it grabs me right in the center of my chest? That I don't know how to make it work or how to give her something I don't have? That on top of it all, I love this place, love you guys, and sometimes I'm convinced it's all going to end? One bad batch, some random asshole falls in the bathroom and sues us. Is that what you want, Cade?"

"Yeah. Well, I don't want your big hairy head on my shoulder, but yeah, I want all of that. You need to get that crap out of you." He hit Boyd's shoulder. "Don't you feel better?"

Boyd sat, put his face in his hands, and wondered how his brother missed out on the memo that life was complicated. For once, he'd like to see the world through Cade's optimistic eyes.

"Well?" he said.

"Well what?" Boyd put his hands down.

"Do you feel better?"

"No."

He took the seat next to him. "Oh, well then let's figure it out."

Boyd snickered. "Just like that?"

He nodded. "You love her, she loves you and your son. I mean this is practically a slam dunk. All you need to do is work through the whole thing with Claire dumping you and leaving you with a kid stuff."

"She didn't leave me with Mason. I wanted him."

"Sure, you did, but she still left you. Packed up and basically told you to shove your 'let's be a family' idea where the sun doesn't shine."

"That's not quite how it went. We came to an agreement that I was going to keep Mase."

"Damn it, bro. You need to quit being so amenable."

"Amenable?"

"Like that? Picked it up watching *Jeopardy*. It's another word for agreeable or doormat in your case. I like the way it sounds."

"Older. Brother. You don't get to call me a doormat."

"If you admit it sucks that your college girlfriend left you with your newborn son then you can get on with it. Move forward and love someone else all the way. If you can't do that, then you're going to be a sad man who tries to Skype his kid in college."

"That seems extreme."

Cade raised his eyebrows. "I'm stating the facts. Let it go, man. Like the song in that snow movie." His brother stood and started singing a song Boyd had heard because it was everywhere since the movie came out. When he twirled, Boyd laughed.

"Who the hell are you, and what have you done with my brother who barely knows how to use a napkin?"

Ella fell asleep with the afternoon sun on her face and woke to the tinkering of her wind chime. It seemed like she'd closed her puffy eyes mere minutes ago, but looking up at the swaying branches of the tree overhead, she realized she must have been sleeping for at least an hour.

She loved naps. When she was little, she craved the quiet and the cool sheets on her face in the summer or the warm blanket during the colder months. As she grew older, sleeping turned into a coping mechanism. When she was frustrated or sad, she napped. It felt like a reboot. Everything, no matter how awful, seemed to improve after a nap. It was interesting that she hit a point in her life after medical school when she rarely rested. She should figure out what that meant, the symbolism of it all, but she was tired of thinking. Tired of trying to figure out why she did the things she did.

Showering, Ella got ready for the next weaving class with Vienna. They had reached the next level now and it was time to make a place mat. She dabbed eye cream on, hoping to look less like a woman who cried over a man. How cliché, she thought and was about to come down too hard on herself one more time when she realized everything had changed from two years ago. She wasn't running this time. She no longer had a cardboard life she could fold on the dotted line and run away from.

This time she had a home, friends, and a job she was good at. She would attempt to dangle from silk again next Tuesday, and today, before working a double, she was going to let Sistine teach her how to make a place mat. She was human now, heart fully melted. There was no turning back, and she didn't want to anymore. She liked hugging and connection. She loved Boyd and Mason more than her heart could take, but if Boyd wasn't capable of giving her his whole heart, she would move on.

Heartbreak was far from the end of the line this time around. Ella's life would never again revolve around half of anything. She was simply too full of life for that now.

Chapter Twenty-Nine

Boyd handed Mason the last four quarters in his pocket and finished his beer. Claire sat with her legs crossed and her dark skirt in place. Boyd had not been able to sleep. He didn't know how to fix things, wasn't even sure what exactly went wrong. Claire tapped away on her phone and met his eyes. He rarely thought about the past these days, but now that she was sitting across from him, Boyd found he was curious. Maybe Cade was right and the way to Ella was moving through his past.

"Mason asked me if you missed out by not being with me."

"What did you tell him?" she asked.

"Standard answer."

"We love each other, but we're not in love with each other," they both said in concert. Boyd's chest hurt, not for what they could have had because the older they got, the clearer it became that he and Claire were not meant for one another. He hurt for Mason, for what he sometimes felt was selfishness on their part.

"What are you doing, Boyd?" She huffed and set her phone on the table.

"Oh, hell. What did Mase say?"

"That you love Ella and that she loves you. She loves him too."

"He has no way of knowing that."

"Are you kidding? He's smarter than both of us put together."

Boyd said nothing.

"Do you ever notice that martyrs are never happy?"

"I'm not a martyr."

"Oh but you are. You've got this whole single-dad thing going on. I'm grateful you're raising our son, you know that, but let's not overdo this, okay? You love that woman. I know you well enough to state that as a fact with or without our son's input. You have never looked at anyone that way, including me."

"Claire, I'm not going to sit here with you and discuss my private life."

"Sure you are." She sipped her beer. "I'm the only person you can talk to who isn't invested."

"How can you say that? Treat it like an analysis?"

"We all have our strengths." She snickered. "I may not be a great mom, but I know how to assess a major mess. Your problem is you don't like change. Never have."

"You're way off. Raising a kid is all about change, being adaptable."

"When they're little, absolutely, but you're struggling now. Now that you can't have it all your way."

"Not true."

"True. That's why you make beer."

"Oh, this should be good. Tell me, Claire, why do I make beer?"

"Because you can control all the ingredients. You go to your happy place, growl at anyone who comes near you, and you create what you want."

He had no words. How was it that he saw this woman twice a year and she was suddenly qualified to be his shrink?

"Mason was your biggest change to date. You had a baby with a woman who left you and her son."

"I never blame you for that."

"I'm not saying you do. You are the best person to raise him, but he's getting older. Unless you want to make a complete ass out of yourself, you need to find a life outside of his calendar and blossom-ing interest in girls."

"I have a life. I'm fine."

"Be more than fine, Boyd. Let the doctor love you. You deserve to be loved." She pushed the rest of her beer aside as if remembering she needed to leave. After applying her lipstick using a small mirror she pulled from her purse, she wiped some of it off with the napkin.

The pinball machine dinged from the back room and Boyd could barely make out the muffle of other people as he stared silently at a woman he'd known since college.

"By the way, you need to change your answer the next time our son asks you that question."

"What?"

"The answer is yes. Yes, I did miss out by not being with you. I think it hurt and changed you and for that, I am so sorry. That's mine. I have to live with the fact that I chose me over you, over both of you. I'm working on making peace with that, but in the meantime, be more than fine, Boyd. You are..." Her eyes teared up and Boyd instinctively reached for her, the mother of his son. "Don't." She held up her hands. "Listen to me because I'll never say this again. You are an exquisite man, a truly good human being. I will be forever grateful to you for loving our son. So yes, Boyd. I did miss out. Don't you do the same. Go love that woman for crying out loud. Accept the craziness that might bring. Haven't you spent enough time keeping the peace?"

Boyd swallowed a lump in his throat as feelings he didn't even know he had flooded to the surface.

"There's so much of you in him."

The tears spilled down her cheeks and she nodded, quickly brush-ing them away. "I have a flight to catch."

He helped her with her coat and kissed her softly on her forehead. She wrapped her arms around him.

"Be kind," she said.

His chest tightened and he understood why he shut some things out. Not because Claire broke his heart, but because they'd shared so much, been through so much. The fact that nothing other than Mason worked out, didn't mean there wasn't history and the pain and sweat of trying.

"Be strong," he said.

She pulled away and quickly wiped her eyes. "Do you still say that with him?"

"Yeah."

"Does he know it used to be our thing?"

He shook his head. He couldn't speak.

She grinned, the past and the ache right there on the edges. "Keep it that way. Keep it alive with him."

By the time Boyd exhaled, she got into a taxi and was gone.

Chapter Thirty

Summer was just getting started and Boyd was back in the emergency room. This time he was sitting across from his son. Arms resting on his knees and hands to his temples, Boyd took a deep breath. He had to have known the teenage years were going to be more challenging than playing with Legos, hadn't he? Looking up at Mason's bloody nose, he tried to remember what it was like to be thirteen. Lately it seemed so long ago. When had he become the frustrated dad on the other end of the aisle? Boyd scrambled for something to say. Mason hung his head, ice pack on the top of his nose.

"I think you're supposed to hold your head back," Boyd said.

Mason grunted. "Google said forward. Keeps me from choking on the blood," he mumbled through the muffle of cloth and what Boyd knew had turned into nasty swelling.

"When did you have time to Google this?"

"While I was sitting outside the coach's truck."

"Oh." Boyd sat up. "Well, I guess that was a good use of your time. Damage assessment."

"Huh?" Mason peeked around the ice pack.

"Nothing. You gonna tell me what happened?"

"Coach said it all."

"You jumped some kid on the second day of summer league, pulled him off the field, and dragged him into the grass. You yelled something about an apology and then you punched him. While the coaches broke you apart, the kid, Jeff, Jake?"

"Joel, Joel Mitchell."

"Right, Joel got in one last shot and busted your nose."

Mason's nod was barely noticeable and he said nothing.

"That's it?"

"Yup."

"Help me out here, Mase."

As his son lowered the ice pack and Boyd got a clear view of the damage, a baby squirming in his mother's arms began to wail. The mom stood and attempted the "shh, shh" dancing bounce Boyd vaguely remembered. He longed for that simplicity now.

Christ, were they ever going to see a doctor? This place was never busy. Figured today there'd be a wait.

"Why'd you tackle him?"

Mason shrugged.

"Cut it out. Why did you want him to apologize?" As soon as the question came out of his mouth, Boyd figured it out. She, all of this had to do with Chloe Stropp—Mason's crush supreme and only daughter of his baseball coach.

"What did he say about Chloe?"

"Dad!" Mason pulled the ice off and checked the waiting room.

"She's not here. What'd the idiot say?"

Silence. Boyd huffed and stood to walk around. He was getting nowhere.

"I was catcher and he pitched. He always pitches." The ice came back down and Boyd sat. "He's good. I mean good good."

"Okay."

"She sometimes comes to practice with her dad, more now that it's summer."

Yeah, that explained the growing disinterest with baseball. Mason had used every excuse—his height, his lack of playtime. None of that mattered as much as not being a star player in front of the coach's daughter.

"I dropped the ball and he said she, well he used her name and said she was never going to give me—" Mason gestured for Boyd to sit next to him.

He did and leaned in so his son could whisper what Jake or Jacob had said. When he was finished, Boyd sat back. "This kid is your age?"

Mason nodded.

"I guess I need to catch up more than I thought. I had no idea kids in your grade even knew those words."

Mason scoffed and Boyd put his arm around his son.

"I would have kicked the crap out of him too."

"Not exactly what I did."

"He was in worse shape. Did he apologize to... she?"

Mason pulled the ice off again, his eyes watered, and Boyd's heart broke. It never occurred to him when he was researching the best baby food and struggling to get his toddler to go in the potty that one day he'd have to watch his son go through all the crap he'd barely escaped. It was hard to watch such a large piece of his heart trying to navigate the world.

"I'm sorry. I'm not even in love with her anymore. We're friends, but still," Mason said.

Boyd shook his head. "Don't be sorry. You don't need to apologize for being decent, Mase."

"But I broke the rule."

Boyd tilted his head in confusion.

"Be kind." A tear slipped down his son's bruising cheek, and Boyd gently wiped it away.

"Listen to me, Mase. You are kind. Sometimes we need to back up our kindness, enforce it a little." He gestured for Mason to put the ice back on his nose.

"Is that a new rule?"

"No, old rule. It's in Man Book Two."

"Oh, hell, there's more?" Fun returned to Mason's voice.

"Yes, sir. I've got volumes of man advice."

"Great."

Boyd squeezed his son's shoulder as the nurse called them back.

Ella was in the break room when Boyd and Mason arrived. Trudy gave her the chart and when she saw Mason's name, her heart jumped. She scanned the triage sheet. Possible broken nose. Without even thinking, as she often did with these two guys, she pushed through to Exam 1. She came up short when she saw Mason sitting on the bed, blood on the compress he was holding, and what tears remained still rimming his eyes. Dear God, when had she started loving him too? Something inside her nearly broke open. This connecting business was going to kill her one of these days. Ella quickly glanced at Boyd and decided she only had room in her head for one McNaughton right now.

She moved closer and gently pulled back his dirty hand and the compress. She didn't touch, only checked to see if she could make out anything through the already aggressive swelling. It was likely a hairline, but his nose wasn't displaced and she let out what felt like her first breath since seeing his name on the paperwork.

"What happened?" she asked, setting the chart down and washing her hands. She'd asked that question thousands of times in her career, and somehow those two words only brought back the moment she'd met his father. How was that possible with all her patients?

"Joel punched me in the nose."

Ella whipped around, again not thinking. "The kid from baseball? The pitcher?"

Mason nodded.

Ella tried to order her brain. She was a doctor, here to assess a patient. Mason already had a mother and a father. It had been made crystal clear that there was no room for her in their lives.

"Okay, well I bet there's a story in there for your parents."

"What does that mean? You don't want to hear my stories any-more?"

"I didn't say that. I meant that times like this call for family."

"Family is what you make it. Right, Dad?"

Boyd nodded, and Ella assumed this topic had come up before. Not where she was concerned, of course, but it seemed like Boyd and Mason had dealt with the exceptional circumstances of their family before. Ella saw Boyd out of the corner of her eye. He flinched a bit in the awkward silence.

"How long ago did this happen?"

"About two hours ago," Boyd said.

Ella turned to her computer.

"Is Joel taller than you or shorter?"

"Why does that matter?" Mason asked.

Ella fought a smile. "Did he punch up, bending your nose, or down and kind of clumsy."

"Down, he's taller," he said.

"Good. Down is better. Less impact. I'm going to need to look at your nose now, Mase... Mason."

"Don't call me that. You already called me Mase. You can't go back. What the hell is going on, Dad?"

"Language," Boyd said.

"Heck, why the heck does everything feel backward? Did you mess this up?" Mason asked and then hissed as Ella carefully took the pack off his nose and noticed his eye was already turning black and blue.

"Did he hit you across your cheek, or straight at your nose?"

"I don't remember. I was on him and then Coach pulled me off and he got in a last shot. I think he was in front of me. I don't know. Is it broken? Are you and Dad fighting?"

"Well, it's not dislocated. It's still in line, which is good news for you because putting things back in place is usually the most painful part."

Ella saw a tear escape his eye and her heart squeezed. She couldn't answer his questions about Boyd and wondered which frustration was making him cry. Being a teenager was difficult on all fronts, Ella thought. She set down her instruments and carefully wrapped her arms around him. She didn't think about it; it felt like the only thing she wanted to do. His chest pulsed and she rubbed his back.

"You're going to be fine. We all are, Mase. Please don't worry about anything right now. I'm going to get you some ibuprofen now and then you'll go home with your dad, elevate your head on the couch, watch movies, and eat ice cream."

His tears slowly morphed into a laugh as he sat back and she let him go.

"Ice cream? Are you allowed to give that to patients?"

"Absolutely." Ella turned back to her computer and quickly wiped her own eyes. "Ice cream is definitely in order, and I'm thinking I need to prescribe a Netflix marathon or since this particular case involves an obnoxious kid who has a fake tattoo, Harry Potter. All of them."

Her eyes met Boyd's and held. She wanted to tell him too that everything was going to be all right. That even though his son was growing up, she would be there to help him move forward. That they had both changed her life and she hoped she'd changed theirs. That she loved them both more than she ever thought possible. She wanted to say all of that and so much more, but she typed a few more notes into the computer and sent in Bri to finish up. She wasn't the right woman for them, no matter how right it felt, no matter how much she wanted it. If Boyd couldn't let her in, she wasn't going to beg. After handing everything over, Ella went to the on-call room, dropped to the chair, and cried.

Ella was already dreading the weekend and it was only Wednesday. She had Saturday and Sunday off and nothing on her agenda save rewashing her bedspread and going to the grocery store for food she didn't want. She couldn't shake the sadness, but there was no way she was getting out of dinner with the girls, so she didn't bother trying. Besides, Vienna and Thad were moving in together and she had orders for three wedding cakes in four weeks. Her friend was over the moon personally and professionally. The least Ella could do was put her weeping heart away for one night.

By the time the second or third round of laughter filled her living room, she was better. She meant what she'd said to Mason. They would all be fine. She didn't know how long that would take, but spending time with friends was a start.

"Do you think you could make Twinkies?" Aspen asked as Ella came back from the kitchen with a bottle of champagne. What started as dinner had turned into a celebration for Vienna and Thad. Ella filled the crystal flutes her aunt on her mother's side gave her years ago. It was nice to use things that had been tucked away in a cabinet for most of her life. Ella allowed herself a half glass even though she worked the next day. Living on the wild side, as Bri's expression said across the room.

"Can I make Twinkies," Vienna scoffed. "I make yellow sponge cake and cream filling. You'll forget you've ever tasted a Twinkie. Twinkie, what? That'll be you."

They all laughed and clinked glasses. Ella had not had champagne since her parents' anniversary party. This was joy, she thought as she set the bottle on her coffee table.

"I would like to make a toast." Vienna unfolded herself from the couch and her eyes took in the space. "To my friends. My sisters in crime."

"And yoga," Ella said.

Vienna nodded. "And bendy time. Thank you for having my back and eating your weight in sugar and flour to keep me from eating cat food. I love you." She raised her glass and they all joined her.

"When do you move in?" Sistine asked, grabbing a chocolate chip cookie off the tray on the coffee table.

"I don't, he does. I have the better house, so he gave notice and we'll be living together next month."

"All in," Ella said without even realizing it.

Vienna nodded. "Well, he can still move out. I can still throw him out, not that I'm thinking about it."

"You won't," Ella said.

"Personal experience, ladies. Even after the ring and the fancy dress, it's never all in, not all the time," Bri said.

"What does that mean?" Aspen asked, pouring more champagne.

"Sometimes it's seventy-thirty, other times it's fifty-fifty, but life isn't one hundred percent of anything all the time. No one is perfect. Now my marriage got to be like ninety me and ten him for about a year. That's when things start to crumble. But neither of you are in that situation."

They all sat staring at Bri, silent.

"You mean I'm not in that situation. Wait, are we talking about me still?" Vienna asked.

Bri looked at Ella.

"Don't start," Ella began to raise her hand in a gesture her friends rarely tolerated these days.

"Oh, put that thing down. Bri has something to say. The bubbles are flowing, sister, let it out," Vienna said.

Bri shrugged. "Boyd is a great guy. His life is complicated, but he loves you, and so what if things are a little lopsided right now? They'll ebb and flow. That's real life, Ella."

They were all still quiet. Ella couldn't recall a better woman-the-hell-up speech. Bri was right, probably because she'd been through a lot. Ella, on the other hand, was only recently dealing in real life.

She stood up and brushed the cookie crumbs off the front of her sweatpants.

"Oh no, let's not let this ruin the night. Bri, back out of Ella's ice den, will ya?" Sistine said.

Ella's eyes met Bri's, and for not the first time, she saw the pain of loss, the disappointment of a failed fairy tale. She leaned forward and kissed her friend on the cheek.

"You better be right."

Bri's teary eyes turned to sarcasm. "I keep trying to tell you, I'm always right."

Ella nodded. "Probably true." She took in her cluttered living room. She was so glad she had her friends over, but in that moment, she needed to be somewhere. "I need an Uber."

"Yeah, you do," Aspen said, high-fiving Vienna.

"I think we have better Lyft coverage this time of night, but I'll try both." Sistine was already typing on her phone.

They all laughed, and Ella was filled with an urgency to fix things that had nothing to do with the physical body for the first time in her life. Her heart leaped in her chest and she liked the way that felt.

Chapter Thirty-One

E lla was tucked into a Lyft and on her way to Boyd's house when she got the text that he needed to see her right away. At first, she thought something was wrong. She'd bumped into him a couple of times around town in the last few weeks and while they were back to "pleasantries," as her mother would say, Ella certainly wasn't his go-to person in an emergency. She gave her driver the new address and tried to quiet her enthusiastic heart.

The Tap House was dark as she walked up. Closed at 9:00 p.m. on a Wednesday? She stepped across the threshold and called out. Nothing. She checked her phone to confirm he'd said The Tap House and then what sounded like a shuffle of feet cut through the space. Before she had a chance to panic, a string of lights illuminated the darkness and Boyd walked in from the shadows. It seemed like he was moving through stars. Her breath caught and she wondered how long it would take before the sight of him dulled, before her heart learned its place again.

"You know when you ask people how they are and they say they're fine?"

Ella nodded.

"I think when Mason was born and Claire bailed, I loved him so much that nothing else mattered. If he was healthy and had what he needed, I was fine."

"That makes sense. I understand. Please don't—"

"Cade says fine is like barely living."

"He says a lot of things. If you're happy being fine then—"

"I'm not."

She met his eyes, and Boyd hesitated as if he had lost his place.

"I don't want to be fine anymore." He stepped closer and she forgot everything she'd planned on saying.

"I'm not sure if it happened the minute I met you, or when you became Mason's friend, no questions asked. I have no idea when it all happened but my heart." He swallowed. "It's never going to be the same if I can't fix this. I love you."

He was inches from her face now. She closed her eyes because the tenderness in his eyes was too much. She wasn't going to be able to say a word, make things right, if he kept looking at her that way.

"I'm absolutely out of control here, Ella. Mason has a busted nose and suddenly seems smarter than I am. Claire emailed me asking what I thought if she adopted a 'little baby' now that our kid is getting older. Nothing makes sense anymore."

"I'm sorry."

"Don't be. In fact, stop saying I'm sorry altogether." He took her face. "I'm in love with you. I was in love with you when you first told me, but I'm not as brave as you are. You're brilliant and gorgeous. You're everything I never imagined walking into my life and now... Now I find that you are the calm in my storm."

"Boyd." Her eyes welled.

"Now, if you've decided that you can't handle all my baggage, I get that, but I'm still going to try to convince you I'm worth a chance because here's the thing: I can't find my way back to fine. I need you more than I have ever needed anything in my life. You want all in, you want to be my one person. You are."

"I know. I wanted to tell you that..."

Boyd dropped to one knee. "It is never going to be better than you, Ella. It never has been and it never will be. You are my one shot at more than fine and I'm going all in." He opened the small velvet box.

"Dad?"

Boyd's knee was killing him as he turned to find his son at the front door.

"Mason, go away. I'm busy. Wait, what are you doing here?"

"Are you down on one knee? What the hell? Do people even still do that? Aren't you supposed to make some grand gesture? Like adventure proposal or a flash mob?"

Boyd stood. The floor was hard and the moment was now ruined. Mason walked toward them.

"Let's try that again, why are you here?" he asked, sticking the ring box back in the pocket of his jeans.

"Uncle Trick had some 'work flair, work flow' he had to do. He was pissed. I... mean he was perturbed."

Ella laughed.

"So, I told him to drop me off here so I could try to beat Aspen's high score in Galaga before I was supposed to be home."

"We're closed." He gestured to the emptiness. "The whole place is closed early so I could... I mean I wanted this to be. You thought you'd pop by a bar alone, at night?"

"I've got a key."

"Wow, not the point. Okay, well I'm trying to do something here, so wait in the truck."

"No Galaga? It's in the back and I'll be out of your way. Can't I play a few rounds while you try to get Ella to marry you with your old-school knee thing?"

"You are so over the line that I might have to ground you forever. Maybe you should join Sistine's book club, because that will be your social life in high school."

"Is that a no on the Galaga?"

Boyd turned to Ella as if to say, "Are you seeing this?" She had wiped away any tears and now couldn't stop smiling. It was so good to see that smile. He wanted to give her everything, starting with a ring, damn it.

"Can I play Galaga, Ella?"

"Why are you asking her?"

"She's nicer and the way she's looking at you, I'm guessing she's going to say yes."

"How do you know?" Boyd hoped like hell his son was right.

"I told you like forever ago. She broke eye contact. She likes you, probably loves you by now and besides, girls go for clumsy and nervous, remember? You're in, Dad. She digs your weirdness."

Boyd closed his eyes. "Two rounds, that's it."

"Then can we get pizza on the way home?"

"Oh, yeah. I'm starving," Ella said.

Mason beamed and the impossible happened: Boyd loved her more.

"Finish strong, Dad. She's the best."

Boyd turned to her as Mason disappeared around the corner. Pulling the ring from his pocket, he gave up on the steps. Life wasn't a series of do this and you'll get that. He should know that by now. He wanted to marry her and he needed to ask her his way.

Letting out a slow breath, he opened the ring box and all but leaped into her beautiful eyes. "I love you. Please share my life, our life."

She smiled, slow and gorgeous. "I've missed you."

"Is that a yes?"

"Give me a minute. I want this to last as long as possible."

"Great. Well, at least if I have a heart attack you'll know what to do."

She laughed and then grew serious. Touching the sides of his face, she gently kissed him. "I love you."

"I love you too." Was she going to look at the ring? Maybe this was a bad sign. Enough with the signs, he thought and instead focused on what he knew. She loved him and he was open and letting her in.

"I was on my way over to your house when I got your text."

"Why?"

"I needed to tell you something."

Recoiling was dramatic—he didn't truly recoil, but it was something close to that. He had a ring, she'd seen the ring, but before all of that she needed to tell him something? Yeah, he felt a heart attack coming on.

Ella wrapped her arms around him. "I don't need you to be one hundred percent all the time. That's not what I meant."

"Okay."

"Sometimes it can't be that way. We need to ebb and flow. Keep things loose and flexible. I get that now. I think that was most of it."

He tried desperately to order his thoughts. What the hell was she saying? Ebb and flow? Christ, had she been talking to Cade?

"Ella, I just got up off my knees. I have a tiny box in my hand. I'm not looking to ebb and flow with you. I want to marry you. One hundred percent, all in. That's what you said you needed and I'm here... giving it to you. Don't go all Zen on me now."

She laughed and then she started to cry. He wiped away her tears and practically drowned in her smile. Her face glowed under the soft string of lights. God, it was a miracle he'd lasted this long without her. No way in hell he was ebbing and flowing ever again.

He opened the box and her eyes went to the ring.

Patrick had helped him pick it out. It was a square stone set low into a platinum band. Simple and perfect, his brother had agreed as they stood there getting all choked up. At first the jeweler had shown them larger solitaires, but Boyd knew she would not want over the top and he wanted a ring she could wear at work. The ring had become more important than he imagined. He wanted her to carry the memory of him asking for her heart every day, even when their lives returned to the normal rhythm.

"It's incredible," she whispered as if there wasn't enough air in her lungs.

"Ella." He lifted her chin. "Marry me."

She nodded. "Thank you."

"For what?"

"For everything. For sharing your son with me. For loving me."

"Oh, it's my pleasure, Doc." He kissed her.

"That's right, cry home to mama, you slimy bastards," Mason roared from the back room.

Ella smiled, her lips still on his, and she eased back to laugh. Boyd should have told his son to watch his mouth like he had at least a hundred times before, but he'd let this one slide. He knew there would be endless family moments ahead and he wanted a little more time. A few more beats before pizza, twenty questions, and discussions about which jeans were cooler for high school. He wanted to be a guy who had asked a beautiful and smart-as-hell woman to marry him, and she'd said yes. He pulled her in closer, kissed her deeper, and knew the rest of his life was going to be so much more than fine.

Epilogue

The autumn brew had been a "piece of cake," according to Boyd. He'd gone with vanilla and praline, flavors that "remind me of my fiancée," he told her right before she'd had a taste. They named it Golden Lace. The man was more romantic than he knew. Ella stepped onto the back porch of Boyd and Mason's home, soon to become their home, to watch the sun set orange and pink over the river. She had cleared the dishes and the two of them were loading the dishwasher, so she stepped out into the cold December dusk. Pulling her sweater closed, she questioned if it was possible to be too happy, to have too much love. She'd spent a good portion of her life needing approval and pushing away when her ego or her heart were left wanting.

Home, she thought, looking back at the glow of light from the kitchen window. This was what it felt like to be home. It wasn't perfect; perfect was stifling. This was real joy sprinkled with bits of angst and frustration to keep things balanced.

She remembered Boyd's words—that everything needed good and bad. She knew there would be challenges in their life together. In three months, she was marrying a man with a teenager, whose mostly absent mother recently adopted a baby with her new husband. Ella's parents were not invited to the wedding, nor was her sister. They were joy suckers and she wasn't having that on the day she was set to stand in front of her chosen family and swear to love, laugh, and protect her favorite person. She would walk herself down the aisle, give the woman she'd worked so hard to become away to a man she knew would cherish her work. Her family would still be in their future and the drama would, of course, continue, but not on that day.

There were plenty of trials ahead, but in that moment, as the black of night took over the sky, Ella smelled popcorn. She heard Mason arguing with Boyd over which movie they were watching—all seemed right with her world. Christmas was less than a week away and she'd never felt more connected.

"Help." Mason slid open the back door. "Dad wants to watch some documentary on... What was it again?" he called over his shoulder into the house.

"Sea wolves in British Columbia. Your famous uncle said it's awesome." Boyd was still out of sight, but his voice came through loud, deep, and clear. She loved that voice.

Mason turned to her, wide-eyed. "Help," he mouthed without a sound. She laughed and turned to go into the house.

"Why are you out here?" he asked. "It's cold."

"It's beautiful."

"Yeah, but cold as—"

"Do not say the next word," Boyd said, appearing in the doorway and putting his arm around his son.

"I was going to say cold as... icicles or snowmen or... tiny little sea wolves."

"Smart-ass."

"You see it's that kind of bad language that led to my downfall."

"Oh really?" Boyd rolled his eyes.

Mason nodded. "No, not really. I'm a saint compared to half my high school. Balls is the least of your worries."

Ella, still laughing, walked between them into the warmth of the house. She was used to what she now called microbursts between father and son. In the beginning of her relationship with Boyd, she worried that messing with their life might change things. There was nothing to worry about—the Boyd and Mason Show went on despite any female distraction. She sat on the couch and put the popcorn bowl in her lap. Boyd sat next to her, kissed her until Mason cleared his throat, and took a handful of popcorn. Mason sat on the other side of Ella, suddenly serious.

"When do you guys think you'll have kids?" he asked, staring into his lap.

Boyd glanced at Ella. They had already discussed what their family would look like going forward. Boyd shrugged, indicating now was as good a time as any to share their news with Mason.

"We have kids," Ella said. "Well, a kid."

Mason looked up at her as if she'd spouted some complicated prophecy.

"You're not... I mean, don't most married people want to..."

The idea that Mason would ever think they needed more than him broke Ella's heart. She let Boyd take it from there.

"Are you kidding? Now that you're the next big thing on the high school field hockey scene, there will be practices, and I can't even begin to think about driving."

Ella raised her hand. "I volunteer."

"Good news. It's probably a good idea to have a doctor in the car because I've seen what this kid is like on his bicycle."

They all laughed, munched popcorn, and joked a little more until Boyd's eyes welled.

He reached behind Ella to rest his hand on his son's shoulder. "You are all we need, Mase. Best thing that ever happened to me."

"Me too," Ella said, her eyes glassy.

Mason beamed, looking back and forth between them. When the love became too much, he broke eye contact and propped his feet on the coffee table.

"So, I guess it's the three of us," he said, a smile in his voice.

"Guess so," Ella said.

"That's good because three is a perfect number for voting. All in favor of the wolves?"

Boyd raised his hand. Ella could feel him pleading for her vote, but she kept her eyes on the popcorn bowl and tried to control her laughter.

"All in favor of *Fantastic Beasts*?" Mason said.

Ella slowly raised her hand and winked in jest when she met Boyd's eyes as Mason cheered and grabbed the remote.

"I love you," Mason said, not for the first time, and leaned over to kiss her on the cheek. Ella hugged him and couldn't seem to let go. Hugging meant more than bad memories to her now, and she wanted Mason to know how much she'd learned.

"Okay, okay." Mason squirmed and she released him.

"Who's the master Jedi, now?" she asked.

"You are." Mason laughed. "I've created a monster."

Ella grew serious. "I love you too, Mase."

Mason's smile reached right into her heart. He nodded and turned his focus back to the movie.

Boyd, who was still mocking shock at his movie defeat, cleared his throat. "So much for the den of dudes."

"So much for it." Ella took his face and kissed him until the opening movie music started and Mason began tossing popcorn at them.

Life was good. The weekend was almost over and she had to be at the hospital by eight the next morning, but that was fine too. She had the mug Bri gave her for her birthday with black script lettering that Ella now knew was the truth: Mondays suck.

Acknowledgements

I would like to thank:

Katie McCoach for her patience and her ability to somehow always find a clear path.

Nikki Busch for catching that Big Red has artificial sweeteners *before* Ella got on her soapbox.

Erin Tolbert for keeping me from the straight jacket. Every. Single. Day.

All the men and women who step up and show up for the children in their lives. The ones who choose love and define family on their own terms.

The City of Petaluma for honoring its past and making excellent beer.

My family for continuing to call back and forgiving my absent mind.

Every reader because all of this stops without you. It is an honor to share my stories.

Tracy Ewens shares a beautiful piece of desert with her husband and three children in New River, Arizona. She is a recovered theater major who walks her dog Jack, drinks copious amounts of tea, and reads well past her bedtime.

www.tracyewens.com

Made in the USA
San Bernardino, CA
11 March 2018